continued ...

"Fast-paced, sexy, and hilarious. . . . Run, don't walk, to get a copy."   —*Romantic Times*

A Bride Unveiled

"Sizzling sexual chemistry and rapier wit . . . a thoroughly romantic literary treat."   —*Booklist*

"Hunter draws the reader in with a compelling plot and engaging characters in this smoothly written tale of love lost and found."   —*Publishers Weekly*

A Duke's Temptation

"A sinfully sexy hero with a secret, a book-obsessed heroine in search of her own happy-ever-after ending, a delightfully clever plot that takes great fun in spoofing the literary world, and writing that sparkles with wicked wit and exquisite sensuality add up to an exceptionally entertaining read."   —*Booklist* (starred review)

"With humor and charm, sensuality and wickedness, Hunter delights."   —*Romantic Times*

"This is the first in what looks to be a very promising, and extremely seductive, new quartet. Few can resist a novel by Jillian Hunter!"   —Huntress Book Reviews

More Praise for the Novels
of Jillian Hunter

"One of the funniest, most delightful romances I've had the pleasure to read." —Teresa Medeiros

"An absolutely delightful tale that's impossible to put down." —*Booklist*

"A sweet, romantic tale . . . full of humor, romance, and passion. Historical romance that is sure to please."
—The Romance Readers Connection

"A lovely read." —Romance Reader at Heart

"Enchanting . . . a fabulous historical."
—*Midwest Book Review*

"[It] bespells, beguiles, and bewitches. If romance, magic, great plots, and wonderful characters add spice to your reading life, don't allow this one to escape."
—Crescent Blues

"Romantic and sexy. . . . Read it—you'll love it!"
—The Romance Reader

JILLIAN HUNTER

A Boscastle Affairs Novel

The Countess Confessions

A SIGNET SELECT BOOK

SIGNET SELECT
Published by the Penguin Group
Penguin Group (USA) LLC, 375 Hudson Street,
New York, New York 10014

USA | Canada | UK | Ireland | Australia | New Zealand | India | South Africa | China
penguin.com
A Penguin Random House Company

First published by Signet Select, an imprint of New American Library,
a division of Penguin Group (USA) LLC

First Printing, February 2014

Copyright © Maria Hoag, 2014
Penguin supports copyright. Copyright fuels creativity, encourages diverse voices,
promotes free speech, and creates a vibrant culture. Thank you for buying an
authorized edition of this book and for complying with copyright laws by not
reproducing, scanning, or distributing any part of it in any form without permission. You are supporting writers and allowing Penguin to continue to publish
books for every reader.

SIGNET SELECT and logo are trademarks of Penguin Group (USA) LLC.

ISBN 978-0-451-41533-2

Printed in the United States of America
10   9   8   7   6   5   4   3   2   1

For Gordon,
with my deepest love and gratitude

Chapter 1

1820
England

The fortune-teller's tent was the talk of the party. It stood beyond the reach of the light shed by lanterns that twinkled in the trees. Even the footmen positioned in the garden wondered whether it had been pitched illegally or was there to entertain the guests. Judging by the chattering young ladies and gentlemen lined up on the footbridge to the dark hollow where the gypsy fortune-teller had encamped, no one cared why she'd appeared. Upon her arrival she had allegedly announced she would give readings tonight that pertained only to romance.

Few of the well-heeled guests would have found the courage to approach her if she hadn't come to the party.

"What an enchanting surprise. Lord Fletcher's wife or daughter must have talked him into hiring her. She's reading for free, I heard."

"Well, I hope she doesn't run out of inspiration before my turn."

Inspiration? It was patience the fortune-teller needed.

So far Miss Emily Rowland had predicted only happy outcomes for the lovelorn, and those had exhausted her talent for deception. Each snippet of excited chatter that reached her ear only made her heart sink lower. She was doing all of this in the pursuit of love, to predict romance for one particular guest at tonight's ball, although as the evening progressed, it seemed more likely this scheme would bring about her ruination.

She sat up in her squeaky cane-backed chair, cringing as the tiny bottle that sat on the table wobbled precariously to one side. Emily had no idea what substance the green glass contained. She had borrowed it from her brother, Michael, to use for atmosphere after overhearing one of his Rom friends whisper to him over the garden wall, "Use this when all else fails."

Emily didn't believe in magic. She doubted she'd have the courage to sprinkle it on her heart's desire when he appeared. She couldn't imagine what the results would be if she dared. When the time came, she suspected she wouldn't have the nerve to use the potion, whether or not it was imbued with any power, on the gentleman she hoped would offer her a marriage proposal.

"Are you ready for me?" a man asked at the door.

"Yes. Enter." *And be quick about it,* she thought as she moved her wobbly bottle to a safer position on the table, away from the flickering oil lamp, about which her brother had said, "For the love of heaven, Emily, whatever you do, don't let the light fall to the straw."

The fifth person to seek her services happened to be a cad whom Emily disliked too much to hide it. He whipped his horse to show off, treated his servants like lumps of dirt, and was staring with vulgar fascination down Emily's bodice while she feigned interest in the palm of his hand.

"I fear, Mr. Prickett, that your palm reveals a short life line." She drew her hand away from his and slid back into her creaking chair.

"Nonsense," he said in an indolent voice. "Longevity runs in the family. Give me the name of the next lady fortunate enough to share my bed."

"Toad!"

"I beg your pardon." His face portrayed the conceit of a man who refused to believe he had been dealt an insult. "Did you say, 'Miss Todd'? I don't believe I know anyone by that name. Is she here tonight? A lady I've yet to meet?"

"How should I—"

A loud cough from behind the tent reminded Emily that a fortune-teller told her clients what they wanted to hear, not the truth. But honestly, what did she know of palm reading and French tarot cards?

She could not have been in her right mind when she had allowed her friend Lucy, Lord Fletcher's daughter, to talk her into this strategy. Once Emily had seized upon the idea, she had turned to her half brother to employ his help. She should have listened to Michael's warnings instead of letting Lucy's enthusiasm for matchmaking erode her judgment.

"You are desperate, Emily," Lucy had untactfully reminded her.

"I am desperately in love, yes."

"With a gentleman who does not realize you exist," Lucy said, her bluntness meant to motivate Emily before she became officially known in Hatherwood as an eccentric spinster.

"Perhaps it's for the best," Emily had suggested. "He notices other ladies. I've tried to make him notice me.

I've done everything but turn cartwheels on the cricket field when he plays. I've dropped my reticule on his foot. I've bumped into him twice in the churchyard. And all he ever does is apologize and go on his merry way."

"You might have been too obvious."

"So in your opinion, wearing a curly black wig, tinting my skin, and telling omens are subtle ways to draw his attention?"

"You will not be yourself. You shall be a fortune-teller who slips Emily's name into his thoughts as his future beloved. As soon as you're finished, you will disappear, remove your disguise, and become Emily again. And this time when he sees you, everything will be different. He won't know why he never noticed you before. He'll wonder how he could ever have missed such a charming—"

Mr. Prickett's voice startled her back into her role. "Where am I to meet this lady?" he asked, apparently unaware that his plans for a lustful evening were of no concern to the fortune-teller.

Her brother bumped up against the tent in subtle warning. Michael was invigorated by his Romany blood, which came from the secret affair their mother had carried on a month before she married Emily's father, the man who had once believed himself to be Michael's sire as well. When the young baroness was dying, she had revealed the truth, cleansing her conscience and breaking the baron's heart by forcing him to realize he had been cuckolded, that his only son and heir was not his own.

Mr. Prickett's voice jarred her again. "What else do you see for me and this woman?"

"Separation. Woe. Perhaps even a lawsuit."

He frowned. "Why don't you give the cards a try?"

"The reading is over," she said. "I have lost contact with the other side."

"What other side?" he demanded with a doubtful look.

The other side of the tent. Or the side of me that claims some link to sanity. He can take his pick. "Go," she said, rising from the noisy chair. "Unstable elements are interfering with my ability to read or influence the future."

"But—"

"Next!"

He started to protest until a cloaked lady entered, forcing him to either make a scene or an exit. Fortunately he chose to leave. The lady who hurried into the tent perched herself on the stool in front of Emily's table. "Well?" she asked, biting her lip as she swung her cloak up from the straw. "Is our little fortune-teller ready to meet her fate?"

Emily stared across the table at Lucy's cheerful face. "Is Camden still outside?" she whispered.

"He certainly is."

"How does he look?"

"No different than usual. Well, are you going to read my cards?"

"Not again. We spent all last night reading them, and Michael has given me so many details about the deck that I'm afraid I don't remember what all the inverted positions mean."

"Make them up. None of us at the party know. There's only one person who matters. Read the future in my palm." She held out her hand. "Practice for your next customer."

"I can predict your future if, against all odds, I manage to convince Camden that he and I belong together. You will be a bridesmaid at our wedding."

"How lovely!"

"But if by any chance he recognizes me, you and I will be found out and sent to our aunts for discipline. We shall spend the next season in disgrace."

A pleasant male voice called from the line outside the tent's entrance. "Are you almost done in there? The band is tuning up in the ballroom, and champagne is being served. We don't want to miss the dance."

"That's him," Lucy said, as if Emily would not recognize the voice that haunted her dreams on a nightly basis. "The seventh in line. I'll slip out the back and listen. Or do you prefer privacy? I wouldn't want to inhibit your performance."

"Privacy? You must be joking. Michael has his ear to the tent in the event that I make an utter fool of myself and need his intervention. You might as well return to the party before your father finds out what we've done."

"Don't worry about him. He's too busy entertaining—"

A commotion of raised male voices, one of them Camden's, diverted Lucy's and Emily's attention. It sounded as if he and another man were exchanging words. But Camden never quarreled with anyone. His even temper was one of the qualities Emily adored.

"Are they arguing?" Lucy whispered, her eyes wide with disbelief.

"Hush. I think so."

"Well," Camden said, more placating than combative, "I *have* been standing in line a dashed long time, sir, but if you are in a hurry, I suppose I—"

Emily could not make out what else Camden said. A deeper voice responded, and there followed a shuffling of feet and silence.

"I shall investigate," Lucy said before Emily, prompted by instinct, could ask her to stay.

She reached down for the handle of her basket. In it several decks of tarot cards, labeled in French and English, sat neatly tied in red silk ribbons. "Michael?" she said over her shoulder, but he gave no answer.

Had he left his post to investigate the disturbance? She turned her head to glimpse Lucy escaping the tent. No sooner had her friend disappeared than the seventh person stepped inside.

Seven. It was a mystical number from ancient times. When Michael had suggested that assigning Camden a number in line would give Emily time to prepare herself for his reading, she hadn't realized that she would become such a popular attraction at the party. She hadn't dreamed that the man she desired and one she did not know would argue over who would be the next to sit before her. No one had ever fought to be with Emily until now. If anything, she was the last girl to be invited to a party or a picnic, and often she wasn't asked at all. Now Michael was gone.

And the stranger standing before her in all his charismatic arrogance did not resemble the man she had expected, in demeanor or appearance. His hard face might not have disconcerted Emily if she had met the man before and had developed a tolerance to the impact he wielded. Under ordinary circumstances, she might not have found herself breathless from his unadulterated masculinity. High cheekbones and hollowed contours defined his face. A handsome man, to be sure. One whose vitality of presence, whose self-possession, a woman might encounter once in a lifetime. Emily realized that it was rude of her to stare. But she couldn't help herself, and he *had* made a scene to be the next man in her tent. What did he intend to conquer? Surely not a vagabond girl.

She waited for him to speak. He appeared to take her response to his magnetism for granted. Emily would have dearly loved to summon Lucy back to the tent to whisper, "Look at him. Where did he come from? Is he as attractive as I think?"

Lucy had gone, however, and some vital instinct in the back of Emily's mind set up a warning cry. *Flee. Run now or live to rue this moment.* But a dreadful suspense weighted her to the chair. His presence rendered her incapable of movement. And, really, what was there to fear? What was the worst that could happen with others outside the tent?

Seven.

Seven was a lucky number.

There were the Seven Hills of Rome. Seven Sisters of the Pleiades. Seven days in the week. Seven archangels. Seventh heaven. Shakespeare's seven ages of man.

The number did, however, possess some dark connotations. An English gentlewoman visiting London would never want to explore the stews of Seven Dials. And wasn't there a fairy-tale giant who wore seven-league boots?

Emily leaned back in her chair and stared at her seventh customer as he sat down casually on the stool. He cast an enormous shadow in the candlelit tent. She felt swallowed in darkness. He was wearing boots, too, with a long black evening jacket over a white shirt, and a pair of black pantaloons.

She had *never* seen him before. She would not have

forgotten those impious blue eyes and the smile that somehow hinted he knew she was an imposter and that he fully expected to be forgiven for ruining her scheme. His impressive physique, combined with his longish dark red hair and light beard, would have made him stand out at any function Emily was likely to attend.

"Really, sir," she said breathlessly, the admonishment too restrained for a man of his presumption to respect. But who had stolen her voice?

And why had he stolen Camden's place? A true rogue rarely needed an introduction to romance, which made Emily wonder why he had ducked into the tent when she had been expecting another man.

"I hope you don't mind my switching places with the other man in line," he said, his gaze taking in her appearance as if he sensed there was something odd about it but he wasn't sure what it was. "I ran into a spot of embarrassment at the party. I noticed a person I wasn't quite ready to encounter yet. I needed shelter to hide out and collect my thoughts. I'm sure someone with your experience will understand. You must be used to keeping secrets."

Experience? Secrets? Never in her twenty-five years had Emily been confronted with the type of man the vicar had always warned the ladies in his congregation to avoid. Hatherwood produced one or two scoundrels a century, if that.

She was instantly drawn to the playfulness in his eyes, delighted and appalled by his unabashed male authority. So, a stranger had thrown her off course. She would simply have to recover and resume her role before the gentleman he had usurped, Camden, was sitting before her.

"What happened to the man who was next in line?" Emily asked, refusing to acknowledge his aplomb. The nerve of him. Supplanting Camden for his convenience.

"Who?" She realized then that he spoke with a deep Scottish brogue. "Oh, *him*. He was kind enough to give me his place."

"But . . . did he leave? Voluntarily, that is?"

"I've no idea. Does it matter?"

Obviously it didn't matter to this interloper. Poor, polite Camden must have been too intimidated to object. After all, what kind of person pushed ahead of guests he didn't even know at a party? Who did he think he was?

Perhaps she didn't want to know.

She realized then that there were seven deadly sins, and that the man who stared back at her with false guile looked prepared to commit at least one of them before the night came to an end.

Chapter 2

"My name is Sir Angus Morpeth," he said, looking around the tent as if to make sure he could make a quick escape if necessary. "I'm a wool merchant from Aberdeen."

"How nice of you to impart that information to me, but I must be honest. I'm not in the market for any woolens, thank you, and I'm not as practiced as your typical Scottish soothsayers."

"Which typical Scottish soothsayers are you referring to?"

She gave him a narrow glance. Why did he have to be a talker on top of everything else? "Oh, I don't know. The witches in *Macbeth*, for example."

"Witches?"

"Those weird sisters."

His gaze cut back to hers. What had she blurted out? Had she just admitted she was a complete fraud? "It's all in the spirit of the party," she said before he could denounce her. "You might say that I am here solely to entertain."

"Then entertain me. I have a few moments to spare."

"I've a feeling that you and I won't agree on what defines entertainment."

"Is this your maiden voyage?"

"Excuse me, sir?"

"Your first time in a tent?"

She flushed at his impertinence. "That has nothing to do with telling your future."

"Pity. I was beginning to enjoy myself."

"I predict that will not last long."

He smiled in a way that said he knew she was trying to get rid of him but he wasn't going to make it easy on her. "Interesting that you make reference to Shakespeare," he said. "I've been out of the country for some time, but I must confess I'd no idea that gypsy women had been allowed schooling."

"You don't have to go to school to learn to read people," she muttered, resenting the fact that what he said was still true.

"Can you read me? Don't look at my hand. Just give me your impression. What do you make of me?"

"Sir, I would say you are determined."

He laughed. "Yes, that's right. Or ruthless. Most men who push to the head of the queue are."

"I might go so far as to say you could be desperate."

He bent his head closer and she could feel the whisper of his breath along her cheek. His eyes held a dark fascination that made her pulse jump. "So could you. Anything else?"

She waited, remembering Michael's advice. *Some customers only want to trick up a fortune-teller. It makes them feel superior to make you confess you're a cheat. Stand your ground. Sooner or later the weakest will break. Don't let it be you.*

It was evident that he wanted only to while away time. Her precious time.

Lowering his voice, he spoke again. "Do you consider the ability to look into a person's future a gift?"

"I've never given it much thought." Which, to her shame, was the only truthful thing she'd said to him since he sat down. "Do you?"

"Not particularly. If you knew that I would die in the next hour and told me, I might interpret your warning to have been a curse."

Emily attempted to draw a deep breath. It didn't help much. His presence had not only begun to make her feel light-headed, but had also distracted her from her intentions. His eyes penetrated her thoughts and invited them to follow a new and dangerous direction. She needed to regain control before she lost her opportunity to speak to Camden. Before this man crowded into her awareness and incited unseemly ideas.

"That is a lurid association," she said after a moment. "Who would think of death at a country ball? It must be the Scotsman in you. Where in that wild country did you say that you were from?"

A smile played about the corners of his mouth. Emily might have thought that was the reason she'd started to shiver had she not known it was because of the wind piercing the back slit in the tent, where her brother had promised to stand watch. Had he wandered from his post? It would be just her luck to be left alone with the one gentleman at the party she couldn't manage.

"Aberdeen," the man answered, his alert eyes moving past hers again.

Again she lost her focus. Something was very wrong. He had not pushed to head of the line on a whimsy. He admitted he was hiding. From whom? A lady he hoped to elude? A gentleman he intended to challenge? Lucy had mentioned that her father had invited a new set of friends to the party, men involved in some vague business he refused to discuss with his family. Was this Scotsman one of them? Wool trading wasn't what Emily considered to be a risky affair. She couldn't understand why Lord Fletcher wouldn't talk of it, unless he was afraid that his wife would consider trade too common for an aristocrat.

All Emily knew for certain was that Sir Angus was stealing the last few moments she had left in the evening to spend with Camden. And as desperate as she was to speak to him, she was even more desperate to get rid of this man—which she suspected made him perversely more intent on staying.

The distinct stomping of footsteps behind her broke the uncomfortable silence.

The stranger stared over her chair to the back of the tent. "What was that?" he asked, his manner alert, diverted.

"What was what?"

"The footsteps that said it has grown too quiet in here."

"Oh, *that*. He's my . . . pony."

"Is that right? A jealous pony that stomps the ground when he cannot hear you? Not a lover?"

Emily felt as if her hair band had tightened around her temples. "If you insist on prying into my affairs, that is my brother."

His broad shoulders lifted beneath his long black jacket. "I'd rather offend a jealous lover than a protective brother. As to prying into your affairs, it's supposed to be the other way around. However, if your pony is listening, I shall try to behave."

"Thank you."

He lowered his voice. "Unless we meet alone at another time, in which case I might be able to entertain you."

"Do not count on it," she said with a certitude that defied his effrontery. To her chagrin, she couldn't deny the blush of pleasure she felt at his presumption. Had a man ever flirted with her before? Certainly not like this. It flattered her, and she wouldn't be surprised to find that he had entered her tent to flee a lady at the party who had pursued him.

"Kindly give me your right hand."

"What if I'm left-handed?"

Emily suppressed a sigh. She wasn't the least surprised, although what his handedness meant to his future she couldn't guess. "Are you?"

"You're the fortune-teller," he said, giving her his left hand.

She hesitated. His hand looked so much larger than hers, elegant and strong, but warm to the touch as he laid it upon hers. It seemed that everything Michael had taught her fled her mind. She frowned in concentration.

"This is your heart line," she said in a detached voice, sweeping the tip of her forefinger across his palm.

"I'm surprised you can find it. Everyone who knows me well insists that I am heartless. I should have you write a letter of testimony in my favor."

"Has anyone ever told you that you are a contentious man?"

"You can see that in my palm? You have an amazing talent."

"I think your time is up," she said, half rising from the chair, his hand still in hers. "The next person in line will be getting impatient."

"That's too bad," he said without a suggestion of sympathy. "You haven't read my cards yet. I demand the same privileges that you have offered others."

She struggled to find her voice. "This isn't a business or institution where you have a right to make demands."

"But I'm demanding, nonetheless. As you were unable to find anything of interest in my palm, you might as well give the cards a try. And don't tell me you're no good at reading those, either. You said yourself that you are an entertainer. Well, you've managed to entertain me longer than I expected, and I'm not easy to please."

The cards. She sank down into the chair. Reading the cards could take forever, especially since he looked like a man with a wicked history, which of course indicated troubles to come. And all she knew about divination she had learned from Michael. In fact, she was tempted to call her brother to have the audacious rogue tossed out of the tent. The only thing that stopped her was the Scotsman's size and temper. He might take Michael down in a fight, and Michael was rather like a bull himself when enraged. Moreover, her identity would likely be uncovered during a melee, and then she would be exposed to all her friends at the party for the hopeless dreamer and schemer that she was. She couldn't take the chance.

She shook his hand from hers, his touch suddenly more intimate than she could bear. She blinked, aware that he was staring at the overturned bottle on the table.

No. *Oh no.*

His gaze lifted to hers in accusation. She reached for the empty bottle, then stopped. "You spilled it," she said. "You—"

"What the devil did you rub on my palm?" he asked in annoyance.

"My finger," she said, insulted at the suggestion she would resort to anything devious, which, of course, she had, but not with him in mind. "What is wrong with your palm?"

"It throbs like the dickens. It burns as if you had touched stinging nettles to it."

Now that he mentioned it, Emily's fingertips also felt as if she had run them across a candle flame. "Perhaps you ought to go outside and stick your hand in the brook."

His mouth flattened. "I did mention I was trying to be discreet. Advise me what you see in those cards and leave off palm reading for a while. I seem to have an odd reaction to your touch."

No sooner had he finished than she heard Camden's familiar voice call from the line outside the tent. He might have been miles away. "How much longer is this going to take? The wind is rising something fierce."

Emily restrained herself from answering, aware that the Scotsman had leaned across the table, his face close to hers.

"Do you want your basket?" he asked.

"What for?" Emily said, not trusting his motives for a moment.

"I don't know. In case you meet a wicked wolf in the woods."

"I believe I've already met him."

"But he hasn't eaten you up yet."

She snatched the basket he dangled before her. "I don't think you know your fairy tales, Sir Angus."

"No?" he asked, his quiet voice more intimidating than a growl.

"The wolf gets done in at the end of the story."

"Not all wolves are that easy to do in." He studied her in a long, unnerving silence. "But you are delicious."

"I am *what*?" she said, shocked and, to her shame, amused by this aggressive and inappropriate conversation.

He lifted his forefinger to her mouth. She lowered the basket to her lap, her pulse throbbing in anticipation. "I could eat you up at one meal," he mused. "Some men would find you to be a threat. Others, like me, would consider you a challenge. There's something delectable and devious about you. If only I had a little more time."

Emily reminded herself that her brother was only a shout away. "You have stolen my time, sir, and if you see deceit in me, it is only because I, with my supernatural gifts, am reflecting *your* wretched soul."

"What a mouthful," he said, breaking into laughter. His forefinger circled to her bottom lip. "What a tempting mouth. Now lay out the deck, darling. Amuse me a little more in the time we have left, or I shall be tempted to divert us in other ways."

She released her breath and reached her hand into the basket on her lap, carefully feeling past the beribboned packs that she and Michael had assembled. There was one deck meant for Camden, if she ever had the chance to be alone with him tonight.

The last deck was a hodgepodge of cards removed from the other sets. She expected it would reveal nothing of significance. She laid twelve cards facedown in a cross upon the table. Sir Angus did not even glance at the first card she turned up. Hopefully, the Scotsman would return to whatever dark pleasures he had planned for the duration of the party.

"If you're not interested in your future," she said, "why should I be?"

His eyes kindled. "Do you see anything of interest?"

She looked down, frowning in surprise. Michael had been careful to cast aside any cards that would not further her cause.

The provocative illustration that stared up at her from the black velvet cloth covering the table had not been meant to appear.

Passion

She felt his gaze lift from the table to her face. "It's a mistake. I don't—" she said without thinking.

He put his hand down before hers to reveal the second card, a beautiful depiction of a man and woman exchanging vows at an altar before a priest.

"*Mariage,*" he said in perfectly accented French. "You're right. This must be a mistake. Marriage is most assuredly not in the cards for me."

Emily could not pull her gaze from the ten cards left unturned on the table. She had given the basket to her maid, Iris, while Emily fussed over her disguise. But the cards couldn't have gotten mixed up, because the others remained tightly bound by their ribbons.

A lady's cry outside the tent jarred her concentration. "One more raindrop and I'm heading for the house! Silk shows water spots, you know."

She shivered lightly. What had happened to her carefully laid plans? Rain and a determined rascal, for a start. There hadn't been a cloud in the sky this afternoon.

He pulled out his watch, rising before she could say anything further. "Here." He reached into his other pocket for several coins and tossed them into her basket. "I predict a short future for you as a fortune-teller. You're too easy to unsettle, for one thing, and too pretty, for another.

"What's your name?" he asked, casually striding around her chair to bend over her.

She stood, coming to a stop several inches below his square-cut jaw. She hoped that Michael's great-aunt would forgive Emily for borrowing her name. "Urania."

"Good grief."

"You can't go out the back way."

He looked down slowly into her face.

She made the mistake of meeting his gaze.

Why had she never heard Lucy mention his name before? She and Lucy discussed *everything*, had shared all their hopes and worries for years. Was he one of the men with whom Lord Fletcher had recently become involved?

"Don't stray far from your pony tonight," he said in a soft burr that sent a chill coursing through her.

"What do you mean?"

"There are other men like me about."

He was teasing her again, but there was a warning in the warm tenor of his voice.

"Thank you for giving me shelter," he added, but made no motion to leave. "I think you would be wise to forget that we ever met."

As if he were a man whose memory a woman could banish as easily as that.

Unmasked desire shone in the depths of his eyes. She wasn't sure what had ignited this temptation between them. It would be up to her to dampen it. Instead, she braced herself against the table and hoped he would quietly end the inexplicable attraction she felt before she fell back in the chair and knocked over the lamp that could easily set the tent on fire.

Claim me.

Kiss me before I change my mind.

He seemed to be reconsidering, prolonging the suspense that had quickened her breath. Perhaps she had only imagined that he wanted to kiss her. He had been playing with her before, had admitted as much without a hint of remorse. She didn't have to be held captive by her curiosity. But when he bent his head, her heart raced, and when his arm reached around her waist, she felt her wits abandon her. She let him draw her into the folds of his long black coat and the hard torso beneath without a murmur of complaint. How wickedly sweet to be caught in his game when she was playing one of her own.

He hadn't bothered to ask for permission. He took. The sudden heat that flared between them scorched the air she struggled to breathe.

For an instant she felt utterly lost. She didn't know which way to turn. He had trapped her without even trying. A moment later she was found, claimed, her indecision melting as his mouth slanted over hers. She had no inkling of what he intended to do next. Was this a standard prelude to passion? Would he dare attempt anything indecent with her brother standing outside?

This was no tender peck between sweethearts. It was a full-bodied, hot-blooded kiss to seduce a woman's will. His tongue stroked the shape of her lips, delving inside her mouth just as she drew a breath. His hard, intense face said he wanted more. What that might be, she hesitated to speculate on. His hand moved up her arm to grip her by the shoulder and draw her into the core of his body.

Should she shout for help? Not quite yet. Perhaps she should give him another few seconds to redeem himself.

Yet it was impossible to keep track of time with his mouth plundering hers. She had waited years to be kissed. She might wait forever for a kiss like this.

She knew intuitively he would have demanded other pleasures from her if they'd met in another place or time. Her heart pounded at the thought. And still she couldn't bring herself to move or utter a word. His hand gripped her harder. His fingers lightly traced her hip through her skirts and lifted away before she could scold him.

He deepened the kiss. He raised his straying hand to her nape of her neck. She ached for his blissful caress to continue, for another chance to revel in the sensations he had awakened in her and left wanting.

Her breasts pressed against the black wool and white linen of his evening dress. Heat stole slowly through her veins. His kiss was persuasive and dangerously pleasurable, designed for maximum effect on a female's senses. She must have been one of many who waged no resistance.

Hadn't she asked the fates to show her what passion was?

He was the wrong man, and she knew she would never see him again.

But for this moment she was in his arms.

The kiss would end. Reason would return. And in the next moment, before she was ready, it did, although he was the first to break free. She stood, shaking, and suddenly she could breathe.

She opened her eyes. He was gone. So were two of the cards, including the last one she had cast on the table. Had he taken them or knocked them over in his departure?

She gathered up the empty bottle and the other remaining cards, still puzzled by their appearance.

Secrets

She straightened with a rueful smile. *Mariage* had disappeared, of course. To judge by the hollow ache inside her, the Scotsman had given her a mere taste of what passion meant in his world. Undiluted. As potent as any love potion.

I think you would be wise to forget we ever met.

As if that were possible.

Chapter 3

He left the tent with as little warning as he had entered it, while Emily sat breathless, recovering, and quite disgusted with herself. If she hadn't been in disguise, she would have given him a piece of her mind for kissing her, intriguing as the experience had been. Then again, if she'd been dressed as ordinary Miss Rowland, he wouldn't have tried. She would have been her usual invisible self. But what would she have done if another guest had entered the tent at the wrong time?

He'd have jeopardized her chance to convince Camden that she, underhanded and unladylike though she might be, was an ideal candidate for marriage. How was she supposed to appear aloof and mysterious when she had spent all her energy surviving a stranger's kiss?

She would never wear wool close to her skin again without remembering that blue-eyed rogue. She should be furious instead of feeling slightly wistful about their encounter.

Sir Angus had taken so much of her time, she doubted many of the guests had chosen to stand in line when they could be sipping champagne or dancing in the warm, bright ballroom. She could hear the wind puffing at the tent, perhaps even a raindrop or two splattering on the canvas.

Camden cared too much for his creature comforts to stand in the wind for a reading. She might as well sneak back to the tower where she and her maid had hidden their cloaks and gowns. She dreaded facing Michael, having to admit her plan had failed. He had only been home for a week, and she had taken up most of his spare time with her attempt at romantic intrigue.

"Emily!" he hissed from the back of the tent. "Have you fallen asleep in there?"

"Where were you when I needed you?" she demanded, glaring at the dark face that appeared between the back flaps of the tent. "I've been held prisoner by that arrogant Scotsman you permitted to barge in and overstay his welcome."

"What Scotsman?" Michael asked, staring first at her and then the odd display of cards in her hand. "What was his name? What did he look like?"

"He introduced himself as Sir Angus Morpeth. He had a dark red beard and blue eyes full of wicked intentions."

"You were supposed to be looking at his cards, not into his eyeballs."

"Really? He was number seven, you know. *You* were supposed to make sure that I was alone with Camden, not with a sinister albeit attractive stranger who refused to leave, no matter how many hints I dropped that he should do so. I don't know how you could have missed him. He was even bigger than you. He was full of himself, too. He shoved Camden out of line in order to hide from someone at the party."

"Why?"

"I've no idea, Michael. He wouldn't tell me, and I've a feeling I'm better off uninvolved. I assume he is leading on two ladies at once and had no idea they would appear at the same party."

"That would make him sneaky, not necessarily sinister. What gave you that impression?"

She bit her lower lip. "I can't remember exactly. The cards, for one thing. And then I spilled the potion all over—"

"What potion?"

"The potion I took from your room—"

"Sssh." He stared past her with that preternatural instinct she had always envied and that had been absolutely useless when Sir Angus had taken Camden's place in the tent.

"Michael?" she said, pulling her shawl over her bare shoulder. The temperature in the tent had dropped at least five degrees since the Scotsman's departure. "Should I pack up—"

"It's Camden," he said succinctly, pushing her down into the chair. "I'll stay out back and listen. Or would you prefer I don't listen?"

"I would like a little privacy to make an utter cake of myself if you don't—"

He swept out of the tent before she could finish, leaving her alone with the gentleman who would undoubtedly never speak to her again if he realized her identity.

She turned in the chair, cringing as it creaked like the gate of an ancient crypt. The brown-haired gentleman who had just arrived brushed off his damp coat before her. He was someone she had dreamt of too many times to fall to pieces now that she faced him in the flesh. He was a man she should have welcomed with a blush of pleasure rather than the unexpected sigh of deflated hope that escaped her. It was a bit off-putting to watch him shake about like a wet dog.

Camden, she thought, and stopped herself from blurting out his name—perhaps because his wind-tousled hair and slapped-red cheeks did not match her secret image of him as her one and only.

Here, at last, was the gentleman she had gone to embarrassing measures to impress. How could she blame Camden for her reaction to the brash Scotsman who had worn through her meager supply of defenses? It wasn't his fault that a stranger's kiss had shaken her composure or that he'd given up his spot in line to a man who didn't look like he would take no for an answer.

"Sir?" she said, in what she intended to be a low, provocative voice but that emerged more like she had something caught in her throat.

Camden didn't seem to notice either way. He wiped off the stool in front of her with the cuff of his sleeve and sat. "Dash, it's getting windy out. Will this take long?"

"Why don't you give me your hand?"

"Whatever for?"

"So that I can read our fortune."

"*Our* fortune?"

She lowered her gaze. This deception had unfolded so much easier when she practiced it with Lucy and her maid last night. She should have taken a page from Sir Angus's book of seduction. He had managed to engage her in his game before she realized what had happened.

Camden cleared his throat. "Well, you're awfully quiet. I hope this doesn't mean I have no future to foretell."

Emily stole a look at his face. "You'll need to give me your hand first."

As he complied, she frowned at the gloved fist he held stiffly over the table. "Well, take it off."

"My glove?"

"I can hardly see your palm through pig leather."

His friendly eyes roamed over her face as he pulled off his gloves. "Will you ask me to strip off my boots and socks, next? You can read my feet, but watch the toes. I'm ticklish."

"I think that can wait for another time."

"Another time?" he said in surprise. "You aren't hoping to set up a business hereabouts? If all your prophecies don't come true, you'll be driven from the parish before dawn. Gypsies are blamed for every manner of mishap." He paused. "Haven't I seen you before?"

"Never."

"At the country fair? My grandmama used to buy a tonic every year for her swollen ankles. My father warned her that she was only paying for water and weeds, but she didn't listen."

"Did the tonic help her?"

"She thought so."

He smiled at the memory. There wasn't a sparkle of the rake in Camden. His sweetness had ensnared Emily from the afternoon he'd rescued her and her maid from an attack of wasps during a picnic. Emily hadn't really been bothered by the swarm. Neither had Iris. But both lady and servant pretended great horror at the prospect of multiple stings, a near impossibility as both had been bonneted, gowned, and gloved so that it would take a determined warrior of a wasp to find even one vulnerable inch of flesh.

In fact, Emily had caught Iris covertly pulling up handfuls of meadowsweet to *attract* the pests. It was then that Emily realized she had not only crossed the line of infatuation to desperation, but even her maidservant realized time was running out for Emily to find an eligible suitor.

He coughed in obvious embarrassment. "You're so subdued, miss. I hope you don't see anything dire in my future."

"Dire," Emily murmured. "No. I see . . . fire, perhaps even desire."

He drew back in alarm. "Desire?" he said, examining the back of his hand. "I don't mean to offend you, but you require glasses if you're going to do this sort of thing for a living. That's a mole you're looking at. Perhaps you have a remedy for it. My grandmother swore the gypsies could cure any ailment."

"Oh." Guilt tightened the back of her throat. He was kind, and this was devious of her. "It sounds as if you miss her very much."

"I do," he admitted. "She went a little off in the head at the end, but no one ever minded. She used to give us swords to fight the ghosts in her house when we visited."

"What good is a sword against a ghost?"

He gifted her with another of his endearing smiles. "She said the ghosts liked to think they were still alive and capable of a last rousing battle against the enemy. But I shouldn't have to tell you this. You're a gypsy. You have the sight. Perhaps you could put me in contact with her."

Deception, Emily decided at that moment, would never be her forte. She felt so miserable that she would likely confess all before the party ended. Being the gentleman that Camden was, he might forgive her if she didn't take this any further. But how could she admit her feelings for him had driven her to this extreme? Besides, she wanted more than his forgiveness.

She longed to win his heart. She wanted him to steal a kiss. But she doubted the thought of kissing her would ever enter his mind.

Her face burned at the memory of that other kiss. How unfair. Forever after she would hold all kisses to the standard a wicked stranger had set. Then again, a young lady who put herself in her position should have expected a little retribution.

"I can't put you in contact with your grandmother," she said earnestly. "We are under the influence of Venus tonight, so I'm prepared to give romantic and not spiritual advice."

"Well, all right, then." His voice dropped. "There is a lady to whom I am attracted."

Emily stared down at his pale, uncalloused palm. "Who," she inquired without looking up, "is she?"

She studied his palm while waiting for his answer. His hand didn't give her the impression of either strength or implacable will. She hadn't noticed any scars on his knuckles. Nor did she detect the slightest sprinkling of hair on his wrist. She was tempted to ask him what he used to keep his skin in such pallid condition.

She was tempted to—

"She isn't here, of course," he said. "She isn't invited to fancy affairs. I don't think she's even gone to an assembly or leaves her cottage much. She's the new schoolmistress."

"The schoolmistress?" Emily said in shock, almost

giving herself away. "Isn't she as old as—as your grand-mother?"

"Hardly. Yes, she's a few years older than I am, but I don't see why that has to make a difference."

Emily couldn't envision her gallant young gentleman in love with the sourpuss schoolmistress. As far as Emily knew, she rarely lit a candle at night or even planted flowers in her garden.

"Of course, I haven't met her formally yet. I can't think of an excuse to introduce myself. But tell me—do you see Miss Whitmore in my future?"

She swallowed, staring down at the bottle on the floor. She ought to pick it up before he stepped on it. The potion was worthless now, wasted on a man who was off juggling his lovers like a court jester. "I see a woman who is devoted to you, who has admired you in secret but was afraid to show her feelings—"

"That's her," he said excitedly.

"I'm not so sure."

"How do you know?"

"How can she be devoted to you if she has never confessed her heart? If you've never even met her?"

"But I have met her. I mean, I've walked past her three times on the street and wished her a good afternoon."

"But she didn't smile, did she?"

"That's because she's shy and proper," he said, heaving a sigh. "Her shyness makes me want to . . . it makes me want to protect her."

"From you?"

He blinked. "Do you think I've been too forward?"

"I'm astonished she hasn't slapped you yet for a scoundrel."

He gave her a sheepish grin. "I understand. It's probably hopeless. It will infuriate my father if I marry her. She isn't gentry. She has no wealth."

Emily's tolerance for humiliation had reached its limits. The next thing she knew, he would be asking her for a love spell, in which case she was going to run out into the night with whatever scrap of dignity she could salvage.

He said, "All I wanted was some help on how to approach her about a courtship and perhaps to broach the subject with my father."

Emily heard a gust of wind hit the tent, or perhaps Michael had banged his head against the canvas in exasperation. "Sir," she said to Camden, "I am neither the king to elevate her to the peerage nor a bank to lend her a dower."

He frowned, as if the crossness in her voice or the thought of losing Miss Whitmore was more than he could endure.

"Write her a letter," she said in resignation. "Although you must consider that it could ruin your life. Or embarrass your family. But you will not be the first person in love to do so, I assure you."

"Just answer me. Can you tell from my palm if she'd want to marry me? Do your powers suggest I tender a proposal?"

First, she would have to concentrate on his palm and not allow his boyish appeal to distract her. Of course she didn't need palmistry to realize that their lives, their *hands*, were incompatible. The schoolmistress probably wore gloves to stir her tea. Emily's hands, with her tint and scratches from playing with the housekeeper's new kittens, looked like a field laborer's in comparison.

She traced her nail over the cross beneath his index finger. "According to this mark, you are destined for a happy marriage."

"But with her?" he insisted.

"The lines don't go into that much detail." She sighed, suddenly anxious to escape the disappointment she had brought on herself. "I'd have to read the cards, and there are people waiting in the wind—"

Which, right on cue, blew against the sides of the tent and whacked loose the wooden poles stuck in the shallow pits of dirt. The canvas walls sagged inward on Emily and Camden. She lurched to her feet, stumbling over the basket that rested beside her chair.

"Are you all right, miss?" Camden asked, pushing up the poles to little success.

She bent to grasp her basket.

The table pitched forward, cards scattering in the rush of wind that swept around her. She grasped the oil lamp and extinguished the light. If not for the rain in the air, the straw that Michael had laid around the tent might have caught on fire, the perfect denouement to an evening of disaster.

In the wavering shadows she watched Camden throw her an apologetic glance before he hurried outside to his friends. The wind carried dramatic shrieks of dismay into the night. She heard footsteps running across the bridge toward the manor house.

"Ladies," Camden shouted to the gathered crowd, "one at a time, and give a gentleman your hand! We don't wish for this rickety bridge to deposit us in the brook."

She waited another moment and then slipped through the back of the tent, her head bowed.

She wouldn't be missed at the party by anyone except Lucy. No respectable gentleman wanted to dance with a bookish girl whose father drank to excess. Certainly no eligible man desired a wife who challenged the five centuries of solid tradition that made Hatherwood the predictable and uneventful parish that it was.

No one would be overly surprised if Emily found herself in trouble tonight. Her downfall was long overdue. She'd been a person of controversy since she was six, the year before her mother died. The fact that Lady Rowland had encouraged her daughter's love of reading and forays into the woods with her brother to study nature only made Emily appear more unconventional.

"My girl is full of life," the baroness would respond whenever anyone criticized Emily.

"As if her excessive activity were a desirable trait," the village matrons murmured. "Is that why you've never kept a governess longer than four months?"

"They were dismissed for boring her" was her mother's usual answer. "And some of them were, frankly, stupid."

After her mother's death, the villagers stopped pretending to discuss Emily in well-meaning terms and gossiped about her in the market square.

Emily Rowland and her brother have been sighted together in the woods after dark.

Young Mr. Rowland is teaching her to ride—bareback.

Why does the baron allow Emily into his billiards room? Why does he act as if he doesn't know she is hiding inside his carriage when he goes to the tavern? Why doesn't he remarry, for the girl's sake?

All Emily could think was, *Thank goodness Hatherwood never learned who Michael's true father is.*

She felt the start of a reluctant smile.

Sir Angus had paid her more attention tonight than any other man in Hatherwood. Yes, she did realize that scoundrels didn't make reliable husbands. She decided that they gave lovely kisses, though, and should be forgiven a few sins on that account.

Chapter 4

*D*amien Joshua David Boscastle, Viscount Norwood, the first Earl of Shalcross, resisted looking back at the hollow where he and the gypsy wench had crossed words. Fortune-teller, his arse. She hadn't even been able to keep her hands steady as she'd laid out the deck for a reading. She also hadn't been able to hide the intelligence in her eyes or the fact that she was a literate fraud. Perhaps she *was* an actress hired to amuse the guests. And even though other men must find her as appealing as he did, she'd kissed like an innocent.

Only one thing was certain: Damien's kiss had not only disconcerted her, but had also proven that he wasn't as immune to temptation as he liked to think. He hadn't emerged as unscathed from their flirtation as he should have.

He tended to regard all forms of divination as utter rubbish. Perhaps tonight he had thumbed his nose at fate. It wouldn't be the first time, but unless he was careful, it might be the last.

He'd lost twenty minutes in that tent before he realized he'd overspent his stay. And now, only steps away from the shallow crossing at the brook, his skin prickled in warning.

He turned his head, glancing once at the wind-battered tent. As he'd suspected, there wasn't a pony in sight, but there *was* a tall man leaning against a willow tree with a casual demeanor that did not deceive Damien for a moment.

The man was measuring every step Damien made, and while Damien did not acknowledge him, he reached inside his jacket for his gun and walked calmly on until the man began to follow him. Damien had been prepared for possible violence tonight, but not this early on. Had his ruse been uncovered?

"By damn," an incredulous voice said at Damien's shoulder. "That red beard threw me for a moment, ugly beacon that it is. But I've known only one man in my life who had the bollocks not to turn around when he's being followed. I consider myself lucky to have made it this far alive."

Damien did turn then, matching the sardonic voice to a face from his distant past. It was a long-ago friend and trustworthy soldier who had served under him in Spain. He drew his hand from his pocket. "Michael Rowland," he said with a rueful laugh. "Still sneaking up on men and surviving to brag of it. Please don't tell me that you are you are Urania's pony?"

"Urania?"

"She's very pretty," Damien said, grateful again that he had not followed his baser instincts when he'd had the chance. "And unintentionally entertaining. I assume that's the purpose of her presence here. To entertain."

Michael ran his hand through his unruly hair. "It's a long story. I'm only a party to this embarrassment. What are *you* doing here? And in that odd disguise? I didn't recognize you at first."

"It's a longer story. Dear God," Damien said with a laugh, taking in Michael's mop of black curls and garish scarlet cloak that came halfway to his gold-striped trousers. "Why are *you* dressed up like a gypsy vagabond? No one mentioned to me that this was to be a masquerade party."

Michael crossed his arms, looking Damien up and down. The curved silver knife he had pulled from his boot rested against the crook of his elbow. "I'm dressed for a private affair. And you? I hope the red fungus growing from your chin and that girth are not the genuine Boscastle. Is this what wealth has done to the man who slipped unnoticed through a crack in the family door?"

Damien grinned. "I don't have time to explain, but let's just say that I'm on a mission that called for a disguise tonight."

"A mission?" Michael stared across the brook at the candlelit manor house. "At Lord Fletcher's ball? It must be personal."

Damien shook his head, turning in distraction as another gust of wind threatened to tear the tent from its poles. "It isn't."

·Michael stepped out from the shadows of the willow. "I'd offer to help," he said with a glance of resignation at the muffled thud that arose from the tent, "but I've got my hands full for the moment."

Damien looked back at Michael and laughed. "So the fortune-teller is really your—"

"Sister."

"Thank God."

"Excuse me?"

"She mentioned her brother in a threatening manner,

that's all. Of course, I never guessed she meant you. Do me a favor?"

"Name it."

"If you run into me later in the evening or during the next few days, we do not know each other. Obviously my disguise isn't as foolproof as I intended, or you would not have recognized me."

Michael flashed him a grin and slipped his knife back into his boot. "Then again, you and I spent weeks on battle trails together. I saw you unshaven and covered with dust and blood more than once."

"If I play my cards right, no one else will recognize me tonight. And there will be no blood."

A splatter of rain hit Michael's cheek. "Your life is at risk?"

"More than mine, I'm afraid."

A panicked female voice drew the men apart. "Michael! The tent is falling down on my head, and *he's* abandoned me! Hurry! The cards are escaping all over the place, and I can't chase after them and hold off this pole at the same time."

Damien placed his hand on Michael's shoulder. "A sibling in distress. Go. I'm glad to have seen you." And gladder still that he'd found the control to stop at robbing an old friend's sister of a tantalizing kiss.

For an instant Damien envied their game. Surely it involved promises of passion and not political motives that would end in wholesale death if Damien did not remember that he had a previous engagement for the evening.

Soldiers kept one another's secrets. He assumed he wouldn't be blamed for ruining her plans when the wind was really to blame.

He'd been away from England for more than a decade. He had spent years fighting a foreign war for the regular army, and a longer stint in the East India Company, plundering and amassing wealth. He had been contacted by one of his Boscastle cousins and asked if he could locate a missing relative, one whom the family refused to believe was dead.

Why not? He was rich, and the woman he'd intended to marry had betrayed him. He had money in London banks, investments that had prospered him beyond his dreams.

What would it cost him to hunt down young Brandon Boscastle and his friend? Damien had never done a damn thing to help anyone except himself.

So he'd set out for Nepal, and within a month of travel was imprisoned under false charges and cut off from the rest of the world. His only good deed had landed him in hell, where he might well belong. But he'd been determined he wasn't going to stay, especially since he'd found evidence that Brandon and his partner were still alive.

He lifted his face to the wind. Freedom. How good it felt.

Perhaps, in a month or two, after he'd foiled another plot that had nothing to do with sweet liaisons but everything to do with deadly conspiracies, he would cross the fortune-teller's path again and have a chance to take more pleasure in the acquaintance.

Chapter 5

*E*mily listened to Camden's voice fade away, to the feminine giggles and male guffaws that accompanied his escape. Her shoulder ached where the pole had hit her. And yet that was the least of her immediate injuries. Sighing, she resisted the urge to run outside to follow her friends, who would *not* welcome her for a minute if they realized what she had done. Her heart wasn't in attending the party, anyway. She knew she would recover. But not tonight. After all, she had just learned Camden loved another woman. Emily wasn't sure why she didn't feel worse.

Where had Michael disappeared to? She couldn't drag the tent off by herself, but he wasn't anywhere to be seen when she heard Lucy calling her from the bridge.

Cross, her shawl scant protection against the wind, she emerged from the collapsed tent to ask whether Lucy had seen where Michael had gone when the look on her friend's face stopped her. "The reading was a disaster. Please spare me the humiliation of explaining how it went. Camden and I are a lost cause. I hope it rains basins of freezing water on his head. Or on mine. Obviously I need something to awaken me from my dreams."

"Whatever happened here?" Lucy whispered with the wide-eyed shock of a person who had stumbled into a battlefield and not merely across a bridge.

"The wind blew everything over while I was inside. My brother was here one moment; in the next he abandoned me. Have you seen the rogue? Is he flirting with a lady in the garden?"

Lucy glanced over her shoulder. "He was talking to a gentleman I'd never met before. I didn't want to interrupt and get us all in trouble, but I'm afraid it's too late. Your father is at the party, Emily. He was looking for you and Michael everywhere. He's swilling champagne like water, and even asking the footmen if you'd been seen."

"You didn't tell him anything?"

"I raced off across the ballroom before he could spot me. I heard him questioning my father, and he's disappeared, too. There's something unusual about this evening, Emily, and I am not referring to our innocent deception."

"The stars are misaligned tonight."

Lucy's voice lowered to a quaver. "My father's new political allies are beginning frighten me."

"All political men are frightening." Emily shrugged, distracted as the wind whisked a tarot card through the grass and into the brook. "But why are they here tonight?" Dragging Lucy by the hand, she slipped down the embankment to catch the fleeting card. It sailed past her reach, the taunting image suspended in a cold moonbeam.

Passion

She would recover that card if it took an hour. It *meant* something, although exactly what was no longer clear. It could turn out to be a memento of the only kiss she would ever know. She released Lucy's hand and snagged the corner of the card. Oh—and there, in an updraft, went Virtue.

She chased that one until she lost sight of it. Whether it was worth the price of her wet skirt and stockings, only Michael could decree.

She stood, at least twenty cards collected in her basket, but double that number escaping like prisoners determined to inflict the acts of fate to which they had been assigned. "I promised my brother I would return every single one of these cards intact."

Lucy stared as one soared over her head. "Some of them are already sailing downstream. There are a few flying like butterflies toward the house. They look ever so enchanting. The guests are going to think we had trained cards unleashed for their entertainment. They're like party favors. Besides, Michael *will* forgive you. Your father won't."

The Past flew beyond her grasp. She watched it go with no regrets; she had the most unexciting life in the annals of English history. But along with it went its reverse, the Future. And that indicated that Emily might be trapped in the tumultuous present she had created, a fate she was not about to settle for.

Another card tangled in her hair. Lucy plucked it free, her expression amused as she lifted it into the moonlight. "What is it?" Emily asked impatiently.

"'Secrets.'"

Emily shrugged, snagged the card, and tucked it securely in her basket.

"You were looking at it upside down."

"It still reads 'Secrets,' even in French."

"For all the good it does."

"I can't argue that." Emily sighed in surrender. "Is Iris still waiting for me at the tower?"

"I assume so. Emily, listen to me. I'll walk you there in case anyone approaches you, and then I'm rushing back to the party. What shall I tell your father if he confronts me? I can't hide from him all night. I thought you said he had passed out before you left your house."

"I thought he had. Tell him the truth—that I was here and meant to attend the ball but felt unwell. Tell him Michael took me home."

"But what if he encounters Michael first?"

"Michael will—"

"Who is it I have to encounter now?" Michael said, materializing from the other side of the bridge.

Emily wheeled around, her basket knocking her brother on the hand. "I've gathered up half of the cards, but the others escaped. Please don't hate me. It was out of my control. Lucky seven turned out to be a rogue."

"Don't go on like a goose," he said, backing away to dismantle what remained of the tent in quick, confident motions, as if he could do so in his sleep. Perhaps he had at war. "Why are you in the water?"

"I'm gathering up all the cards."

"Never mind the cards." He took a long look at her. "Are you all right?"

She bit her lip. "Honestly? My heart is shattered. Please don't make me talk about it, or I'll cry, and then the dye will wash off my skin if the rain doesn't do it. I spilled the potion on the wrong man. Thank goodness it was only a few drops. It felt peculiar. The flush still hasn't gone away—"

He was staring at her with a bewildered expression that touched a place inside her that felt as tender as a fresh wound. "I'm asking about the tent, actually. Did any of the poles hit you on the head when it collapsed?"

"No."

"Go with Lucy, then. I'll hide the tent in the bog in the woods."

"The chairs and tables need to be returned to the house."

"Never mind the furniture," Lucy said, shivering in her thin green silk gown. "Nobody will ever miss it."

"I'll meet you and Iris in the woods behind the tower with the horses, as we planned," Michael said, rolling the canvas onto the poles.

"If you see Father first—"

"I'll deal with him, Emily. You stood up for me often enough in the past."

She nodded uncertainly, letting Lucy drag her to the bridge.

"Camden is a horse's bum," he said under his breath. "And that's an insult to the horse."

Chapter 6

"The night isn't over yet," Lucy said with a wan smile of encouragement. "You could still find true love."

"Or utter disgrace."

Lucy turned resolutely. "That's it. I am going to take you to the tower to ensure that does not occur."

"I don't know what I would do without you. You are a true friend."

"So are you. Let's make a dash for it, shall we?"

She ran behind Lucy until the bulky tower loomed in view. The ivy that draped its wall shone like dull emeralds in the moonlight.

Emily had always said that her friend Lucy could have made a career in espionage, based on her experience with manipulating love matches between unsuspecting couples with the subterfuge of a master spy. Lucy was the one who had sparked the romance between her father and her stepmother. Lucy had also convinced Cook that the head footman in her father's house needed her care more than the household needed boiled tongue for breakfast every morning.

And for months Lucy had volunteered her services to

make Camden realize that he loved Emily. She had invited Camden to every tea party that her stepmother gave, and Emily had always lurked in the background. Tonight was the culmination of Lucy's dedicated work on her behalf.

"He appears to have his mind made up," Emily explained as she and Lucy paused, panting, beneath the shadows of the tower that sat isolated from the rest of the house.

"That's nonsense."

"That he has a mind?"

"That it can't be changed," Lucy said, looking back at the moonlit walkway. "There are people wandering about again now that it isn't sprinkling. You'll have to go up the stairs and through the trapdoor to fetch your clothes. I hope Iris is still waiting."

Emily stared up at the thick ivy vines that embraced the tower to the arched window aperture. "Oh, no. Please tell me I'm seeing things. I hope that isn't smoke wafting out the tower window."

Lucy turned, colliding against Emily in breathless horror. "Is it possible," she whispered as she looked up to follow Emily's gaze, "for two people to imagine the same thing at once?"

"Only if they're a pair of idiots like us. You swore that nobody ever visited the tower. You swore it was safe."

"Perhaps it's your maid," Lucy said. "She might have gotten worried that you'd lost your way and couldn't find the tower in the dark, where you'd hidden your clothes. She knew it would be late and you'd be anxious that no one recognize you in your gypsy costume."

The answer made sense, but Emily did not believe it for a moment. "Iris would never light a candle to draw attention to our hiding place. I still say there's something wrong."

Lucy's forehead creased in lines of strain. "What if my father is committing adultery behind Diana's back? What if he's hosting a gambling party at which he could lose huge sums?"

Emily reached back to grasp Lucy's hand. "Did you see that?"

"See what?" Lucy asked, putting her arm protectively around Emily's waist.

"I counted five tiny red balls of light."

"Rats?" Lucy guessed, shuddering.

"I was thinking more of cigars."

"That leaves out Iris," Lucy whispered. "But you're right. There does appear to be some sort of meeting taking place. Why on earth would anyone choose such a lonely place?"

"For the same reason I did," Emily retorted. "So they could plan in private and not be caught."

"How are you going to fetch your clothes without any of them seeing you? The trapdoor is right under the table. You can't expect to pop up like a jack-in-the-box, race across the floor without a 'pardon me,' and not be seen."

Emily pondered this problem. "I could climb the ivy at the back where it's tough and hasn't been trimmed."

"Except that there isn't a window at the back of the tower."

"Then I'll have to crawl over the wall and wait until whoever is there leaves. I hope Iris found a safe place to hide. Maybe she's waiting for me in the woods or in the stairwell."

"I think I'd be more afraid of your father than I would

of a group of strangers," Lucy said, biting the knuckle of her glove. "After all, *my* father must have offered to let them meet here."

"And I'd be willing to wager that one of them sells black sheep," Emily said, thinking of the Scottish merchant who had flustered her in the tent. Could he be part of this mysterious group of gentlemen? "Aberdeen is a long way to come to meet in a darkened tower. Whatever they're up to can't be any good. I wonder if they are spies."

"But we're at peace with France."

"What could a man possibly spy on from a secluded tower this late at night?" Emily murmured.

"Perhaps they're a bird-watching society," Lucy said dubiously

"And which birds would they be watching in the dark? Owls? You can't believe that any sensible gentleman would travel to Hatherwood to catch a glimpse of an ordinary barn owl."

"Maybe they're smugglers," Lucy said. "There are plenty of waterways leading in and out of the village. Do you think they might be smuggling stolen sheep?"

"That would be rather awkward, wouldn't it? I imagine we'd have heard a bleat or two by now."

"Well, I don't see any lurid shadows engaged in decadent acts or hear cries of help from women held there against their will," Lucy said.

"It's most likely some manner of business meeting," Emily said after a moment.

"Which could have been held in any of several rooms inside the manor proper," Lucy pointed out.

"Unless your stepmama said that this was to be a party for entertainment only, and business must be conducted away from the other guests."

"That's probably what it is," Lucy said in relief. "She and Papa have been quarreling a lot lately over the associates he's brought home. Diana said they seem rather intense and not always polite."

Emily frowned. She wished her father would find a business interest to fill his hours instead of drinking himself to death. If he'd had an occupation, their family might have traveled and broadened their circle of friends. "I'm going to take my chances on the trapdoor," she said decisively. "At least I might find Iris. And who knows? She might already have my clothes and be waiting for us to meet Michael in the woods."

Lucy looked back at the manor. "I'll hold your father off as long as I can. You'd best make it home before he does."

"Don't worry. I'll be washed and reading a book like a perfectly bored young lady when he sees me again. He'll never dream I left the house. And tomorrow, well, when I wake up I'll have a cry, but I won't mope forever."

"It was worth a try," Lucy said, backing away in hesitation. "We could—"

"No. We can't. But thank you. Camden wasn't meant to be mine. And maybe that's for the best. If he knew what I'd done tonight, he would never talk to me again. Deceit is not the best way to spark a love match."

"Probably not."

"Go, Lucy. I'll be fine. Even if I can't fetch my clothes, I have to get Iris. This was so much easier when it was light. It's only the dark that gives the tower that haunted look."

"If the tower is haunted, it would only be my mother," Lucy said, sighing. "And she would never hurt you."

*   *   *

The mansion had been built on the grounds of a grand but dilapidated Jacobean estate that the first Lady Fletcher had inherited but despised. When she married Lord Fletcher, he had rebuilt it to please his delicate wife, whose dark moods had seemed to be aggravated by the original architecture.

She had demanded an elegant tower instead of the bulky pepperpots that dominated the back roof of the estate.

Years earlier Lady Fletcher had spent most of her days in the east tower, mourning the loss of Lucy's younger brother, who had been killed by a constable during a street riot over the rising price of food. The magistrate insisted it had been an accident. Lady Fletcher refused to believe that and sank into a melancholy.

Even during their earliest years of friendship, Lucy had managed to explain it all in a simple, if distressful, way.

"Mama will kill herself if Papa won't build her a tower of her own."

"Why?" Emily had asked, wondering if the answer would help her to understand the reason her own mother had died prematurely, certainly not of a suicide, but of a languishing spirit. "Why would a tower make her happy?"

In the end the tower had not made Lord Fletcher's first wife happy, and as the years passed, Emily grew to realize that grief over losing both his wife and son had turned him bitter inside.

Emily felt a newfound pang of empathy for him. She had lost her belief in true love, too.

Chapter 7

She squeezed under the drapery of ivy and pried open the iron-barred door to the stairwell, hoping the faint squeak it gave did not carry. She heard the rumble of unfamiliar male voices from the room above. The aroma of tobacco drifted through the trapdoor into the dankness of the space below. *So much for Lucy's rats.* She remembered to avoid the cobwebbed tangle of old leaves and crumbled mortar on the lowest step. Then something shuffled against the stone. She braced herself.

In disbelief she looked up and recognized the two figures on the steps above her. One was the Scottish merchant who had impertinently kissed her while the wind rose outside her foolish tent. Now, as if to rub salt in the wound he had inflicted, he was holding her maid, Iris, in his arms—

No. He was holding one hand over Iris's mouth to silence her; his other arm anchored tightly around her torso. "This is your mistress?" he whispered in Iris's ear. "Michael's sister?"

Iris nodded, her green eyes filled with glassy tears.

Emily could have committed murder in that moment. "Let her go, please."

"Be quiet," he hissed at Emily. "If those men up there suspect you have heard one word of their conversation, you will not leave this tower alive."

The truth that glittered in his eyes stilled her even as she wondered who this handsome fraud thought he was to terrify her maid and hiss dire warnings about her death in Emily's face. After kissing her, no less.

She opened her mouth. "I—"

He slid down the steps, one hand still holding Iris immobile, the other sliding up Emily's shoulder to her chin. He pressed his cheek to hers. Her heart beat so hard in her throat that she would have cried out if she thought it would help. He gave her no choice but to relinquish her control to his.

This wasn't the same man who had charmed and provoked her such a short time ago. "I beg of you," he whispered, "do not scream."

Footsteps punctuated the ensuing silence.

"The greatest challenge," a man said from the tower room above, "is to murder Deptford and make it look like an accident. The more witnesses, the better."

Emily could not make out the reply to this statement. Her captor's body pinned her to the stairwell wall. She held her breath and let her shoulders slump, closing her eyes until darkness beckoned.

"What is the matter?" the Scotsman whispered urgently.

"I'm trying to faint," she whispered back.

"How the devil do you do that?"

"Close your eyes very tightly. Hold your breath until you know you are about to die. Then submit to a darkness so complete that no one can find you."

He swore softly, considerate soul that he was. "Are

you prone to fainting spells? Do you have a medical ailment?"

"I have never swooned in my life."

"Don't start now, darling." He placed his fingers to the erratic pulse in her throat. "Breathe. Be still. Listen to me. It is so important that you trust me now. Michael trusts me. Do not panic."

Of course she would not panic. Had she gone hysterical when he'd kissed her? Imminent death was no reason to lose one's head.

She glanced at Iris, who nodded in complicity, as if anything he'd said made the least bit of sense. Michael. He knew her brother's name. That meant something.

His low voice caressed her cheek. "If any of the men in the tower realize you have been here, they will not hesitate to kill you."

"But I—"

"Quiet. It is enough that you *might* have overheard their plans. I want you to leave this estate, and after that you must not return or be spotted in the vicinity for at least a month. Is it possible to make your people understand that they must not send the two of you out again?"

It was more than a possibility. It was an absolute. Her father was the only person Emily and her maid would have to plead understanding from tonight. Clearly Sir Angus assumed she belonged to the band of gypsies who had left the area a fortnight ago. Michael had not given her identity away.

"Listen to me carefully." His voice heightened Emily's anxiety even as she clung to his every word. "I am going upstairs to the meeting. Let four minutes pass. No more. No less. Promise me you will keep count."

Emily nodded again, too numb to offer another response.

He frowned at Iris, who was stuffing strands of her light hair back under her cap. "You, Goldilocks, did you hear what I just said? No, don't answer. I'll tap my foot twice against the trapdoor. That will be your signal that it is safe to flee. Now, ladies, if you will excuse me, I must leave your company. I strongly suggest that you forget this night ever happened."

Emily, her face lifted, took Iris's hand and drew her down the steps. "How do we know you aren't their ringleader?"

He shrugged. "There is no time for either of us to demand letters of character. You read my fate earlier. Now I shall determine yours."

Emily dabbed a tear from Iris's cheek with her knuckle. "There's only one flaw in your plan," she whispered.

Exasperation flared in his eyes. "What?"

"I left a red satin ball gown in the corner of the tower, and my companion's clothes are folded underneath it."

He stared past her. "I assume the dress is stolen or is part of some other scheme of yours to deceive. You did not leave anything *with* the gown that would identify you?"

Emily felt truly light-headed then. "Only a letter." To Camden, confessing her affections. "With my signature on it."

"My God. Now I am to hide women's clothing for the good of— Well, so be it."

"How will we know if something goes wrong with your plan?" Emily whispered. "What if one of those men catches you with a lady's ball gown and thinks you're up to no good?"

A beguiling smile ghosted his face, only to be followed by an answer that elicited gasps from both Emily and her maid. "You will hear a gunshot. Correction: you will hear several gunshots."

"And what are we supposed to do then?" Emily asked in an unsteady whisper.

"Run as fast as you can for cover. Stay in the shadows, if possible, until you find your brother, a footman, anyone. Do whatever you would have done had you never met me."

Chapter 8

$\mathcal{D}$amien would have burst into laughter at the challenging look in the young gypsy's eyes if he did not understand the remorseless instincts of the seven men—three former army officers, a farmer, two noblemen, and a journalist with a brilliant mind and a black heart—assembled in the tower chamber. Each man either held a grudge against the Crown or had deluded himself into believing that anarchy and upheaval served some greater good. Personally Damien thought all but three of them to be irrevocably deranged. Damien did not for a moment believe that their grievances justified the killing of innocents in the street.

He pushed open the trapdoor with one arm and waved his other arm over his head in a prearranged signal to indicate that the arsenal aimed at his forehead should not be put to use. "It is Sir Angus," one of the conspirators muttered, "and high time, too. Where the devil have you been?"

All but one of the various firearms disappeared inside greatcoats and evening jackets. The pen in the journalist's hand remained poised above the table. Damien climbed into the tower with a sheepish grin, allowing the trapdoor to thud with a clatter that made several men seated around the oaken table cringe at his apparent disregard for secrecy. He could almost hear the women underneath the room cursing at the thunderous noise.

Still, to have exhibited tender manners at this point would have only awakened suspicion. The clatter, he suspected, would give the gypsy woman and her companion a chance to breathe and stretch their muscles.

These men did not even trust their own mothers. As a relative newcomer to their conspiracy, "Sir Angus" must measure his every step.

"My apologies, gentlemen. The damned thing slipped."

"Where the hell have you been?" demanded the farmer, in his white hat and high-topped boots.

Damien stroked his mustache. His lips itched under the annoying accessory. He wondered if he'd rubbed any of that caustic potion on his mouth without thinking.

"Waylaid by a maid?" guessed the impoverished and clearly inebriated Lord Brewster of Shropshire.

Damien pulled a chair from the table to the corner, where a glimmer of crimson satin peeked out from beneath a moth-eaten blanket. A letter. A gypsy who made reference to *Macbeth* and wrote letters? His instincts argued again that she was more than she appeared to be.

"Your silence condemns you," Lord Ardbury said with disdain. "Could you not control yourself when everything we have planned is at stake?"

"There's more to it than that," Damien said, his demeanor deliberately unapologetic. "One of us should take measure of our surroundings in the event of discovery."

The former army major at the table grunted. "It was a sacrifice, I assume, to sleep with a woman on our behalf? I hope you didn't strain your back too much for all the actual riding you'll need to do soon."

"Did I admit that I slept with anyone?"

"Sit down, Sir Angus," the journalist said, glancing up from the map he had drawn of contingent forces across England where a slew of riots were to occur.

Anarchists.

Damien had intended to return to London to reunite with his family; instead, the moment he set foot on British soil he had been asked by a high-ranking family member in the Home Office to become involved in a countrywide conspiracy.

"I prefer to stand with my eye to the window," he said. "I remind you that we are purportedly enjoying a country house party. A guest could wander this way at any time."

Lord Ardbury nodded in reluctant agreement. "Lord Fletcher was to make sure that did not happen. Where is the man, anyway? Did he indicate to you at the party that he might wish to become one of us?"

"He gave me the impression that he has no idea of our true intentions," Damien said. "And, in my opinion, he is not reliable enough to even consider."

"What do you mean?"

"From what I learned tonight, he isn't the one who held a grudge against the government. It was his first wife, and she wanted revenge for her son's death. He built this tower to ease her grief. I don't believe he has the spine to help us."

Chapter 9

*E*mily nudged Iris from her reverie, whispering. "It's been four minutes, and I heard two taps. Are you ready?"

Iris gave a firm nod, and they turned together to descend to the door, Emily praying it wouldn't creak and betray their presence.

"It's stuck," Iris whispered, pushing her shoulder against the iron-barred oak. She shook her head, frantic, as Emily lowered her basket to join in the effort.

It had to open. For several moments Emily struggled against the panic she had promised to fight, terrified of the airless confinement, of being caught by the radicals in the tower. God help the devil who had braved their revenge to warn her. He had entrusted an unknown woman with knowledge that would endanger many lives if she did not keep his secret. And she had trusted him, neither one of them having much choice in the matter.

The heavy door opened with a force that knocked it against the stone wall. The echo resonated in the stairwell. Emily heard the clatter of heavy boots above the trapdoor. There was no time to think. She picked up her basket, took Iris's hand, and plunged into the evening dark.

The seven conspirators at the table froze in the aftermath of the reverberation. Damien had returned to his chair. Attuned to the slightest noise from below, he doubted he would have reached the trapdoor again before the others and made no effort to try. With everyone diverted, he reached into the corner, felt for the hidden letter, and tucked it inside his shirt. Then he withdrew his pistol from his waistcoat and aimed it at the bolt that lifted open the trap.

"Stay here," he ordered the other men in the room. "I will take care of this. I have already been seen about the estate. I won't raise the suspicions that rest of you will."

Lord Ardbury had removed his own gun from beneath his greatcoat. He glanced at the farmer who had reached the trap before Damien took a step. "Go down as fast as you can, Weltry. Do not let whoever that was escape."

"What if it was Lord Fletcher?" Major Buckland asked, his pigeon-chested figure stretching over the table.

"Then he was spying on us and has written his own death warrant."

The journalist rose from the table and pushed aside the chair that Damien had drawn to the window. "I think I see two people running for the woods."

"Find them," Ardbury said, his voice fading as Damien drew the trap bolt and descended into the stairwell. "Give chase, or all we have planned is lost."

Emily practically threw herself at the slight figure hurrying along the secluded walkway to the house. "Lucy!

Lucy, help us. Hide us. Something horrible has happened."

Lucy took one look at them and reached out a hand to calm a case of what Emily realized must appear to be unwarranted hysterics. "What is it? You couldn't find your clothes? It is nothing. I have more ball gowns than I could ever wear. It is your father we—"

"There are men in the tower." Emily paused to draw a breath. "Diana's fears about your father were justified."

"Who are we running from?" Lucy asked in confusion, letting Emily sweep her toward the verge of the encroaching woods. "If—" She fell silent, as if entranced, and stared over her shoulder. "That must be one of them now. He looks very intimidating, I must say, and I believe he saw us—" She broke off to catch her breath. "Wasn't he the man talking earlier to Michael? Emily, hide with Iris in the trees. Let me run back to the house."

"We stumbled upon traitors who think that two gypsy women overheard their plot. They're going to hunt us down. We need a distraction. Can you do something to divert their attention without endangering yourself? And don't repeat what I told you to anyone but Diana."

"But your father—"

"Assuming I am still alive in the morning, I'll try to explain what happened."

Chapter 10

$\mathcal{B}$y the time the two women had vanished into the stygian grove that bordered the manor, Damien spotted several couples strolling along the path, presumably in search of a private spot for a tryst. All, he assumed, had been cautioned by Lord Fletcher against attempting to use the tower for romantic purposes.

He noticed a tall man striding toward him, clearly unmindful of the guests he brushed to the side of the walk. It was Michael, and his grim expression did not bode well for a furtive encounter.

"What happened to my sister and Iris?" he asked without preamble.

Damien did not stop or give any indication that he recognized Michael. He had seen Ardbury standing in the tower window. It would be difficult for Damien to explain how he had become well enough acquainted with a Rom to pause for a chat during a crisis.

"In the woods," he said without breaking his stride. "We are being watched. Your sister's life is in jeopardy. Find her before someone else does. We should not be seen together."

*   *   *

Michael disappeared with a swiftness that Damien admired. He heard Weltry clumping up in the path in his heavy boots, eager to be the one to find the gypsies detested by farmers for unlawful poaching. He glanced once at Damien before slowing to approach the path to the woods.

"What is it?" Damien shouted, appearing to join the pursuit. "Did you see anyone?"

The farmer looked back at him in suspicion. "You did not? There were two women, as far as I could tell."

"I doubt that a pair of females at a party are a threat to our cause."

"Everyone is a threat. A careless word could brand us all as traitors."

"True," Damien said, his muscles tensing beneath the weight of his disguise. The jacket felt as if it had been filled with stones. The longer he delayed Weltry, the better chance that Michael's sister and her companion could escape. Were they well acquainted with the woods? It seemed likely that young women who tricked others for a living would know where to hide in the event of trouble.

"I'm going after them," Weltry said.

"Don't be a fool. In those old breeches and boots you look neither like a guest nor a servant. I say we return to the tower and organize a discreet search. You must remember that there is a party in progress and we can't afford to attract attention."

The farmer turned with a final look into the trees. Damien did not deceive himself into thinking that the two women would be safe from discovery because of his decree. But he had bought a little time for them to escape.

"Sir! Sir!" a male voice shouted in his direction.

The figure hurtling toward Damien wore the frocked coat of a footman.

"Have you seen them?"

"What is the matter?" Damien asked.

"Lady Fletcher and her daughter have just discovered that the house has been robbed by gypsies. Several valuable pieces of jewelry are missing from their rooms, including the sapphire necklace that belonged to Lady Fletcher's mother. Have you noticed any vagabonds, sir?"

Damien frowned. "I visited the fortune-telling tent earlier. I would start by searching there before running willy-nilly in the night."

"The tent is gone, sir."

"Gone?" He suppressed a grin of admiration for what was no doubt Michael's handiwork.

"Vanished as if it never were. There's not a trace that it ever existed."

If Michael could make an entire tent disappear, he could certainly find a way to hide his sister.

The footman muttered an apology for his abruptness before he excused himself. Damien was no longer paying attention. A rectangular white-edged object with an intriguing design had caught his notice. He placed his boot over the card and waited for Farmer Weltry to look away before picking it up and slipping inside his thickly padded shirt.

Urania had left another calling card—*Mariage*. He

shook his head and turned to walk back to the tower to report to Lord Ardbury. She wasn't going to survive long enough to predict anyone's wedding if she left a trail like this to follow.

Emily and Iris knew every bridle path and secret route through the woods, having traversed them with Michael for years. However, neither Emily nor her maid wished to escape without Michael's company as protection. The dense thicket would serve as a hiding place for only so long.

"I want to go home," Iris whispered. "I hate the dark. I hate the rustling I just heard behind me. And right now I even hate—"

"Iris, please. We have to wait for Michael."

"All night?"

"He will not be all night. You know we can depend on Michael."

"And the Scotsman? He acted as if he knew you, miss. Is he a man to be trusted? How could you have met him and I not hear of it?"

Emily wavered. "I hope we never see him again. From what I can gather, his only valid credentials are that he and Michael are known to each other from their military days."

"Mr. Rowland is a good judge of character," Iris said after a moment.

Emily heaved a sigh. "Yes. But I'm not. I made a mortifying misjudgment tonight, and it has brought me nothing but disaster."

Iris stared at her in sympathy. "It didn't go well with Mr. Jackson?"

"He's in love with the new schoolmistress."

"Her with the face that could curdle mother's milk?" Iris said in shock.

Emily laughed reluctantly. "I think he might want a woman to take care of him."

"Well, that would not be you, miss," Iris said pragmatically. "You can't even take care of yourself."

Chapter 11

When Damien returned to the tower, he answered Ardbury's interrogation as dispassionately as he could. "I took refuge in her tent to avoid a guest at the party I did not wish to meet. The fortune-teller had black curly hair held back in a blue headband. Her skin was the color of light tea. She had a basket at her side. And there was some nostrum on the table that she knocked over."

"She robbed the house?" the journalist asked for the third time.

Damien shrugged. "So I was told. For all I know she may have robbed the guests who came to her tent to have their fortunes told." He slipped his hand inside his vest. "My watch is still here. She is obviously not a professional."

"You should have done us a favor and taken her to the brook to make sure she would never remember your face again," Lord Ardbury said.

"The authorities aren't going to care about anything except that she robbed the wealthy citizens of the parish," Damien replied. "It would astonish me if she heard anything incriminating or that she possessed the wherewithal to turn evidence against us."

He threw Damien a thunderous look. "She overheard enough to have us all dancing in air."

"One of us needs to go after her," the major, seated at the table, said. "Angus, you had the closest look. Search for her as you would one of your lost sheep."

"The rest of us will be on the lookout in the other directions of the compass, in the village outskirts, and away from the party," Ardbury said. "It can't be that hard to find two gypsy maidens."

The journalist laid down his pen. "I have made a sketch based on Angus's description. Perhaps, Lord Ardbury, you can ask another guest for more details."

"We have this." Lord Ardbury reached beneath his chair and lifted the card that had apparently blown across the floor when the trapdoor opened. "What does it signify?" he asked, flicking it in the air.

Damien's expression did not change as he caught the card in his left hand. "It is written in French and English. Four Hearts. I've seen a few suits like this in my travels. I believe it was part of an old court game played in France. The original cards came from Egypt, as I recall."

"How did it get in here? If the gypsies had only theft in mind, what lured them to the tower?"

Damien shrugged. "Perhaps they hoped to hide themselves or their loot. As to this card, it is used for divination and in private parlors. Some members of the royal family are said to request a secret reading before they make any important decisions."

"Divination." Ardbury drew on his cigar. "One of us needs to divine whether the fortune-teller was invited here tonight or invited herself. If Fletcher paid her to entertain, she should not be difficult to trace."

"I am not returning to the party," Damien said, resisting the impulse to make sure the clothing was still covered. He had the signed letter and another card in his possession. That was enough.

The farmer surged to his feet, moving to the window at some noise outside before Damien could intercept him. "Shit and damn," he said. "It's only another couple from the party. Sooner or later a pair of lovers are bound to wander up here for privacy."

Ardbury studied him through a bank of smoke. "Lord Brewster, Major, I will give Fletcher your regrets. The rest of you know what has to be done. Mr. Dinsmore, you will notify our contacts and send out our messengers. Now find those women before Viscount Deptford's assassination, Angus."

In one moment Michael appeared on his gelding and ordered Iris to mount behind him. In the next Sir Angus trotted his horse to the thicket from which Emily had emerged. He spoke to her in a tone that forbade resistance.

"Give me your hand."

She looked up, dumbfounded, into his bearded face. Her brother and Iris had vanished without a word into the woods. Why had Michael abandoned her to this man of dubious credentials?

And why was he staring down at her again as if he realized something was off? Had he noticed the bare patch on the scalp of her wig? No—he shook his head in obvious exasperation at her refusal to obey. "It is an inconvenient time for an explanation." He swung around in the saddle, offering her his hand with impatience. "You can either trust me or meet the men in the tower."

She wavered another moment before she lifted her

hand to his. There was no other choice. "Where are we going?"

"To your encampment. It must be hidden somewhere in these woods."

"My what?"

"Your encampment. Your camp. Isn't that what your people call the place where they park their wagons while plying their trades? Or would you rather admit the truth now and tell me who you really are?" he inquired, his voice soft and yet underlaid with iron. "I can find out myself. But as a courtesy I'd prefer you spare me the time and be honest."

"I can't," she said in hesitation. "I'd get into so much trouble."

"You're in trouble now, my darling."

"Are you going to take advantage of my innocence on the back of a horse?"

He laughed. "It hadn't entered my mind—the part about the back of a horse."

"Oh. And the other part?"

His deep laughter was an alluring sound in the dark. "It entered my mind, yes."

"I wanted to dance tonight," she said ruefully. "I wanted to drink champagne and twirl around in—" She broke off. Camden was banished from her dreams.

"In . . . ?" he prompted.

"The arms of a handsome gentleman who did not see me as an undesirable."

"You enjoyed my kiss. Don't deny it. You don't need to admit it, either. I'm not trying to put you in an embarrassing position. I enjoyed it, too."

He was so full of himself that she couldn't help laughing. "I am accustomed to embarrassment."

"But not kissing?"

"And I've never been in the position of having to flee for my life."

He breathed a sigh into her hair. She was terrified he would notice it was a wig. "I'm sorry," he said at last.

"For what?"

"Not for the kiss. I'd have asked for more at another time. I'm sorry that you're no longer safe because of our association."

"I thought England was at peace with her enemies."

"But not within her own lands."

"Will you send me a wool shawl when you go home?" she asked quietly. "Something to remember you by?"

He frowned. "Why on— Oh, of course. A brightly patterned paisley?"

"Oh no. That would look awful with my hair."

He was silent. She knew he was thinking about what she had said. "You aren't a gypsy, are you?" he said at length.

"All gypsies don't have to act and look a certain way."

He nodded, considering her confession. "You wanted romance and—let me guess—it had not come into your life, so you thought to give it a push."

"More or less," Emily said, lapsing into silence.

"Which path should I take here?" he asked, his rough voice giving her a jolt. "Gather up your thoughts, girl. My associates have already put together a description of you. Believe me, you have no desire to meet one of them in these dark woods. Nor do I."

"I had no desire for any of this."

"Young fortune-tellers who prey on the romantic delusions of others take their chances, don't they?"

"Go to the left, you odious wool vendor. Follow the

moonlight and guide the horse with care. And I've taken all the chances tonight that I had on my list for eternity." She glanced back at him, wondering whether it was her imagination or whether his left shoulder seemed narrower than the other. "Riding to who knows where with you was *not* one of them."

"A decent fortune-teller would have seen this coming."

She shook her head. "I didn't need to look at the cards to know I would have been better off had we not met."

"You feel quite sorry for yourself, don't you?"

"Yes," she said. "I do."

"Why?" His voice was museful.

"Because instead of dancing in a red ball gown with the gentleman of my dreams, I'm slung over the horse of a dangerous stranger who just witnessed, if not accelerated, my complete social decline. It would be easier for me to climb the back of the tower than out of the mess I've made."

His hand brushed the cusp of her cleavage. An accident, she was sure, but it put her on the defense. "You aren't dropping any more of those accursed cards, are you?" he asked dourly.

"What if I am?"

"Do you not understand me? Your life is as nothing to those men."

The horse walked slowly past a landmark that Emily recognized as a deserted vixen's den. The Scotsman hooked his arm around her ribs, an awkward captivity that challenged her concentration. She gripped the basket to her lap.

"I see a barricade of blasted tree stumps ahead," he said, slowing his mount.

"Veer around the blackest end of the last trunk. I wish I had gone with my brother. I resent him for rescuing Iris and not me as well."

"You'll be safe soon," he said distractedly.

But was she safe now, with him?

"Oh no!" She wriggled from his loose grasp to the ground, aware he had drawn a gun. "I've lost another card."

"For God's sake." He dropped to his feet beside her. "You do realize you've left a trail for the entire village to trace?"

"I've got it now. Do you have to raise your voice?"

"I am not raising my voice."

She hooked the basket over her arm, reached up to grasp the pommel, and lifted her foot to the stirrup. He gave her an undignified boost in the behind, which she refused to acknowledge. He mounted from the other side, wasting no further time arguing with her. Uncomfortable and cold, she kept one eye on the basket and the other on the path for guideposts.

Her half boot slid off her heel and sat dangling on her toe until it fell in the dirt. "Sir Angus," she whispered in hesitation, afraid of his anger.

He dismounted, sighing, and wedged the boot tightly back on her foot. He vaulted up behind her before she could explain that the boot could fall off again. She had borrowed the pair from Lucy, and she might be wiser removing them for the duration of the ride. But Sir Angus didn't appear in the mood to make any concessions for fashion, so she refrained from comment. Until the other boot came off.

"Heaven help me," he muttered. "What is this preoccupation you have for shedding various belongings at the most dangerous moment of your life? A ball gown, a deck of cards. Anything else?"

She wanted to answer, *Yes. This hideous wig. It's going to droop to the side of my head at any moment.* But again she managed to hold her tongue, slipping the boots back on in reflective silence.

He grunted as he settled back in the saddle. "Under normal circumstances I would encourage you to disrobe to your heart's content."

"Would you?" she said, not at all surprised.

He laughed. "Shameful, isn't it? I'm not impartial to a beautiful woman, dishonest though she might be."

A beautiful woman. Was that what he said? Ordinary Emily Rowland, a beauty? *Lies must come as second nature to a spy,* she thought.

Besides, she was the one who should feel ashamed instead of oddly flattered. But, then, neither of them had started out on the right foot. Or feet. One of her boots had fallen off again, and she knew he'd noticed. She shivered under her shawl as he jumped from the horse, this time removing both her shoes and handing them to her before he remounted. "I am sorry," she said. "I suppose you could accuse me of ruining your plans, too. It wasn't on purpose. I didn't set out to deceive you."

He blew out a breath. "What did your scheme involve, anyway? It had to be more than romance. Plain jewelry theft? A few coins from a gullible guest? You didn't try to rob me. Are there others in your group? I cannot believe that Michael would be a party to such a low-class crime. What did you hope to gain tonight?"

She decided to ignore his questions. His mind was sharp enough that eventually he would find the answers he sought without her help. "Stop a moment, Sir Angus," she said, gesturing to a pattern on the path of twigs around the crop of toadstools. "Do you see that signpost?"

"What signpost?"

"Are you telling me that with your highly trained senses you cannot see what is arranged around those toadstools?"

"The toadstools? Oh yes. It's obvious. How could I have missed them? Surely they were there last night when I pranced naked through these woods, playing my reeds."

"Are you finished, Sir Angus?"

He took some time to answer. "I was going on like an ass, wasn't I? It is a habit I'll have to break if I'm to travel through England."

Emily didn't care if he traveled to Prussia and back in a bad temper. She wanted to go home. "As I was about to say, just beyond the toadstools is a passageway concealed between those juniper and aspen. It's an escape route the gypsies use when they're blamed for a sickness in the parish."

"Show me." He sounded serious, if not contrite.

"It's right in front of you," she said, pointing to a stand of silver-gray branches. "We'll have to walk your horse the rest of the way."

"Is it the fastest route?" he asked hesitantly.

"It's the safest that I know. We don't want to ride across an open ridge with only furze as cover. In the moonlight we'd be too easy to spot."

He hesitated, then slid to the ground, holding out his arms to catch her. She fell into his arms and against his chest, which felt strangely uneven. What was *he* hiding under his coat? He pulled away. It was clear he was anxious to be rid of her, and she had no particular desire to become further involved in his life. "We have to arrive home before my father," she said. "Once I'm back I assure you that you will be absolved of all responsibility for me."

"I hope you are right." He frowned. "Where did you put the stolen jewels?"

"The jewels— Oh. Iris has them."

"So you are the decoy, and a good one at that," he said, with a dark smile. "I might have been one of your victims."

Chapter 12

For most of his life, the Honourable Michael Rowland had managed to live between two worlds. Then one day he realized he didn't have to make the choice. Society harbored deep prejudices toward his natural father's people, but also a fascination for their wandering ways. Baron Rowland, the man who'd raised Michael as his own son and heir, had come to terms with Michael's heritage the year after his wife had died. The baron had adored her. He would never marry another. But he wanted a son, and Michael was an easygoing child who never gave him a spot of trouble, unlike his sweet younger sister, who had been a magnet for mischief from the night she had climbed out of her cradle.

The baron had his failings. He drank to excess. He grew distressed if Michael showed an interest in his gypsy ancestry. But Lord Rowland had never told anyone that Michael was not his. Emily was the one who seemed to have been sired by a wild seed.

"If I think we've been followed," Michael said to the maid sitting immobile on his saddle as if rigor mortis had set in, "we won't return to the house. We'll go along the hollow ways."

"The hollow ways?"

"Tracks that have been made by rain or wagons transporting goods by drivers who don't want to be spotted. Try to lean back against me and relax. You're jumping at every twig that snaps. If you don't stop, I'll have to—"

"Do what?"

He'd thought to answer *Kiss you*, but a kiss would ruin their camaraderie or initiate a romance that had no chance of survival. Iris was three years older than Emily, and he had always known that while he was at war or reacquainting himself with a purposeless life, he could count on Iris to take care of Emily.

"How do you know you can trust that man with your sister?" she said quietly.

"I've seen him on the battlefield. He never thought twice about his own life when it came to his troops. That kind of decency and sacrifice means more to me than how he stirs his tea."

"When was the last time you saw him?"

"I don't remember exactly. Men don't keep track of their social encounters like women do. I'd say it was six or more years ago in Spain."

"Six years, sir. And prior to that how well did you know him?"

Michael nudged his gelding forward. "I knew other men who served under him, and that was good enough for me. He was a brave and honorable solider during our acquaintance. What more can you ask of a man?"

"He could have become a dishonorable philanderer since then," Iris said not unreasonably. "It isn't as if he keeps good company."

"He's an agent for the Home Office, and if you repeat I said that, I will never speak to you again."

"He's a spy?" She sounded relieved that there was an explanation for Damien's behavior. "That was what he was doing in the tower? He didn't make up his story to frighten us away?"

"I don't know the entire story myself," Michael admitted. "But I doubt that the earl would—"

"An earl! A Scottish earl, he is now? He was supposed to be a wool merchant. I've heard of noblemen investing in trade, but not of an earl who deals in sheep."

"Be quiet, Iris. Your voice carries in the woods." Michael said, dismounting at the end of the narrowing trail.

"You'll have to change your clothing and cut your hair the moment we get home," she said thoughtfully. "Whether you like it or not, this isn't the time to attract undue notice, if I haven't misunderstood the gravity of the situation."

"I will admit one thing," he said with a reluctant smile, "of all the schemes in which you have served as Emily's henchman, this is by far the most heinous."

"Not that either of us have ever been able to refuse her. Still, she respects you more than she does me." She slid down before a cloak of creeping vines that hung between the trees. The reassuring shape of the baron's modest country house showed through the foliage.

"You could have stopped her if you'd been so inclined," he said.

"Lucy thought up the idea," she answered. "I was only trying to be helpful. My mistress believed that this was her one chance at happiness. Did you discourage her?"

"No," he said, shaking his head. "I wanted her to be happy, too."

Chapter 13

*E*mily was braced for the sadness that submerged her whenever she returned from Lucy's estate to her own home at Rowland Hall. No matter how many years had passed since her mother's death, Emily still searched the apple orchard in hopes of glimpsing Mama playing with the dogs before bed. But the orchard was untended and lonely, as was the country house that had once been a refuge for the baron's beloved family. The only sign of new growth, of life, was the sunken rose garden where the double-petaled roses the baroness had planted still thrived. The baron and the gardeners lavished all their love and attention on this fertile plot.

The roses flourished. But the baron had never found the enthusiasm to finish the stables or the conservatory.

"What is it?" a low voice asked behind her. "Is there anyone in that orchard?"

"It's only a gardener picking up snails. Or a ghost." Emily shook off her memories and turned to glance up into the Scotsman's face. What would her mother think of him? Emily couldn't decide herself. In a few more hours she hoped it wouldn't matter.

"Are you sure there isn't anyone in that orchard?" Sir Angus asked again.

"They don't mean us harm if there is." Emily decided that Mama would approve of his conquering-hero character, especially if he kept her daughter safe. But he wasn't a gentleman that a lady would have *chosen*, given his profession.

"I have to hurry inside and change before—" She caught herself, but not in time.

He stared across the lawn at the house, his face pensive. "It's a nice house, from what I can see. I don't understand why a gentlewoman who lives here has to go about in a disguise to steal jewels."

"I *didn't* steal any jewels," she said in exasperation. "My friend made that up so I could escape."

"I thought as much."

"Then why did you ask?"

"I wanted to understand whom I was saving and trusting with my secrets."

"Now I've told you mine."

Something wicked glittered in his eyes. "I'd like to see you safely inside before I go."

"I can find my way from here. You should go. I've no doubt you'll save the day for England. I apologize for interfering in your work. I hope all goes well. And that your mission is more successful than mine was. Please don't get yourself killed. I'll try to behave myself from now on, too. The only towers in my future will be the ones I read about in fairy tales. She drew a deep breath. "Thank—"

"I want another kiss before I go."

She felt the horse nudge her against the Scotsman as if encouraging her to obey his master. "You had your kiss. We kissed."

He locked his arm around her waist, drawing her away from the horse. "I kissed you. It's your turn to kiss me."

"A good-bye kiss?"

He bent his head and brushed his mouth over her swollen lips. "As you wish."

"But we already—"

She stared up into his face and couldn't concentrate on anything except what he had asked of her. Kiss him? How? She felt herself slipping into some forbidden world. She closed her eyes, rising on her toes to better reach his mouth. His arm molded her to his body. She shivered and lightly touched her tongue to his.

"Damn me," he muttered, his breathing harsh. "I was the one who had to ask."

He took control then and slowly deep-kissed her mouth until the pleasure that lanced through her shocked her back to herself. "Passion," she whispered, opening her eyes to stare at him. "This is what it does to a person. I've always wondered."

"Aye," he laughed. "And it doesn't come along like this very often."

She edged around his unmoving frame. "I'll have to take your word on that," she said, her voice firm. "And you have to leave. I'll explain this to my father. Don't ask me how."

"I intend to be gone before you meet him. I should have been in the next village an hour ago. I wish *you* luck with your father. Is he violent?"

She shrugged. "Sometimes. But don't worry."

She'd run out of breath, and yet she felt a deeper appreciation for what he had done for her than she could put into words. She would remember this night, this man, for a long time to come. He had given her her first kiss. He had rescued her from evil and most likely from a humiliation that would have crushed her spirit.

As she glanced up again at his face, she realized that her sheltered life had never prepared her for a man like this. He was a scoundrel to break hearts, yes. But somehow he had given of himself to protect two women he could easily have dismissed as worthless. That was a different kind of passion than he had shown in his kiss.

"You can go now," she said, her voice softer.

He frowned. Obviously his thoughts had run off in a direction different from hers.

A soft footstep in the grass stopped Emily's heart. Sir Angus heard it, too, and drew her and his mount deeper into the orchard. Another horse whickered softly. Emily leaned back against the gnarled trunk of an apple tree in relief.

"It's only my brother."

"Good. Then I can leave you with a clear conscience." His dark eyes traveled slowly from her face to the hem of her skirts. "Be careful."

"And you," she whispered, her throat suddenly dry. "Thank you for bringing me home. You kept your word. I admire that."

He laughed. "It was an experience I won't forget in a hurry. None of it. From the tent to this place. You are entertaining, Urania. You made me lose my sense of time and responsibility. I suggest, however, that you take your talents to the stage, where you'll have a genuine chance to find a protector. Don't undervalue yourself. Make those who vie for your company earn your devotion."

"A protector?" she said, unsure whether he considered this to be an insult or a compliment. Well, this wasn't a convenient time to set him straight. He would disappear soon enough.

"Another thing," he said. "Your guardian should provide you with jewels in the event that you are tempted to steal."

Emily turned her head. She had never heard such a lovely load of nonsense in her life. Why couldn't she have met a charmer like this in Hatherwood? Perhaps she should suggest a holiday in Scotland to her father, if men there appreciated young ladies desperate for affection.

"You'll make some fortunate gentleman a fine mistress," he added. "And who knows? You could be offered a decent marriage proposal."

"Do you think so?"

"I do not lie."

She smiled. "Except to traitors."

"That's right," he said, leaning into her. "Now stay out of trouble."

"The same to you, I'm sure."

Michael strode up behind them. "You'll have another unforgettable experience with my father if you stand chitchatting all night." He glanced at Emily. "Run inside and bring out a bottle of brandy for our friend. Iris, make yourself and my sister look respectable and ready for bed."

Damien shook his head in refusal. "I'd rather take my horse to the stable for water. I'll have a drink when I go back to the inn."

"You have a few minutes to rest," Michael said. "I've locked the gates. It takes ages for a servant to hear anyone calling for entry at this time of night. We'll know if he arrives. We can all breathe a little easier until then."

"Father will be furious," Emily said. "He has no patience at all these days."

"Is it any wonder?" Iris said under her breath. "Come, miss, into the house before you frighten anyone in that costume."

Emily wavered. She couldn't help noticing the detached expression on the Scotsman's face. He was back to playing his role. Only moments ago he had been staring at her intently, not only as a woman to seduce, but because they had forged a fragile bond tonight. Or was that her wishful thinking again? He would forget her by tomorrow. It wasn't as if he had nothing else on his mind.

She'd meant it when she wished him well. Only now did she realize how quickly he had acted to protect her. Maybe in a few months she'd laugh about their escape. But she would still be alone.

At any rate he was the most dangerous gentleman she had ever met, and she ought to be grateful to escape his company with nothing lost but a kiss or two. Her infatuation with Camden was tarnished as if it had been only tin all along. But, then, a man like Sir Angus tended to put other gentlemen to shame.

"One thing I would like to know," Sir Angus said, his eyes locking briefly with hers before he looked at Michael. "What was it that Urania spilled on the both of us in the tent?"

"Who?" Michael said, running a hand through his unkempt black hair.

"Never mind," Emily whispered.

"She knocked it over and it splattered on us both," Damien said. "Does that mean we are destined for each other?"

Emily bit her lip. "I told you, Michael, but you weren't listening."

Michael grinned as Emily looked away. "I hate to admit it, and I know I shall not ever be forgiven, but considering that it didn't come in contact with the intended victims, I'll tell you the truth."

"Do hurry, sir," Iris urged, tugging at Emily's hand.

Michael shrugged. "Emily must have eavesdropped. Jasper told me that it was to be used—"

"When all else fails," Emily said, her eyes still averted. "I know. I shouldn't have eavesdropped. I shouldn't have taken it," she continued quietly. "Whatever Jasper poured into the phial was a caustic and potent substance."

Damien snorted. "It burned like the devil's own breath."

"Well, I don't wonder," Michael said, frowning as if he remembered when Emily had huddled over him in the still room, whispering half-seriously for him to make something potent that would bind Camden to her. He shook his head. "This particular formula was to be used in case of snails. Not when all else fails. But who knows? Magic is mysterious. It might have been the perfect potion even though it was meant for the rose garden."

Emily walked sedately to the front steps of the house, her shawl concealing her hair and, she hoped, most of her face. She could fool the butler and footman into believing she was only staying covered from the storm, but it would be harder to convince the two upper chambermaids who brought her bath and breakfast every day.

"Go up into your room," Iris said behind her on the stairs. "Let's wash that dye from your skin first and dispose of that hideous wig."

"How?" Emily wondered aloud as they reached her room. "There are at least fifty pins left to pull from my head."

"I can cut the wig up and strew it on the road to the village tomorrow when I go marketing."

"That wouldn't look at all suspicious." Emily sat down at her dressing table and untied her blouse. "Bring me a plain evening gown, Iris."

"You're not going out again tonight?"

"Only as far as the garden."

"But what for?"

"Just to make certain I didn't lose any other cards where my father might find them. He'll be in a dither enough as it is. I don't want him thinking that Michael had gypsies on the estate while he was gone."

Iris's eyes clouded with worry. "Those cards are supernatural. You should never have touched them. Palm reading and tea leaves are one thing. But those cards, miss. They are only as reliable as the person reading them. Or so Mr. Rowland says."

Damien couldn't escape her fast enough.

If she'd given him one more hint of encouragement during that last kiss, he would have forgotten who they were and why they could never become passionate with each other.

A smile curved his lips. Why had he met her tonight? Why not the evening before? Wouldn't they have been attracted to each other during an ordinary encounter?

Or had their mutual deception added kindling to the

heat he'd felt the moment he had seen her sitting in that
tent?

She had looked as if she wanted to kill him. He'd
spoiled her romantic scheme. He was a little sorry that
he couldn't stay and make it up to her. He couldn't remember the last time he had felt sexual desire for a
woman while enjoying her company.

To be honest, passion, in its deepest sense, had never
come into his life before.

Emily stood, wiping off the face cream she had plastered
on her throat and arms. "Give me a wet cloth—I just
realized that the boots I borrowed from Lucy are in Sir
Angus's saddlebags. I doubt he'll remember to return
them to Michael."

"Well, he can send them by post."

"No, he can't." Emily rubbed off the cream with the
damp cloth Iris handed her.

"Send a footman instead."

"Dare I? We had better not. Michael hasn't changed
yet and we don't want anyone asking him what happened tonight. Sir Angus ought to know what to do with
a pair of boots that are half his size."

Iris sighed. She had removed her colorful costume
and restored herself to her usual neat-as-a-pin appearance. "It's not over yet. Your father will return from Lucy's party any minute, and let's hope he's by himself."

"Do you think he'd lead the conspirators here?"

"Only if they figured out who we were and where
we'd gone, and that is unlikely unless Lucy or Lady
Fletcher gave us away."

"That won't happen. They're too good at making up
stories. Lucy swore to me she would keep my father at

the party for as long as she could. She isn't going to tell him that I spent half the evening as an unsuccessful fortune-teller and the other on the run from anarchists. He wouldn't believe it."

"Lucy and I also swore that you would be dancing in Camden's arms the entire evening, didn't we?"

"Maybe Papa hasn't even left yet. He took the carriage, and that means the long way home."

Iris tucked and pinned her bright hair under her cap. "And how are you going to explain walking in the garden this time of night when he arrives?"

"I always walk in the garden when I miss my mother. So does he." Emily shook her head. "I lost at least half a deck of those cards tonight. They took off in the wind."

"Well, why didn't you sprinkle golden sovereigns all the way here from Lucy's house? It might have lit up the path to the house and made it easier for that nest of traitors to find us."

"Iris, we're home. We are only what we appear to be— an innocent young lady and her maid. Who could recognize us?"

"They'll certainly recognize Sir Angus if he hasn't left," Iris said, stuffing Emily's skirt, bangles, and blouse in the false-bottomed drawer of her armoire. "There. Now I'll pop downstairs, pretending that I can't breathe, and run out to the stables to explain about the boots. Sir Angus, or whatever his actual title is, will not want to be caught with lady's footwear."

The crunch of carriage wheels from outside drew Iris to her feet. "If that is your father, and the Scotsman isn't gone, then we are doomed."

Emily glanced away from her reflection to her maid. She had wiped most of the tint from her skin and slipped into the silk dress she had worn earlier in the day. "Not necessarily. Go through the front way, apologizing that we locked the gates on him before we realized he had not gone to bed as he'd told us he would earlier."

"And then?"

"Dash around to the stables to warn Michael and Sir Angus that my father is home, in case they didn't hear him clattering down the drive."

"The Scotsman should have gone by now," Iris said. "I can't think of any reason to explain why he is in our house. I've changed my mind. I'm not leaving this room again tonight, miss. Mr. Rowland knows better how to deal with his lordship."

Chapter 14

$\mathcal{M}$ ichael helped Damien brush down and resaddle his horse. "I would like to be part of your operation, my lord. I'd be honored if I could expose those traitors to the Crown. I'll go mad if I stay in Hatherwood for the rest of my life."

Damien nodded. "No one else must know what you learned tonight. You'd have to alter your appearance if you become involved."

"How?" Michael asked, laughing.

"Shear off the pretty curls that the girls ask to touch. Different clothes. You were brought up as a gentleman."

"My blood doesn't agree."

"Then do what you are meant to— What was that noise?"

Michael glanced across the barn into the moonlight arena. "A carriage. His Drunkenness is home, and that means a quarrel is imminent. Don't let him see you. If you need me, I'll be here. Thank you for taking care of my sister."

"I wanted to ask where she—" Damien broke off. "Never mind. Keep a close eye on her for the next few months. Take her away for a seaside holiday, if you can."

He patted down his saddlebags. "God, she's left her boots with me."

"I'll take them. There's a small track that leads around the hills to the old Roman road. You can follow it until you reach the village. Watch yourself."

"I will." Damien cleared his throat. "Guard your sister. She seems to have a penchant for trouble."

"You don't know the half of it."

Their luck held for about twenty seconds before both men heard the rattle of a small carriage coming up the inner driveway.

"I thought you locked the gates," Damien said, leading his horse into the backyard, where the arena and outbuildings sat in misty moonlight and one could mistake a fence post for a man.

"I thought I did, too," Michael said as he reached into his pockets. "He must have used his own keys. Most nights he's too foxed to find them. I never dreamt he would go to the party. He does little but stay home to drink and roar nowadays."

A man's bellow broke through the night. Michael groaned. "That's him."

"Emily!" the man roared from the front steps. "Michael! I will see you both downstairs in the hall, or there shall be hell to pay! I am too old to allow your antics."

"Hush a moment," Damien said. "I thought I heard another voice between his bellows. He isn't alone."

"That's only the footman, talking to himself." Michael closed the stall door, his face grim. "I'll take care of this. Use the distraction to escape. Everyone in the house who was sleeping will be awake and in the entry hall in a minute."

Damien frowned as Michael strode through the stables to the manor house. The baron's temper was a distraction, all right. It would alert the curiosity of any men in the area who happened to be hunting a gypsy girl who had wandered into the wrong place at the wrong time.

Had she admitted that sometimes her father was violent? Damien cringed to think of anyone marring her soft skin. But, then, he shouldn't be thinking of her at all.

She was deceitful.

She was undeniably sweet.

She had brought most of this situation on herself with her scandalous behavior.

Hadn't she insisted he leave?

Didn't he have a few uprisings to prevent, a viscount's life to save?

He should never have asked for that last kiss.

And she should never have kissed him back.

The front doors flew open with a force that sent Iris scurrying for cover in the dressing closet. "Lock the door, miss. He must have been drinking again at the party. Or on the drive home."

"Or Lucy and Diana were forced to reveal all. I can't hide from him forever."

"You could try until he's sober. What if he's brought one of those men with him?"

Emily backed out of the room. "What if my father *is* one of those men?"

"He couldn't be."

"He's been talking all month about taking a chair on the council."

"The *parish* council."

Or had he been referring to a position that had nothing to do with alleviating the suffering of the poor? "Of course he isn't involved in treason. What am I thinking? He couldn't control himself long enough to be of help to any conspiracy unless it was staged at a tavern."

"Excessive spirits rot a man's brains," Iris said with conviction. "Stay in here until he's sober."

"Don't be absurd, Iris. He might know nothing except that I sneaked out of the house tonight, which is enough to infuriate him. If I hide it will only make it appear I've done more than disobey him."

She pulled the door open, whispering, "At least he didn't see me in that costume. He would have flown right into the boughs if he knew I was telling fortunes just an hour ago."

"Miss, the wig—it's only half unpinned."

Emily glanced at herself in the pier glass. At least she had washed the tint from her skin and changed into an unadorned ivory gown.

She would have to remove her hairpiece before he noticed it. If he noticed it. The horrid thing refused to be freed from the pins Iris had jammed into her scalp.

She hastened down the hall and made it to the last three steps before her father saw her. He strode toward the staircase, brandishing a bundle of wrinkled red satin in his hand. He stank of drink. His silver hair stood from his head.

"Good evening, Father."

"Was it?" he asked in a caustic voice. "Did you enjoy making a mockery of every decent principle in existence?"

Emily gripped the balustrade. She had never seen him this drunk or out of control. Had he found out what she had done tonight from a perceptive guest who had seen through Emily's disguise in the tent?

How much does he know? What is *he clutching in his hand like a shroud— Oh. Oh.* He advanced to the bottom of the stairs.

"I can't blame this defiance, this shameful behavior, on Michael, because he has only recently returned home. I can't fault Lucy, though I wonder why Lord Fletcher tolerates your friendship with the girl when it is obvious you have an indecent influence on her."

She dropped, barefooted, one step at a time to answer him. She saw a shadow slip through the door into the darkened hall. Her throat closed. Michael and her father in this mood created a deadly combustion.

"What is it?" Michael asked in accordance with the plan that Iris and Emily had agreed on in the case that they were caught. "I was in the stables, looking at the foal, sir. She—"

The baron did not turn around. "Be quiet, you young bastard. You have helped her to disgrace my name."

"Disgrace?" Emily could only echo his words, afraid that her father and Michael would come to blows.

She had to intervene. She deserved her father's wrath. "I can explain," she said, inching down another step and motioning Michael back into the hall. She knew she was breaking her promise to her brother that she would not confess, but she couldn't allow him to take any blame for her reckless judgment. "It was an innocent folly, Papa. I went to the ball without your permission."

"Innocent?" he said slowly, opening his fist to unravel the red satin ball gown she had hoped to wear when Camden asked her to dance. How naïve her masquerade seemed now. Yet even if she hadn't believed in her heart it would lead to a marriage proposal, she could not have imagined the dark turn it had taken.

"You were with a man tonight," he said in disgust. "I forbade you to attend that dance, and not only did you defy me, but you apparently met a man alone in the tower and spent the evening with him and without your clothes."

Emily shook her head, realizing he would never believe the truth. To all appearances the red gown condemned her. She would need hours to explain the sequence of events, and even then she couldn't deny that she *had* deceived him.

"Who found the dress?" she whispered.

"I caught young Lucy trying to sneak it past her father."

"She was not with a lover," Michael said, his voice low and furious. "I took her there and made sure she came safely home."

The baron held up the evening dress by its rumpled sleeve. "Then explain this."

She stared past him to Michael. "I took it to Lucy's house and intended to change there before the dance. I made Iris come with us. She didn't want to be part of it. I'd no idea you wanted to go, too, or we could all have traveled together." Which would have crimped her plans for romance, but in retrospect that might have been better for everyone involved.

"You are a liar. Like your mother," he said, his voice hoarse with drink and disillusionment. "I've confronted you with the evidence, Emily, and you are still lying to me. You never went to the party at all. No one saw you there. Not one person witnessed your appearance."

"That's because I—" She lifted her hand to the atrocious wig and tugged.

Her father stared at her. He was too upset to even

comment on—or notice—that her hair was not its usual style or color. "I've always known you were a hoyden," he said. "But I would never have thought you would become loose."

"That's enough," Michael said, coming forward to place his hand on the baron's shoulder. "We can discuss this with cool heads in the morning."

The baron shrugged off Michael's hand. "What do you say for yourself?" he asked Emily, blocking Michael from her path.

"We *did* go to Lucy's. But—"

She read the warning in Michael's eyes, the reminder that if she mentioned the word *gypsy* in her father's presence, he would only blame her brother for encouraging her unladylike attempt to impress a man. She couldn't admit the truth.

The baron threw her dress back across the hall. It slid into the path of the man who stood in the doorway, unnoticed until Emily looked past her father to the spot where her dress lay.

Him again. Back to bring her more bad luck.

Was he out of his mind? Did he hope to see her banished from her home? He must have heard her father shouting. He had to understand his appearance would only make her dilemma worse. He lifted his gaze from the floor and stared until she realized that he was studying *her* as if he had no idea who she was.

Was this to be another act on his part? If she were in his place, she'd refuse to become implicated in her fall. What was he doing in her house? Why didn't he leave awful enough alone? She would never have accused him or dragged him into her affairs.

She begged him silently to go. Nothing good could

come of him confronting her father. What could he be thinking? She couldn't guess, even though he hadn't taken his eyes off her.

He closed the door and walked quietly into the hall. Michael either sensed his presence or was alerted by the dread on Emily's face. Her father appeared too deeply in his cups to detect the sudden menace in the air. His voice shook when he resumed his tirade.

"This is the last time," he said. "Lucy and her young stepmother might think I'm stupid enough to believe their lies. Not a single person at the party except those two troublemakers could remember seeing you and even then they would not give me a straight answer."

"I spent most of my time in the garden," she said, her gaze flickering to her Scottish protector. Dear God, what was he going to do? Didn't he realize that anything he said would only make it worse for her? Maybe he wasn't concerned about her at all. Maybe he needed to make sure she never divulged his secrets.

"I did spend most of my time in the garden," she said again to her father. "I came back home when I heard you were looking for me. I—"

"I demand to know the man's name and whereabouts." He raised his fist to her face. "So help me God, I will beat the truth out of you if you make me. Everyone at the party must be laughing at what a fool I looked, searching for—"

"My name is Damien Boscastle, the Earl of Shalcross, and I am standing in your shadow. Your daughter was with me this evening. I take full responsibility for our actions. I led her astray."

"What?" Emily whispered, shaking her head in disbelief, moving forward without thought to what she was doing. Damien Boscastle? Who in heaven's name was this man? An earl? She hadn't believed her maid's prattle.

The unfamiliar voice either failed to penetrate her father's rage or further stoked it. In a blur she watched her father's hand descend, and Damien intercept the blow with his forearm. Her father stumbled back into Michael, who steadied him before stepping forward to act as a shield between the earl and the baron. Emily wouldn't want to stand between them at this moment.

"What *are* you doing here?" Michael asked Damien in bewilderment.

Damien straightened, scrutinizing Emily again before he answered. "The ranting from this house is more than enough to draw the attention of any neighbor passing by. I'd have thought that this would be a night for discretion. It is not necessary to broadcast one's private difficulties, is it?"

Emily swallowed hard, avoiding his hard gaze. There lived only one neighbor who, perhaps if he were taking an evening walk, might have overheard the baron's outburst. That was unlikely. The servants had learned long ago to stay in their quarters when the master had been drinking. And it might be undesirable to attract notice to an unpleasantness at home, but no one had asked for his intervention as far as Emily knew.

Her father seemed to have calmed considerably. Perhaps at last he had made sense of what the earl had said.

"My lord," he said, his manner deferential. "You will understand my distress. I was under the impression that my daughter had stayed home, and naturally I would not have allowed her to go without a reliable escort. Perhaps she even told me and I forgot."

"I understand," Damien said, when it was clear he didn't have the clue what the baron meant.

"I have known that my daughter would be the death of me since the day she started to walk."

Damien's eyes darkened. "I think I understand," he said again.

"She changed the color of my hair overnight," the baron said.

"I can see that happening, too," Damien murmured.

"I do not believe I properly caught your name. Forgive me. And did you or did you not offer her a marriage proposal?"

Emily shivered in the moment of silence that followed her father's bluntly asked question. An earl. A request for Emily's hand. A single indiscretion could be overlooked when accompanied by a proposal from a nobleman. But this was his opportunity to back out of his impulsive offer. Her father would rage, yes, and then he would pass out on the sofa. In the morning everyone in the house would hide in their respective places. The baron would not be certain what had happened during the night.

But he was alert enough now. He coughed lightly, prompting the earl to respond.

Damien shrugged with a detached air that Emily might have admired had she not been the object of his impassivity. "I am Damien Boscastle, Earl of Shalcross. Yes, I wish to marry—"

The baron turned to Michael. "Do you have knowledge of his lordship?"

Michael glanced in Damien's direction. "Yes. I do. He's of an honorable family. You heard what he said. Twice."

The baron expelled a sigh.

"I served under him in Spain," Michael added.

"Then all's well that ends well." Baron Rowland looked shaken but relieved. "Shall we call for a drink to congratulate one another? I had no idea, Emily, that you had fallen in love with his lordship."

Neither had she. Still, the earl, if that was indeed his title, had placated her father for tonight. She expected there would be hell to pay all over again when dawn came and Damien had disappeared. She wouldn't let herself believe he meant what he'd said.

"Come, come," the baron said, motioning to Damien as if he were already the favorite member of the family. "We shall break out a French brandy."

"It isn't necessary," Damien said with a taut smile. "We can celebrate over tea on Sunday while we discuss the details of the marriage."

"Sunday?" the baron said, blinking.

Emily wrenched another pin from her wig. Her father looked as though he might tear off his cravat and tie the earl to the banister before letting him escape this engagement. Not that any length of linen could hold a man of Damien's agility. She had become familiar with the brawn that his evening clothes disguised.

She felt a shudder of relief begin to unbind her muscles. Sir Angus/the earl—whoever he was—would *not* return tomorrow or on Sunday. This was simply the last act he must play before the curtains dropped. He would be gone before Emily rose in the morning. It did not seem probable now that anyone would wish to hurt her or Iris because they had unintentionally overheard a part of some alleged conspiracy.

It also seemed improbable that a man with those unearthly blue eyes had asked her drunken father for her hand with any sincerity.

"Good night, everyone," she said, and turned before the gentlemen below could reply. "Sleep well."

It was too much to expect—to be allowed the last word and a graceful by-your-leave. Never mind what miracles she prayed that the morning would bring.

"What is wrong with you?" her father asked with an uneasy laugh. "You might as well give your betrothed a proper send-off. I see no point in playing coy if you're engaged to his lordship."

A challenging smile crossed Damien's face. Something was different about him. His voice interrupted her before she could work out why he seemed entirely changed. Almost as if he'd become another man. Of course, she had known him for only a few hours. But they had stared at each other in the tent. He had kissed her and brought her home on his horse. He was not a mere Sir Angus. He was a peer. But that wasn't why he seemed different.

He stood as tall and wide-shouldered as before. He wore the same red beard and detailed evening clothes. He looked a little tired, but the fire in his eyes hinted that it would be dangerous to underestimate him.

He was still unlike any other man she knew.

But something had definitely changed.

His voice startled her. "May I be allowed a moment alone with my fiancée?"

No one else said a word.

She shook her head and the wig dropped on the last step.

Damien stared at the mass of black ringlets that had landed at his feet. "This is a surprise."

Michael rubbed his cheek. "At least she revealed her identity before the wedding night. It's your turn now."

Emily wound one arm around the stair railing. "Yes, what about you? I don't know anything except what you wanted me to know."

The baron cleared his throat, unable to follow the conversation. "It takes years for a man and wife to know each other, Emily, and even then they can end up as strangers. How and when did your affection for each other begin?"

Michael forced a laugh. "It was me. I played Cupid, sir. I introduced them through a series of correspondences. Before I knew it, their letters to each other had evolved into an enduring love."

"I never noticed that Emily received any letters," the baron said in puzzlement.

"Well, you wouldn't," Michael said. "She was shy and not certain what would come of their written devotion. But that is why they are still awkward around each other, sir. They're still learning to express what was easier said on paper."

Devotion. Love letters. Emily wanted to weep.

Damien looked up from the step to her face. "You appear to have lost your wig," he said, nudging it aside with the toe of his boot.

She stared back at him with a gasp of realization. "And you have lost your Scottish brogue. That's what is different."

He advanced on her, speaking in a low voice that only she could hear. "I have lost more than that. I do not take surrendering my name and protection lightly. Despite what you and your maid might think of your charade tonight, you have put yourself in a dangerous position."

Emily had only to examine the hard angles of his face to realize that she might be better off taking her chances on staying in Hatherwood than surrendering to Damien's dark sensuality. She wondered if Michael knew of an antidote for a love scheme gone wrong, and whether it would be too late to use it.

Chapter 15

$\mathcal{D}$amien stared up in astonishment at the graceful hand that the woman on the stairs sifted through her long red hair. She had changed into a demure white silk gown in place of her gypsy garb; what lay beneath was a mystery he was growing intensely curious to solve.

Her simple gown graced a body with ample curves and a softness that he found incredibly sensual. She was not the same woman he had brought to this house. She was definitely one who piqued his interest.

Of course, she could still spring a shock or two after they exchanged vows, and he had some surprises in store for her, too. Still, the sight of her now made him hopeful that a passionate future lay ahead of them.

As if he were an expert on matrimony. He was not. His former lover had emptied his coffers before she ended their engagement to marry a business partner. She believed that Damien was on the road to ruin, his wealth depleted. When he discovered who she was at heart, he considered himself fortunate that she had revealed her true colors before he'd given her his name.

At any rate the bride-to-be and her captive groom

would make a commitment to each other before her father, brother, maid, and Damien's valet. It would be easier to escape Newgate Prison than the arranged marriage that must take place in a week if Damien was to succeed in preventing an assassination. He could not afford to let Emily escape, thus risking her life and ruining the culmination of months of covert work to capture the traitors. Of all the sacrifices he had been prepared to make, a wedding had never entered his mind.

The baron could not allow an earl, eccentric though he may appear, to slip through Emily's fingers. In fact, once he had finally recognized the name Boscastle and realized Damien was indeed the Earl of Shalcross, the baron was far less interested in the details of the disgrace than he was in the marriage arrangements.

"May I ask if the wedding date has been set?" the baron inquired, breaking the stillness.

Damien shook his head. "I prefer a small private ceremony in Hatherwood. As soon as possible."

Lord Rowland beamed. "My hopes exactly."

Damien lifted his chin, smiling like the scamp he was. "You don't mind, do you, Urania?"

"Emily," she said through her teeth. "We don't need to use code names for each other now, my dear heart."

"Code names?" the baron said in bewilderment.

"She means our pet names, the silly endearments that amuse only us," Damien said smoothly, leaning against the railing with a lovelorn sigh.

"Do you have a date in mind?" the baron asked again, frowning now.

"Ten days at most. I would prefer to be married and gone within a week."

"A week?" Emily and Michael said in unison.

The baron smiled. "That's rather a whirlwind courtship, isn't it?"

Damien shrugged. "The winds of fortune brought your daughter into my life, sir. I cannot risk them blowing her into the arms of another."

Winds of fortune, Emily thought. Sir Angus—the earl—was a great bag of wind himself. And she would deflate him the next time she saw him. *If* she saw him again.

She glanced at her brother, who seemed pleased by this improvisation. Damien looked, well, who knew what was going on in his devious mind? She'd bet it had less to do with a wedding reception than with chasing rebels for the good of England.

Anyway, she was marrying him for her own protection.

"A marriage built upon a foundation of letters written to each other over a course of time is bound to last," the baron announced. "I am honored, my lord, to accept your proposal for Emily's hand."

Chapter 16

*W*inthrop, the earl's valet, walked his horse out from his hiding place in the woods the instant Damien reached the oak tree where they had agreed to meet. "My lord," he said, "I've had a hard time waiting here tonight. My intuition warned me that you were in grave danger. It is a relief to see you—"

He paused, assessing the condition of his master's disguise.

"What is it, Winthrop?"

"I hope you did not attend the meeting missing a part of your shoulder and a good deal of your torso padding."

"The padding is in my saddlebag," Damien said. "And good riddance to it. I can hardly wait to remove the rest of this disguise."

"Then you were caught out?" Winthrop asked in alarm.

"Not exactly. However, our plans have changed. We'll have to finish discussing them at the inn. I trust you've paid Sir Angus's bill, expressed his gratitude, and found a room elsewhere for the Earl of Shalcross?"

"Yes, my lord, but I do not understand."

"I don't have time to elucidate, Winthrop. I'll fill you

in as best I can as we travel. I need a shave and fresh clothes for the morning."

Winthrop nodded in complete agreement.

The moment the two men entered the room at the inn, Winthrop brought out a razor case and set the towels warming by the fire, while Damien finished removing his Sir Angus costume.

"You will need to dispose of this disguise as soon as possible." He thought of Michael's ingenious method of hiding the tent. "There are quagmires in the area. However, we are amateurs in that matter and I would not want you to go down with the evidence. Leaving our past identities behind does not mean we should literally vanish from the face of the earth."

The valet smiled. He had nursed Damien back to health many years ago. To this day he seemed to believe this action meant that he was indebted to his master instead of the other way around. Damien depended on Winthrop too much to argue.

"I was about to launch a search for you, my lord," Winthrop said. "You are three hours later than I expected, even given an emergency. What went amiss at the party?"

Damien frowned at his reflection in the shaving mirror. "Damn me if I ever have cause to wear a mustache this thick again. What did you just ask me? And this red beard. What irony. My hair was red when I met her. Hers was black and is now red."

"Something went wrong this evening, I assume. I feel as if I am following the moves on a chessboard."

"'Wrong' seems an inadequate word to describe the trap I walked into tonight."

Damien removed from his vest pocket the letter that

Emily had asked him to rescue from the tower. He turned toward the fire. He had no inclination to read her private correspondence. But, then, he was marrying her. He had the right to learn something of her nature.

> *Dearest Camden,*
> *By now you realize what I have kept hidden for so long. No matter what the outcome of my reckless act tonight, I confess . . .*

He crushed the letter in his fist and threw it into the fireplace, frowning as he noticed his valet staring at him in alarm.

Winthrop lowered the stool he had brought to the shaving stand. He lit the two candles in their wrought-iron stand. "You weren't recognized?"

"Sit down while I explain what happened."

"Haven't I stood steadfast at your side during attacks and storms at war? I cannot shave you while sitting down. I have never been prone to hysterics."

"Well, neither have I. But in a few minutes you and I might challenge our history. I was not caught out by the conspirators. Give me credit for at least doing my job."

"Then?"

"I fell into the company of a fortune-teller."

"Good gracious. She was able to divine that you were incognito?"

"She wasn't able to divine her own name," Damien said in annoyance. "She tricked me. Whether it was deliberate on her part or mere carelessness on mine, I haven't reassembled my wits enough to decide."

Winthrop paused. "But if you represented yourself as Sir Angus, you deceived her, too."

"It appears that neither one of us meant to deceive the other," Damien said in disgust. "We were on separate missions. Not that I can use that as an excuse for what occurred."

Winthrop looked appalled. "You were exposed by another operative?"

"I wasn't exposed by an operative, Winthrop. I was forced into an engagement with her. And her father. Anyway, she is not an agent unless the Crown has opened a division called the Amorous Office since we've been gone."

"And you proposed to a fortune-teller?" Winthrop could not suppress the note of horror in his voice. It was no secret that he wished Damien would marry and lead a life befitting his rank, but this was evidently not the match he had in mind. "Can they be trusted?"

Damien pulled another wad of padding from his shoulder. His back looked like a damned bridge. "Her life depends on it. After the wedding she will rarely leave my side."

"Until then?"

"Until then I must contrive to spend as much time in her company as possible. I have to appear to be a man obsessed, unable to tear myself from my betrothed whom, it is to be hoped, won't reveal that we knew not of the other's presence until this portentous evening."

"What about her father?"

"I can only sacrifice myself to marrying one of them."

"Ha, ha, my lord. What I meant is, can he be trusted with your secrets?"

"As of now he doesn't have an inkling that I am anything but a besotted fool who fell in love with his daughter over an epistolary love affair that her brother evidently initiated and encouraged during this past year."

"You are a remarkably driven man, my lord."

"I should be driven to an asylum for accepting this responsibility."

"And now you shall have a wife, a countess." Winthrop looked wistful. "Do you still plan to retire in London when this operation is finished?"

"I have not yet planned how I am to conduct a believable courtship with a woman I've known for mere hours and love for reasons I have yet to invent. Do you have any suggestions as to how I should go about this?"

"You have never lacked for lady admirers," Winthrop said carefully. "I don't think I could give you advice on doing you know what."

"Tossing a willing woman over my shoulder and into bed is not the same as wooing a gentlewoman. There is an interlude between that must be correctly staged."

"I am confused again. Isn't she elated that she will become the first Countess of Shalcross?"

"She certainly didn't throw herself at me in gratitude."

"What did she do?" Winthrop asked, glancing up now as if he'd finally realized that this marriage might not be one made in heaven.

"She threw down her wig."

"Good God. Is she bald, my lord?"

Damien laughed. "She has a mane of flame-red hair, and from what I've seen the spirit to match."

"She'll need pluck to live at your side, my lord," Winthrop said without glancing up. "We shall have to look at the bright side."

"She'll need more than pluck to stay alive. She walked into a hornet's nest tonight."

"May I ask why you feel compelled to become her guardian? Has her beauty blinded you to common sense? Protecting her cannot be more important than honoring your mission."

Damien turned from the mirror. "Marrying her and honoring the mission have become one and the same task, I'm afraid. One of us will have to carry a message to Heath Boscastle in London to warn him about the assassination plot. A slight detour to secure a special license is also in the cards. Canterbury isn't far from here. Show the letter of carte blanche to the clerk in the archbishop's office."

"And you plan to make a few additions to your current wardrobe, I hope?"

"I don't have time for that. Ply your needle if it gives you pleasure. In the meantime let's give Sir Angus a hasty funeral. I hope that we will never see him again."

Chapter 17

"How could I have been such a ninnyhammer?" Emily said as she dropped down onto the end of the bed.

"It's a little too late to ask yourself that now," Iris said. "Perhaps we'll both wake up tomorrow and discover we had a bad dream."

"But I saw the future so clearly," Emily said, staring at the wig that Iris was burying under a loose floorboard. "Camden would realize we were meant to be together during the ball and ask me at the last minute to dance. Afterward we'd stroll out onto the terrace with all our friends, who would say—"

"Come to your senses, miss. Your future is a Scottish earl," Iris said with the subtlety of a wave crashing against a cliff.

"I don't want to marry him, and he isn't a Scotsman." Still, he was a blackguard, and the mere memory of his chiseled mouth on hers made her feel restless and over-warm. She hadn't guessed for a moment he might be deceiving her. It hadn't taken him long to see through her game. "I should at least have been able to regard him in the light before I agreed to marry him."

"The same could be said for him."

Emily smiled, remembering the look on his face when he realized she had red hair. He had seemed pleased. "I suppose you're right."

Iris put on her stern face. "You have no choice. And if I were you, I'd be grateful to him for having the decency to propose. He's heroic, and while you might have drawn a long queue outside that tent tonight, no one else is standing in line for your hand."

Emily frowned. "He doesn't *want* to marry me. If I were him I'd be halfway to London or wherever he lives by now. He doesn't owe me anything, least of all a proposal."

"He came bursting into this house and confessed you had been together all night."

Emily sighed. "True, but he was only trying to placate my father."

"He *confronted* your father."

"That's true, too," Emily murmured.

"He's the most adventurous man we have met in this village. True?"

"Adventurous or not, we don't know the least thing about him. Everything he said could be a falsehood. I might as well marry a stranger."

"But without him you may not live at all."

Emily didn't respond, and watched for several moments as Iris rearranged the perfume bottles on the dressing table according to size. "Dear heaven. Will you stop doing that?"

Iris made an impatient noise. "We shall have to make the best of this."

"I'm not sure."

"Think of it as a fairy tale."

"Not all fairy tales have happy endings. And which

heroine should I be? Rapunzel? No. The earl has already rescued me from a tower. I believe that under his guard, my perils have only begun." It didn't take a soothsayer to predict that the earl would continue to seduce her while they "courted." She would have to prepare herself for a lot of kissing.

"I feel guilty now for the part I played in this imbroglio," Iris confessed as she began to brush out Emily's hair for bed. "I encouraged you to carry out your ill-fated plot, and not for entirely unselfish motives, either. Whatever good fortune you found could only benefit me. If I hoped for love or merely a more eventful life than the dull one we live, it could come only by your social elevation, which we both know means marriage."

"Hush up, Iris. Your chatter isn't helping."

"I didn't wish to watch you wither away as a spinster for the rest of your life. Nor did I want to be the maid to one. But now? Who knows? This could all be a blessing in disguise."

"Do not ever mention that word to me again."

"I was desperate once myself," Iris went on in a reflective voice as she sat beside Emily on the sofa.

"Not to get married."

"No. To escape my guardian."

"You mean your uncle?"

"I'd prefer not to be reminded he's a relation. I don't want anything to do with him, although I still say a prayer every night for his seven children."

"Seven. That number again. How old were you when you left his house?"

"Thirteen. And after I became a companion to the old widow, I swore I'd never let anyone clout me on the head again."

"No one has hit you in this house," Emily said gently.

"I thought there was going to be a fight tonight, miss. I swear I was more afraid of your father and the earl getting into fisticuffs than I was of those men in the tower."

"I know." Emily shook her head.

"Perhaps you have to look at this as fate."

"Fate? That word is also to be banished from our conversations."

"Miss, my dreams didn't come true, either. I'd hoped by now that I'd be a doting nursemaid to your children. Once I even hoped I'd find a man to marry."

Emily smiled at her. "It's still possible."

"It certainly is. I'm about to become lady's maid to a high-ranking noblewoman. I've come up in the world."

She and Emily stared bleakly into the blazing fire that warmed the small bedchamber. "Don't you find him handsome?" she whispered, putting her arm around Emily.

Emily frowned, transfixed by the flames. "You had a look at him in the hallway. I'm sure you could see that he's very handsome."

"Well, for what it's worth, all I noticed was that he was tall and brawny and had red hair."

"And blue eyes," Emily murmured. "I've never seen such a vivid blue before. He took my breath away. And he took away my dreams, too."

"I've never seen a fire burn in the hearth like that," Iris said in alarm. "What did you use for kindling?"

"The rest of that worthless love potion."

Iris gasped, pulling her arm free. "You didn't!"

"I just told you I did."

"Why?"

"What good is it to me now?"

"What good? I've no idea. But burning it might render it more potent."

Emily laid her head against the sofa.

"I lost any chance to win the man I thought I loved. I walked into a den of traitors, at least one of whom wants me dead. I am marrying a man who will resent me forever."

"He will expect something in return."

"Well, any man would."

But Damien wasn't just any man. He'd wanted to hide in her tent, and he had. And even though Emily was no expert, she knew she could travel halfway across England before she'd be so wickedly kissed and aroused *and* rescued by the same man in a single night. And he hadn't once lost his confidence. During their kiss he had been planning what he would do when he returned to the tower. And she hadn't thought of Camden at all. She hadn't been the least bit rational.

She sat up, startled, at the loud hiss that came from the fireplace.

Both women gasped at the large cobalt-bronze flame that danced up high into the chimney and disappeared. "What was that?" Iris asked, squeezing back against Emily.

"It wasn't the Holy Ghost. It looked like—"

"Don't say it," Iris muttered. "Whatever it was has gone. Perhaps the potion contained some ordinary volatile substance that has burned itself out."

Emily exhaled in relief. "Oh, of course. That would explain why when I spilled it on the earl's palm he complained that it stung like mad. It did, too. I tried to rub it off with my thumb and I can still feel a tingling sensation there, now that I think of it. Poor snails. I'd never use anything that nasty to get rid of them."

"It didn't seem to work on the earl, either."

"Never have I known a man less intimidated by a threat to his mortality," Emily said in agreement.

Iris snorted as she rose to fetch a wet cloth from the washstand to place between Emily's fingers. "Never have I known a lady less intimidated by a threat to her morality."

"If he has deceived me and does not appear on Sunday as he promised, I'll have to contend with danger to my mortal life, and my morals will be the least of our worries. Yes, Iris, I said *our* worries. We were both seen last night. Perhaps we should dye your shining tresses a dull brown."

Iris's mouth tightened. Her golden hair was her glory, and Emily felt spiteful that she had suggested such a cosmetic insult. "I'm sorry," she said, staring up at Iris's troubled face. "The earl said that we should expect to make sacrifices."

"That's fine for you to say. You are about to become a countess."

Emily sighed. "You know I wouldn't allow anything to happen to you. Still, as highly as you seem to think of the scoundrel, he is only one man against how many traitors across England, I cannot guess. Must we entrust ourselves to a stranger? He could be as ruthless as the members of that clandestine society, for all we know."

"Except that Michael knows him and considers him a friend," Iris reminded her. "If not for their acquaintance, we would be hiding in the closet together."

"That is still a possibility. It's gone two o'clock, and you have not heard—"

"Hoofbeats?" Emily rose and peered through the window curtains. "I hear a horse in the distance. If you listen—"

"In the distance?" Iris stared at her. "How can you tell if it's coming or going?"

Emily's heart quickened. She was trying to control her nerves, but at this rate, Iris would arouse all her secret fears. "The only way I'll know is to stand here and watch."

"I shall sneak out onto the terrace first," Iris said grudgingly. "I can take a look at the road behind the house."

"That is brave of you, Iris. I admit I'm impressed by your courage." She also found her maid's valor peculiar, but then Iris might have become temporarily unhinged by what had happened.

"Often it takes a war to bring out the warrior in us, miss."

"Thank you, Mrs. Socrates. Did you have a brandy while the drama downstairs was unfolding?"

"The entire night has been dramatic," Iris said.

"Yes. Well, the worst thing we can do is to become hysterical and act as though we have a secret to hide."

"What if the earl doesn't return on Sunday? What if after he's had a good think, he decides to abandon you?"

"Then hysterics might be an appropriate response."

Chapter 18

$\mathcal{M}$ichael glanced around at the young woman tiptoeing across the terrace with a glass of brandy in her hand. That Iris knew he was sitting on the steps at three o'clock in the morning came as no shock on a night like this. Poor girl. He knew she fancied him. She was wrapped up like a mummy, a cloak fastened at the throat over her nightclothes, her cap covering half her forehead.

"Oh, sir," she whispered, handing him the brandy before she dropped down onto the step below. "Why did you allow it to happen? No, you did more than that. Not only did you allow it, but you encouraged it. Passing your sister over to a stranger, a man immersed in things I don't want to believe exist."

He looked down into her worried face. Hard to see how green her eyes were in the dark. "I allowed it because I love her and didn't want her to be without a protector for the rest of her life." The brandy did not appeal to him. He set the glass beside him on the step. "You helped her as much as I did. Why?"

She sighed and fussed about with her cloak. Michael supposed she'd never sat alone with a man except him before. "I'm as guilty as you, it's true. I couldn't stand back and become the maid to a lonely spinster, committing us both to lives of misery. Now look what happened. Murder plots and a sudden marriage. How well do you know the earl? You didn't give me a decent answer in the woods."

He folded his arms over his knees, propping his chin on his wrist. "I know he's a brave fighter. He's ambitious and he keeps his thoughts to himself. I'm not surprised he's involved in suppressing a revolt. He's one of those men who always has to prove himself, and I can't say why."

"Oh," she whispered, shaking her head. "I was afraid of that. You're never going to set down roots, are you, sir?"

"Who knows?" he said with a laugh.

"The lady who wins your heart had best be prepared to make a home wherever you lead her."

"So, you haven't any urge to wander, Iris? No desire to travel and see the world?"

"No, sir. Even sitting out here on the steps makes me long for home fires."

He pulled a gold curl loose from the back of her cap. "Why didn't I ever realize how lovely you are?"

"For the same reason I pretended not to notice that you are a delightful rogue."

He tugged on her curl. "You're like a sister to me."

"You're like the brother I'm glad I never had."

He let go of her curl. "But you aren't my sister."

She pulled off the cap and shook out her hair.

He watched it unravel like a spool of deep gold thread. "Look what you've done to me. I hate it when my hair is untidy and I have no comb."

"You look fetching," he said quietly. "I feel almost like Rumpelstiltskin."

She tucked her hair back under her cap. "A brother would never say that."

He wanted to pull off her cap again and ask her to walk with him in the garden. "But you're not my sister."

"Is the earl— Please tell me again how well you know him."

He took the glass of brandy she had brought him and emptied its contents into an urn overflowing with geraniums. "I know him well enough that he is the last man I would have chosen for Emily."

"Sir!"

"But now that her life is endangered, I can't think of a man I'd rather choose to be her husband."

Chapter 19

$\mathcal{D}$amien struggled to stay asleep. His hands moved over the bare breasts and bottom of the woman sitting on top of him. Her red hair spilled against his chest as she kissed him on the mouth. His body begged for release. She whispered something. He couldn't make out what.

His erection was the only answer he could give her.

She seemed so familiar to him, but he couldn't put a name to the face. Were her eyes green or brown? His hands slid down her back, grasping her ass, urging her to take him inside her. She felt warm and wet against his groin. He raised his hips. He needed her.

Take me.

Why did she keep teasing him?

She lifted herself up, and in her smile there was a promise. His throat closed. He wanted to say that he would worship her if he lived through her teasing. He wanted to kiss her again as he thrust into her, but she was fading.

Emily.

That was her name.

He said it aloud, and then she disappeared.

He opened his eyes and it was daylight. He was as hard as a lance under the bed sheets and unhappy with his predicament. He didn't move, letting the sexual ache recede until gradually he realized that the palm of his left hand still burned from whatever substance had been in that bottle. The whole of his body, in fact, radiated an uncomfortable warmth. He sat up, the dream receding as he recalled the events of the previous night.

Winthrop bustled into the room, ever alert to the moment when Damien awakened. "You have perfect timing, Winthrop," he said sourly.

"Thank you, my lord."

"Why is the mirror of the shaving stand cracked?"

"I believe it broke when a certain person threw his boots across the room. That is seven years of bad luck that we don't need."

"Seven." Damien snorted. "That wasn't supposed to be my number. This entire thing has gotten out of hand."

"I'm sorry, my lord. I haven't a clue what you're talking about. I was referring to a Roman superstition. Other than that, the number seven didn't figure into our plans."

"Nor did a fortune-teller. But one thing we have both learned is to expect the unexpected and do the expedient."

"The fortune-teller being the unexpected and marriage the expedient?"

"More or less. Except that I also have to court her to make a convincing case for our rushed wedding, a novel experience that I would never have chosen."

"I see your point," Winthrop said, emptying the water pitcher into a ceramic bowl. "However, with the exception of your last fiancée, Miss Howell—"

"Don't ever mention her name to me again." Damien got out of bed in his nightshirt and stretched his arms above his head. His back ached. He was about to accuse the valet of sewing lead weights into Sir Angus's shoulder padding. But then he remembered that he had opened the trapdoor to the tower several times last night.

He went to the mirror. All traces of Sir Angus were gone. "The main thing is that we keep them safe."

"*Them?* Your fiancée and her brother?"

"Her brother? No, although he could prove to be an asset to us, and I trust him. My fiancée has a lady's maid who should meet with your approval."

Winthrop's eyes narrowed behind his spectacles. "Not if she endangers the operation."

"She will. I'm sure of it." Damien sat down heavily on the stool. "In all likelihood the maid will become your responsibility. It would seem suspicious if we left her in Hatherwood."

"Oh, my God. Why, I hesitate to ask, should we care about a parish that has a population of fifty-eight?"

"We don't. We care about Lord Ardbury and his associates, who haven't yet left the parish. And don't grouse. At least you're not marrying a stranger. How should I go about courting this woman?"

Winthrop folded and unfolded the towel on his arm. "If you mean to convince others that you can't live without her, then you must show great passion for her."

"Passion? Go on."

"Properly contained, of course."

"Why?"

"In a village of fifty-eight a man of your stature is bound to make a stir. I assume she is fair enough on the eyes."

Damien shrugged noncommittally, although he had been awestruck by the loveliness she'd hidden under her disguise. It would be his turn to surprise her next. Would she be disappointed that Sir Angus was gone? Well, tit for tat.

"I take it by your silence that she's a beauty." It was evident by Winthrop's change in demeanor that he had already begun to formulate a plan. "As far as your courtship goes, I doubt you'll have to do much to impress her. You are not only a titled man, but a handsome one also. Your normal wardrobe is enough to impress any lady with a taste for good tailoring."

"It's debatable whether she entrapped me," Damien said, crossing his arms behind his head, "or whether I led her into a dangerous situation. I don't know if I took advantage of her or if she took advantage of me. I haven't the vaguest idea whether she cares about the cut of my trousers, either. Look, Winthrop, I don't need your advice on how to dress and undress for the woman. I need to give the general impression that I can't live without her. It could be true, if she lets our secret slip."

Winthrop ceased his examination of a long-tailed morning coat for creases and loose threads. "Good grief. This is rather fast work to fit around the conspiracy."

"It is not typical of you to jump to conclusions," Damien said in annoyance.

"It's not typical of you to become engaged."

"Do you have another suggestion?" Damien asked dryly. "If so, speak your mind. Just remember, she holds the fate of innumerable lives in her card-dealing hands."

Winthrop turned white. "She is a *gambler*? You neglected that part in your recounting."

"When I met her she was telling fortunes with cards.

The blasted things have been blown into the next county by now."

"I am confused, my lord. I thought you had proposed to a gentlewoman."

"She was in disguise."

"As a lady?"

"No, you parsnip. As a gypsy."

"Male or female?"

"Female, Winthrop. Her disguise was part of a scheme she concocted to impress her desirability on the gentleman she was hoping would propose to her."

"And you are *not* that gentleman?" Winthrop inquired after a long silence.

"How could I possibly be the damn fool when I only met her last night?"

Winthrop compressed his lips, clearly refraining from suggesting to Damien that he was a damn fool himself. "If the jade deceived you with a disguise, I do not see that you have any obligation to marry her at all."

"As you pointed out last night, I was disguised myself. I forced my company upon her for my own interests."

"Well, that is a different matter. If you behave dishonorably toward— toward— I don't believe I caught the young lady's name."

"Urania."

"I beg your pardon."

"She deceived me into believing her name was Urania while I was disguised as Sir Angus."

"That is far more complicated than I first understood. You were acting on the government's behalf?"

"And she was acting on behalf of her heart. She is not a jade at all. If I believed she was corrupt, I might be tempted to let her take care of herself. Considering the ruthless intentions of the conspiracy, that would be tantamount to her demise."

"I'm beginning to understand," Winthrop said, his lips pursing. "Perhaps I'll ride into the next market town early in the morning for flowers to start off this courtship."

Damien nodded. "I don't think I was my usual self with her last night."

"I'd best make sure to deliver the roses before she sees you again, then."

Chapter 20

*J*ust after dawn the next day Iris caught the scullery girl whispering to the milkmaid at the kitchen door. Iris realized too late what had happened, but one had to expect that the servants had heard the drama in the entry hall. There was nothing to do for it but smile mysteriously when the rest of the staff begged her for more information. She refused to answer. The rumor spread.

It appeared that an earl would step in where others had been hesitant to tread. Hatherwood would never again view Miss Rowland as an on-the-shelf eccentric. Her behavior, her history, and her bloodlines would be scrutinized as usual.

But one would not be analyzing Emily for amusement. The question in everyone's mind asked how it was that she, of all girls, had attracted an earl?

And what could one do to emulate her?

Emily's father met her at the bottom of the stairs early the next afternoon. She averted her gaze and offered no greeting. He took her chin in his hand to force her to look at him. "Emily," he said, as she braced for another confrontation. "I knew you were unhappy. I knew you were lonely. But I never thought you would sacrifice what little standing we have to behave without a backward glance to propriety."

She sighed. "It didn't start out as an impropriety."

"Scandal rarely does. It is one small misstep after another until you're up to your neck in a sea of muck."

"It wasn't what you think it is."

"No?"

No. In many ways what had happened was worse. Society might disagree, but Emily valued her life above her reputation. The failed debutante she had once been would have to die if Emily was given a chance to live. But she couldn't explain this to her father. He sought his solutions in a bottle. And yet he was so different when he was sober. Gentle. Caring. She was ashamed that she had caused him distress.

"I was in my cups last night," he admitted. "You had gone to the party without telling me. I'd fallen asleep," he continued, "and when I woke up and saw you had gone, I went straight to Lord Fletcher's house to find you. On the way a peculiar fancy crossed my mind. I imagined I heard your mother telling me that you were in trouble somehow."

"I suppose I was," she said, too guilty to meet his gaze. But she *had* told him about the party, knowing he was too drunk to understand, knowing he had forbidden her from attending.

"I never dreamt you had disobeyed me to meet a lover."

"I didn't." She edged around him. He followed her to the drawing room.

"How long has this romance been brewing?"

"Well, he was Michael's friend before I met him, and—"

His face darkened. "I wish you hadn't felt the need to keep your romance a secret. Did you learn nothing from the pain your mother caused?"

"I have lived with that pain every day of my life," she said quietly. "I can feel it between you and Michael every time he comes home."

"Then why would you engage in such deception, knowing what the price might be?"

"I was lonely, Papa."

"You have friends. You have that little nitwit Lucy and your lady's maid."

"I wanted a husband."

"Well, an earl is not a bad catch." He shook his head, clearly confused. "You evaded my answer. How long have you known Shalcross?"

About five hours longer than you have, she wanted to shout. And that he was marrying her only for the good of God and country. Instead, she said, "I know him best through Michael."

He sat down on the sofa beside her. "Forgive me for what will surely sound like an insult. But I cannot help wondering why a man of his rank would choose a country maid for a bride when there must be a hundred women who would better fit the bill." He might be a drunk and neglectful parent, but he was not without perception.

Emily shrugged. "I suppose it was in the cards. Destiny, you might say."

"Destiny," he repeated in chagrin. "I assumed you would settle down with a nondescript gentleman like Camden."

"Are you complaining because I am marrying an earl?"

"You have not exchanged vows with his lordship yet.

I shall withhold judgment until he meets you at the altar.
I also think it would be decent of him to call on us today
instead of waiting until Sunday."

"I understand that he had other business plans to arrange. He might have wanted to give us time to settle
down."

Or perhaps he had simply gone.

Damien did not call at the house at all that day. He did,
however, send a messenger to the baron to apologize
and to say he looked forward to tea on Sunday. Emily
hid behind the door as her father hesitated to reply.

What could he do? Emily wondered.

Should he hunt down Damien, who might be on the
road this moment, or should he appear to agree, hoping
that Sunday would bring a desirable outcome?

"Sunday it is," he said after a long pause.

The messenger bowed, and Emily released her breath.
"You don't think he's going to come, do you?"

Her father frowned at her. "He will come, or I shall
lead a chase to drag him back for disgracing you."

She smiled wanly. "With the vicar?"

"And his wife."

An hour later a basket of long-stemmed red and
white hothouse roses arrived for Emily. She pulled out
the card that read:

> *For my beloved from—*
>
> *D*

And behind her she heard her father calling a maid to
put the earl's flowers in a vase that should be promi-
nently displayed on the mantel.

Emily pressed the card to her heart. *Beloved*, he'd written. What a rogue. Still, it was a beautiful word. It went perfectly with his gift of the gorgeous roses, which she decided to enjoy, even if they were only a token gesture.

Chapter 21

Lucy arrived in the escort of a footman early Sunday morning before tea. She and Emily walked to the bottom of the garden before either of them felt safe to talk. Then they plopped down on a bench where they could bask in the sun and breathe in the fragrance of the tiny triangles of herbs planted by an artistic gardener's hand.

"I found out who your fiancé is," Lucy whispered.

"Bluebeard?"

"No one quite that ominous," Lucy said with a shudder. "But bad enough, really, for a girl who has led your sheltered life."

"Do I strike you as sheltered?"

"You've never gone to France for a dress fitting, and you've never sailed to Cornwall on a yacht."

"I've never visited London, either," Emily said, leaning down to pinch off a sprig of thyme.

"I assume that will soon change."

"Why?"

"It's Boscastle headquarters. Your betrothed's family is infamous in town."

"I've never heard of them. But, then, I only met him

the night before last. I don't even know what he looks like in the light."

"You don't exactly resemble Urania, either."

"That's one of the things that worries me. It was bad enough placing myself at the mercy of a brash Scotsman with an ever-so-nice voice. But who does he think he's marrying?"

"He'll have the surprise of his life when he sees you face-to-face," Lucy said, adding hastily, "A pleasant surprise, that is."

"He looked shocked when he saw me without the wig. Is his family *that* notorious?"

"My stepmama says that scandal shadows their every step. That goes for the ladies, too, but the gentlemen are worse. You wouldn't believe their history—*recent* history."

"I might if you would tell me. Besides, I'd believe anything after this experience."

"Abduction, duels, a bride who jilted herself at the altar and is now the family's matriarch. One of Damien's cousins opened the Academy for Young Ladies in London and ended up marrying a mercenary who ended up becoming a duke."

"Which made her a duchess."

Lucy sighed. "Society adores them. You might adore him in time, too."

"There is little I could do to save myself. It isn't as if I can break off the engagement."

"Break it off?" Lucy asked incredulously. "My stepmama only wanted you to know so that you'd keep a tight grip on him. And—"

Emily gasped, rising from the bench. Deep masculine laughter wafted through the garden, and there, greeting her father at the front steps, stood the earl. "He's here! He looks so different. So—"

"He looks so fine," Lucy whispered. "Did he get taller?"

"No. Yes. He's leaner. And his hair—what a sinful shade of black."

"He doesn't have a red beard."

"He doesn't have any beard at all," Emily said, wishing she could see more of his strong bone structure. And his eyes. No. She would avoid their spell today, or she wouldn't be able to concentrate on anything else. "What should I do, Lucy?"

"Ask whether he has an eligible cousin or brother somewhere in England who would suit your dearest friend."

"I will promise you this." Emily tucked the sprig of thyme behind Lucy's ear. "If I am still alive three months hence, I shall summon you to London for a husband hunt."

"You aren't in any *real* danger, are you, Emily?"

"I might be," Emily said, biting the inside of her cheek. Had anyone in Hatherwood's history ever known a moment of true fear?

"Then it *was* gallant of the earl to ask for your hand so that he could protect you."

Emily shrugged, her gaze drifting again to Damien's arresting figure. Not only did he stand out in a crowd, but even the sunlight seemed to pay homage to his appeal. It deepened the hollows of his hard face and glinted on his soft blue-black hair. And even though he appeared to have lost some girth, his elegant jacket displayed the broadly proportioned shoulders that had shielded her last night. Just watching him shrug at someone's remark, hearing his deep laugh at another, electrified her. How unfair that he had become more handsome than when he was in disguise.

How much harder it would be to resist the devilish smile that he turned on her without warning. His eyes traveled over her, from her face to her slippers, openly warm and sensual. She returned his playful smile with one of her own before she could curb the instinct.

He was wickedness and danger in the form of one irresistibly self-possessed gentleman. And suddenly she realized that she needn't worry about saying the wrong thing. Everyone was staring at him and vying for his attention. She would go unnoticed until he formally approached her. At least the respite allowed her nerves to settle.

With a twinkle in his eye that promised trouble, he gave her another smile and turned back to the gentlemen who crowded around him, asking his opinion on everything from the weather to his political views.

She would have loved to eavesdrop.

"He could have had you locked away in some dark Scottish castle if he chose," Lucy whispered. "I daresay that in the long run that would be a lot easier and less expensive than a marriage of inconvenience."

"How morbid of you," Emily said with a tight smile. "Think of your father building that tower for your mother. You should honor her memory, at least. Aren't castles supposed to be romantic?"

Lucy looked so instantly guilt-stricken that Emily wished she could take back her words. "I didn't mean to sound cruel. The tower was an act of love."

"A dark castle isn't. You're right. Maybe he will lock me away, except that he isn't Scottish, which doesn't mean he couldn't lock me up in a manor house."

"Now I shall cry."

"I'll cry with you. I miss my mother every hour of the day." She reached for Lucy's hand. "Forgive me."

"Always. How dull my life would be without your frequent sins to forgive. And now I'm going to lose you."

"I won't go that far away, Lucy. We can visit each other, can't we?"

Lucy sniffed. "There will never be anyone like you, Emily."

Emily took Lucy's hand. She should have apologized more, but all of a sudden a row of vehicles appeared in the drive. Lady Fletcher's phaeton was one of the first to arrive. Lucy gasped.

"I forgot to tell you," Lucy said behind her fan." My father is bringing Lord Ardbury along for tea."

Emily swallowed over the tightness in her throat. "Does Damien know?"

"I assume so. Don't be alarmed if Ardbury asks everyone whether they've encountered any gypsies in the area, or are missing any valuables."

"Gypsies?" Emily said, then she nodded in understanding. "I haven't seen any in months."

"Apparently everyone is convinced that they robbed us last night at the party," Lucy said. "Diana is ever so convincing. I almost believed her myself."

"I didn't realize that there were gypsies at the party," Emily said, slowly strolling forward. "Did you notice any?"

"Oh yes. There was that fortune-teller's tent by the brook."

Emily stared straight ahead, her heartbeat accelerating. "Did you visit it?"

"Of course. She couldn't give me a good reading. The wind blew down the tent."

They glanced up together as the gentlemen who assembled on the steps moved as one into the house. Damien paused. For a moment Emily thought he was about to turn in her direction. Her heart hammered in expectation. But at the same instant, Lady Fletcher and four other matrons emerged from the garden and veered toward the bench that sat beside the stone entrance steps.

"Nothing was really stolen from your house?" Emily whispered to Lucy, relieved and yet disappointed at her reprieve. It was only a matter of minutes before she had to face the rogue and put on a performance to convince everyone he was the love of her life. Somehow she thought it would not be as difficult as she'd feared.

"Diana hid a few things to cover for you," Lucy said softly.

"To make me appear to be a house robber? Thank her for me."

"She did it for us, Emily."

"The gentlemen have abandoned us for their somber conversation," Lady Fletcher said, as Emily and her step-daughter approached the ladies seated before them.

"Is anything wrong in the village?" Emily asked in an appropriately distressed voice.

"Only that you have been deceiving us with your delicious secret, Emily." Lady Fletcher glanced meaningfully at the house. "Wherever did you find him, and how did you manage to keep him to yourself for this long?"

Chapter 22

$\mathcal{D}$amien stared straight ahead as the baron led him and a small group of gentlemen through the hall toward the drawing room. He hoped to appear appropriately concerned over the vicar's warning that a brazen theft at a ball should not be allowed to go unpunished, and that heathens would be murdering innocent citizens in their sleep, the next Hatherwood knew.

He had not been able to keep his eyes from Emily when he spotted her in the garden. He'd stared at her lush figure and fair skin, the copper-red hair drawn back on her neck. She was not the same woman who'd caused so much mayhem the evening before last. This demure young lady looked capable of ruining a man's life.

But she hadn't trapped the young man *she* wanted. Damien was the prey she had caught in her web of deceit.

She had stolen several glances in his direction, hesitating to meet his eyes. When she had, he'd been torn between beating a retreat and striding across the grass to take her in his arms. It was easier to act besotted with her than he'd anticipated. The challenge was in not overplaying their attraction to each other.

He smiled inwardly, wondering what she was thinking. And if he met her approval.

Emily swallowed and tried to compose herself as she settled in her chair. Now the courtship began. The town of Hatherwood was about to meet her suitor. And, apparently, so was she.

She wouldn't have recognized him as Sir Angus when he entered the drawing room. His dark elegance stopped conversation between the vicar and her father. The vicar's wife stared at the earl and then at Emily, not hiding her astonishment that they would soon marry.

She wasn't half as astonished as Emily.

Damien's face, shaved clean to reveal a square jaw and chiseled cheekbones, left her momentarily speechless. Without his beard, he intimidated her in a different way than he had as Sir Angus. His blue eyes, still intense, held hers in amusement.

The guests could forgive him for looking at his fiancée with pleasure.

Emily knew that they would not forgive his thoughts. Nor should she.

He walked toward her chair, uncaring that the entire room watched him in anticipation. The vicar often came for tea. But today he appeared to have brought the entire parish with him.

"I trust you slept well, my dear," Damien said as he reached her side. His low, mellifluous voice bore no hint of Scotland at all. It managed to penetrate her composure nonetheless.

"I slept like a baby," she lied.

"Did you?" The skepticism in his voice revealed that he didn't believe her for a moment.

She glanced up at his shoulders. He was built well enough to make any lady's heart race when he approached her. His lean, muscular torso didn't need padding. Even if—

"You aren't half the man you were when we met," she whispered, hoping to unnerve him.

He laughed quietly to let her know she had failed. "I hope you don't miss our friend Angus. He's gone and is never coming back. He wasn't much of a lady's man, anyway."

She twirled a lock of her hair around a white-gloved finger. "And you are?"

"That depends on the lady. You'll have to wait to find out. Are you impatient?"

Her voice caught. "For the wedding?"

"It's a good thing," he said, glancing up at a passing guest, "that I didn't see through your disguise right away."

"And why is that?"

"I've discovered recently that I have an obsession for red hair."

"Yours or mine?"

He grinned. "Do you prefer Sir Angus to me?"

"I did let him kiss me."

"That's true." He frowned, his heated gaze drifting to the curl she dropped to her décolletage. "I'll have to take that as a challenge."

She swallowed. "I did think your shoulders looked lopsided when we rode through the woods."

His mouth curved. "Are they more pleasing to you now?"

She felt a blush wash across her cheeks. "A lady doesn't admire a man's physique in public."

"Don't worry. We'll have plenty of private moments to admire each other."

"Sit down, my lord," the vicar said. "It's time for tea. You'll have years for your betrothed after the wedding."

Damien bent his head close to hers. His cheek bore the scent of sandalwood soap. "Behave as you normally would," he murmured, taking the empty chair adjacent to hers.

"I've never been in this position before," she murmured as she rose beside the tea table and proceeded to fill his cup until the hot brew cascaded over the rim. "Oh, dash. I am all thumbs today."

Lady Fletcher leaned over the table, lifting the dripping saucer to the footman at her side.

"Have you decided whether you will honeymoon or settle down immediately on your estate, Lord Shalcross?" Lucy asked in a bid to draw attention from the dripping saucer.

Damien leaned against the arm of his chair. "I would prefer to live in the country, but I haven't begun to look for a house. My wife will have a say in the matter."

Envious stares and endless questions were directed at Emily from the parish ladies, who could not believe that the baron's gauche daughter could land an earl when she'd never even attended finishing school. Emily was likely the only person in the room who knew that a school didn't exist that could prepare her for this earl.

Suffice it to say, he made a stir by answering a barrage of questions with a smile or two and several vague replies. By the time a fresh tray of pastries and lemon cake arrived, Emily wished she had laced everyone's tea with gin.

Someone had returned to the subject of the jewel

theft at Lord Fletcher's party. "And to think the vagabonds disappeared without a trace," Lady Fletcher said. "My husband had the woods around the house searched, and all that was found was a card. I'll never see those jewels again."

Probably because most of them had never existed in the first place, Emily thought, not knowing how to react. Fortunately, Damien took the initiative. "Ladies and gentlemen, shall we walk through the garden before another storm ruins the day?"

Emily followed the party outside. How could Damien appear so collected? Her heart was thudding against her breast. But, then, who else knew that his outward urbanity concealed a dedicated agent?

"Pay attention," he said quietly, giving her his forearm.

She blinked, pulled from her daydream. Pay attention to what? If she paid any closer attention to him, she'd melt into a puddle.

He had led the party out onto the front steps. Tiny spears of sunlight poked through a gathering bank of clouds. All at once she felt Damien tense.

"Do not panic," he said under his breath, which naturally made her heart thud all the harder.

Her father brushed around them, mumbling his apologies. "Some late arrivals, my lord. You must excuse our rustic ways. An earl taking a local lady to wife is an event that will be long remembered in Hatherwood history."

Emily sighed. She assumed that their impending marriage would be an event that Damien wished he could forget. But then on the front steps he murmured, "Darling, you've dropped one of your gloves."

"No, I haven't."

He made a discreet motion, tugging the glove from her fingers until it fell at her feet. "Oh, really," she muttered, bending to rescue it, only to realize he had dropped the glove as a ruse to lean over her.

"Remain calm," he said. "Act as if this were any other day. That is Lord Ardbury walking up the drive with Fletcher. You are to behave as if he were any other stranger who came to tea to make your acquaintance."

"Except that he wants to kill me. That does not make him like most other strangers."

"True. You will have to put on a convincing performance. We both know you're capable of it. I heard you giving readings in the tent."

"Listening to a professional consultation? Have you no shame?"

"Eavesdropping is part of my profession."

"Why eavesdrop on me? I'm not a professional anything."

"Perhaps I had an inkling that you would become a person essential to Crown security. Perhaps I liked the sound of your voice." His eyes narrowed in good nature. "I haven't decided whether I can trust you yet."

"Lord Shalcross," her father said behind them. "Two gentlemen have just arrived who would like to meet you."

How the earl could straighten and look Lord Ardbury in the face as coolly as he did amazed Emily. Damien did not betray by his voice or mannerisms that he had been Sir Angus Morpeth, anarchist and enemy of the Crown.

Emily was anything but cool. Her mouth went dry. Her knees shook, and she suspected she had a guilty-as-charged look on her face that was impossible to conceal. And when Lord Ardbury brought up the subject of the missing jewelry, she excused herself from the conversation and promised she would be right back.

There were only a few activities in her normal routine certain to calm her down. A sequester in the library was one of them.

In the clatter and conversation and clinking of glasses in the billiards room, Damien could easily step outside and not be missed. It wouldn't be unusual for a betrothed couple to become separated from the party to steal a few moments alone.

Emily wasn't what he would call helpless. She'd acted with enough audacity to stage a plot that had deceived even Damien on the night he had walked into her tent.

She had gone to great lengths to attract the man she desired. Damien had inserted himself in number seven's place with no thought to the damage he would inflict on either party or on himself.

He roused himself at the sound of Lord Ardbury's voice. "I have business matters that require I leave for London this afternoon. Before I go, I urge you to apprehend this gypsy before she commits other crimes. I brought this sketch so that you can be on the lookout. We cannot allow lawless persons like her to victimize innocent citizens."

He produced from a portfolio a poor sketch of Emily disguised as the fortune-teller Urania. "Pass this to each man at the table," he instructed the footman who was standing in a trance at the sideboard.

"Never saw her in my life."

"I'd not forget a face like that, gypsy or not."

The sketch came to Damien. He considered it carefully, recognizing the revised work of the journalist who worked for Ardbury. Apparently the artist had not received an accurate description from the guests who visited the fortune-telling tent, because Mr. Dinsmore had given Urania eyebrows like arched caterpillars and a tiny mole on her left shoulder.

Or had she worn a false patch last night? Damien had been so startled when she'd discarded her wig that a little beauty mark could have easily escaped his notice.

"Does she look familiar?" Lord Ardbury asked, clearly noticing Damien's interest in the sketch.

"Not in the slightest," he said in a bored voice, passing the paper to the gentleman standing across from him.

His heart thumped against his ribs. Damn it to hell. He had been studying Emily all morning. Had her shoulders been covered by her dress, or had she been wearing a shawl? One slip and her shoulder, marked or not, would draw any red-blooded male's attention. The dream he'd had of her still tantalized him, but then, merely watching her play with her hair had stirred a relentless agony in him that was all too real.

He needed to warn her before she and Lord Ardbury came face-to-face. Although Ardbury was more engrossed in politics and power than in womanizing, he was not likely to overlook a detail as distinct as Emily's mark. Nor would her father, who had just been handed the sketch to examine.

The baron knew only part of what his daughter had done the night of the party. He had witnessed her dramatic removal of the wig. Surely he knew whether Emily had a mole on her shoulder or not. Would he inadvertently reveal who she was by his reaction to the sketch?

To Damien's relief, the baron gave the drawing a cursory glance, muttering, "They all look alike to me—

thieves and vagabonds. The gypsies know to avoid this estate. They'll find no sympathy here."

At that moment another man entered the room. He was tall and properly dressed in a frock coat and light trousers, his black hair cropped short. Damien did not recognize him at first until he said, "I'm sorry to have missed the tea. I was up with a sick horse all night. What have you done with the ladies?" He grinned at Damien. "Lovers' spat already?"

Damien relaxed. Michael looked more like an English scholar than a half-blooded Rom. His devil-may-care demeanor dispelled the tension that had been gathering in the room.

"Thank you for reminding me that I have neglected my fiancée for too long," Damien said. "Gentlemen, it has been a pleasure making your acquaintance. I hope to meet you again. May your jewels remain safe until then."

He bowed as cheers and good wishes for the wedding accompanied him to the door. Several men in the room stated they would leave now, too. Once in the hall, Damien quickened his stride. In his haste he nearly collided with Emily's maid, who backed away from him as if he were the grim reaper come to collect her soul.

"Is something wrong, my lord?" she said, giving him a harsh scrutiny. "Are you leaving the house, or the village perhaps?"

"I regret to disappoint you, but I am here to stay until the wedding." He paused at the relief he saw in her eyes. "If it doesn't offend you, I would like to make a personal inquiry about Miss Rowland, and you have likely seen her undressed more often than anyone else."

"My lord!" she said, shocked. "How dare you ask such a question."

"I dare because it could—oh, never mind. I'll find out myself the traditional way."

He wanted another look at Emily in the daylight, anyway. He wanted to study the ingenuous miss who would become his wife when he had loved only one other woman in his life. If he was going to exchange vows with Emily, he might as well learn the symmetry of her face, her preferences, her favorite pastimes, as she would learn his.

Still, for the life of him he could think of only one pastime whenever he looked at her. Was there anything wrong in longing to possess the woman he was to marry? They were going to be together perhaps forever. How could he not look forward to their intimate life?

No one would think it remiss of him to feign infatuation with his bride-to-be. But if he overplayed the role, Lord Ardbury would notice, and something, perhaps the sight of Emily standing beside Damien, might prompt suspicion.

In the event that Lord Ardbury realized the truth, Damien would not hesitate to wrestle the traitor to the ground and hold him there until the authorities could arrive. Despite having successfully having tricked several people, Emily had placed herself in peril. Damien could only hope she could remain levelheaded enough to throw Ardbury off her track.

Curse the winds of fortune. Had a man and woman ever been tossed together at worse time, in a worse place, or for a worse reason?

Chapter 23

*E*mily had taken shelter in the library, assuming her absence would go unnoticed, as it often had in the past. She might have guessed that Damien would pursue her. Now he had cornered her with her back to the door. There was no escaping him today. Nor after the wedding. Would he always be this attentive?

"I understand that facing Ardbury is nerve-racking for you," he said. "But you're not alone in this. I will stand with you."

She frowned. He was staring intently at her left shoulder, and not with his usual sensuality. "Facing *you* is nerve-racking," she said. "I came in here to escape."

"It wasn't a bad idea. How easily does that sleeve unlace?"

"I beg your pardon?"

"I need to examine you from your left shoulder to the top of your breast."

Her mouth dropped open. "Wouldn't you rather check my teeth and knees for soundness?"

Dark humored danced in his eyes. "I wouldn't mind taking you for a ride around the paddock, but it might look odd at a tea party."

She backed away from the door and toward the corner, only to feel his hand capture her and pull her forward by the waist. She gave a strong twist of protest, just on principle, but unfortunately her heart wasn't in discouraging him. It was too busy beating in her throat.

"Damien!"

"Yes, darling."

"This sort of behavior can't continue."

"It can and will," he said, consoling her, his hand stroking up her arm. "As long as you are with me, you are safe."

"Not if I am required to start undressing in the library."

"But I like libraries."

She clenched her teeth. "So do I."

"Maybe we can read together after everyone leaves," he suggested, although his mischievous smile implied that reading did not figure high on the list of what he wanted to do when they were alone.

It seemed rules were meant to be broken by men of Damien Boscastle's background.

She had a single moment to look up into his chiseled face before his mouth descended on hers. His lips felt indecent and delightful. It took all her dwindling reason to remember that he was kissing her in front of the window in full view of three guests who happened to be strolling toward the carriages parked in the drive.

"Damien," she whispered. "We have an audience. This is a library, which is almost as sacred to me as a church. It's blasphemy to accost a lady in her only port from the storm. Besides, everyone can see us through the window."

"We are supposed to be in love. I think they will excuse us this performance. And I might not be an expert in the social graces, but I don't think it's polite to browse through books when one is giving a tea party."

His mouth claimed hers again before she could ask him to at least close the curtains. And then it didn't matter. His kiss deepened and demanded. It conquered her will and left in exchange a greed as wild as his own. The only difference between the two of them that she could identify was that while her body had softened, his had become hard and unyielding.

Damien was her complete and irresistible opposite.

She broke free for a moment. "Lord Shalcross—"

"You taste like the woman in my dream," he murmured. His tongue sketched the shape of her lips, slipping back inside her mouth, flirting, taunting until her breasts tightened in response. She sagged against the support of his arm. Had she heard him correctly? Was the passion the scapegrace showed her meant for someone else? Had he just said that he was dreaming about another a few days before they would stand together at the altar?

"You shameless, deceitful—" She couldn't find the words to describe what she felt at his confession. It was all she could do to take in air. "You're kissing me like a libertine, and you expect me to be flattered that I remind you of another woman? A woman that you *dream* about? You are as tactful as an ape to mention her to me. I never told you about the man I dream about."

He stilled. "You have erotic dreams about another man?"

"I didn't say my dreams were erotic."

He began to laugh. "The woman was *you*. What I meant was that you—she—was in my bed, about to ride me into oblivion, when I woke up."

"Ride you into—really. I *wasn't* in your bed. And I've never done anything erotic in my life."

"You will soon enough," he assured her, sliding his hand up between her shoulder blades. Her breasts brushed his shirtfront. If she went to pieces when all he had done was kiss her and whisper a few wicked words in her ear, then she would never survive their wedding night.

"I did dream about you the night we met," he said.

"From your brief but vivid description, it was quite a sinful dream."

"The only sinful thing about it was that it ended too soon."

A warm sensation washed over her. She was powerless to resist him. "Was anyone else in this dream?"

His smile was utterly disgraceful. "You *were* the dream. And it was lovely. You and your breasts."

She gasped, embarrassed, but at the same time longing to hear how wickedly she had behaved in his dream. In all fairness, she couldn't resent his dream lover when it had been her.

He drew her closer, his other hand caressing the gap of skin between her glove and the sleeve of her gown. Little by little she dissolved. Her senses wanted to surrender. Her blood clamored for an ending to this confusion. What manner of husband would he make? He was a charming, conniving scamp. Well, it took one to know one.

"The window," she whispered again. "They've seen enough."

"But I haven't."

"We're in the library, my lord."

His voice vibrated with humor. "Are we?"

"Our performance is over—"

"You didn't come here to read," he said, looking around for a book she might have taken from the shelves. Then he grinned at her. "Neither did I. But I want to look at you, and I have a good reason for it. Your hair is truly red."

"Yours isn't," she said crossly.

"You should have seen my valet scrubbing the henna out of it."

"You've lost your nationality and about half your weight. Or is *this* another disguise? For all I know, you'll be a Spaniard tomorrow."

He gave a rich laugh, his gaze lowering from her face to her neckline, lingering there. She felt heat rise to her skin. "I hope you don't think a book will come between us once we're married." He looked up at her. "And I'm not taking a position against literature."

She stared up at him. "Don't you think I understand that ours won't be a real marriage?"

He frowned. "If I were a better man, I might not insist you surrender to me as part of our bargain. We could come to another arrangement for our needs."

"But?" she queried, a hint of hope in her voice.

"But I'm not a better man," he said, smiling ruefully. "I'm one who does what he has to do. And as a man, I find you rather appealing."

"My life is shattered."

He shook his head. "You missed your cue. You were supposed to give me a compliment back. Unless you think I have no redeeming qualities at all."

"You're—" She couldn't admit how beautiful he was and that she was afraid he'd break her heart. She couldn't confess that when he smiled at her, nothing seemed impossible. And that if she had become enmeshed in his conspiracy, there wasn't anyone she trusted more to take care of her. "You are the most courageous man I've ever met."

"And?"

"And I find you appealing, too, and if you use that as an advantage, I won't ever compliment you again."

Silence. Then he took her hand and led her into another corner of the room where the curtains were drawn, explaining over her objections, "I didn't intrude on your solace to kiss you. That was a spontaneous pleasure. What I meant to do was take a close look at your bare shoulder."

"You— *What?*"

He put one hand against the wall as a barrier to her flight. "Can you pull down your sleeve yourself or do you require my help?" he asked with the confidence of a man whose seductive powers he clearly took for granted.

She felt color rise to her face. "Can you control yourself before I pull an entire shelf of books onto your fatuous head?"

He smiled at her threat. "You misunderstand." He brought his hand to her throat, tracing downward until his fingers slid beneath the sprigged poplin of her left sleeve. Her nipples tightened against her undergarments. "I'm doing this for your own good."

Michael had been the first person at the party to notice his sister's disappearance. He had been standing outside the billiards room when she had sneaked off down the hall to vanish from sight. He knew where Emily took refuge when the baron went on a drunken rampage.

But as far as Michael could tell, the baron had behaved like a gentleman, a proud father of the bride-to-be, all day. Something else had sent Emily into hiding, and Michael couldn't take the chance that one of the traitors in the tower had already learned her true identity and traced her to the house.

"Where the hell is Shalcross?" he muttered, backing so erratically to the stairs that he almost knocked Iris into the banister.

"Sir!" she exclaimed in the prim voice that usually made him tease her.

"Where is my sister?"

"She's saying good-bye to the guests, I think."

"No, she isn't. She's gone off alone."

"I'll check upstairs," she said, tightening her apron strings.

"I'll search below."

And below was exactly where he found Emily a few minutes later when he burst into the library and spotted her bare-shouldered in the corner with the man he was going to kill.

Chapter 24

$\mathcal{D}$amien turned to shield Emily from the gentleman who had slammed the door with enough force to unshelve a volume of *Fanny Hill: Memoirs of a Woman of Pleasure*. He raised his hand to catch it, his body serving as a dressing screen while Emily retied her sleeve.

"This is not what it looks like," Damien said, realizing the lanky man who had murder in his eyes was actually Michael.

Michael pushed a chair into the wall. "You rotten sod."

Emily ducked beneath Damien's arm. "He's right, Michael. Stop abusing the furniture. There is a reason for this."

He strode up to Damien, his eyes black with anger. "When a man undresses a woman against a wall there is only one possible explanation for his conduct."

"Michael, you're wrong." Emily snagged his arm before he could take a swing at Damien. "He was only trying to see if the birthmark on my left shoulder was visible in this gown."

"How does he know that you have a birthmark there?" Michael demanded, pulling out of her grasp. "I never noticed it, and I've lived with you since you were born."

Emily took a deep breath. "I *don't* have a birthmark. It was a spot of ink from the quill I was using to take notes on those cards that have caused all this trouble."

"The cards didn't cause trouble," he said grimly. "Certain people did. What does a birthmark matter, anyway?"

Damien pushed away from the wall. "If not for your behavior, I'd take you for a civilized being."

Michael glowered at him over the top of Emily's head. "I'm beginning to rue the day I called you my friend."

Emily placed the book that Damien had rescued on a chair. "*Michael*, listen for a moment. One of the men in the tower made a sketch of me to show the authorities. He drew a mark on my shoulder. The earl wanted to make sure it couldn't be seen in this gown."

Michael, uncomplicated male that he was, looked at Damien for confirmation. "Well, could it?"

"Not that I could tell," Damien replied. "She said she washed it off the night of the party."

"How good is the sketch of her?" Michael asked, calmer now.

"The dark wig obscured most of her features." Damien glanced at Emily's face. "With the exception of her eyes." How the journalist had managed to capture their sultry mischief in such a rush of circumstances was a credit to his skill and of deep concern to Damien. Emily's bright red hair attracted a man's notice like a banner.

He studied her profile, the loose curls captured in a ribbon. She had eyelashes of an extravagant length and a smattering of tiny scars on her cheeks from what might have been a case of childhood pox. If not for all the excitement last night, he would have noticed the dimple in her chin. Thank God neither detail had appeared on the sketch.

She might not resemble the exotic fortune-teller who had intrigued Damien last night, but she had a secret allure that appealed to him a little more whenever he looked at her. He realized he had a long way to go before she would give herself to him of her own volition.

He would have to take, initiate, coax her, one move at a time.

There wouldn't be enough time before the wedding to build trust between them. But he planned to take full advantage of their marriage bed. She seemed to have accepted that her life depended on Damien's ability to protect her.

In fact, she had shown herself to be more levelheaded than any of the ladies Damien had known in the past. He was the one who had gone into a panic over the sketch. It made him wonder whether he had underestimated her ability to adapt to a crisis.

She had risked everything to take her destiny in her own hands. He would do well to remember that he had fallen for her artless scheme and had not even been her intended victim.

Chapter 25

The Earl of Shalcross called on Miss Emily Rowland every morning, afternoon, and evening for four days straight. When he was not visiting her house, he was escorting her to a small supper party hosted in his honor by a member of Hatherwood's gentry, who seemed smitten to have a genuine nobleman in their midst.

In the eyes of the enthralled villagers, Damien's desire for Emily's company reinforced the image of a man desperately in love. An intense courtship was not only a means of keeping watch over Emily, but of passing the hours until Winthrop returned with the special license. Lord Ardbury had taken leave of the village a few days prior. Presumably he had set in motion the cogs of his conspiracy.

Damien wondered how much longer he could curb his impatience to resume his own duty. He had an assassination to thwart. He'd been given only a few details about Viscount Deptford. Three years ago Deptford had been a staunch supporter of the conspiracy. But apparently in the interim he had become disillusioned with the group's leaders, Lord Ardbury among them. Deptford knew the names and connections of secret radicals all over England, some in government positions.

Damien assumed this was why the anarchists wanted the viscount dead and why the Crown had offered to protect him. But instead of rushing to Deptford's castle to persuade him to go to London, Damien was discussing thoroughbreds at dinner with a country squire or imagining what Emily would look like when he undressed her.

In his estimation, her hair, unbound, would reach several inches below her shoulder blades. He pictured the ends curling around her breasts. He tortured himself wondering what sounds she would make when he made her his. He knew that his kisses gave her pleasure. He knew that he desired her. But he was surprised that she seemed so receptive in the moments when he simply had to touch her when nobody was looking.

After all, he was a man who had willingly assumed other identities for his country. It was no burden to feign attraction to her. But, on the contrary, he had to restrain his sensual impulses in her presence. This courtship had begun to feel so natural that it worried him. No matter that he would be her first lover and that taking her virginity was a matter that deserved consideration.

But it wasn't until the fifth afternoon of that week, as he and Emily watched a cricket game on the village green, that he was reminded *he* was definitely not her first love. He would have to be obtuse to miss the quick looks she darted at one of the cricket players, a tall, rather gangly young man who seemed oblivious to everything except the game.

The party guest Damien had replaced in the queue. So this was his competition—the man Emily had dreamt about, schemed to attract.

Did Emily still have feelings for the man? Damien

shook his head. This was what happened when a person forgot his manners—life would have been far less complicated if Damien had not insisted on taking someone else's place in line. Or if the cricketer had refused to let Damien have his way. It was shocking how one small act could alter a person's life.

"Someone you know?" he asked her quietly, noticing that she had let her bonnet slide to her nape, the blue silk ribbons at her throat fluttering in the breeze. An unconscious or openly inviting gesture? And was it directed at him ... or at the cricketer? "Yes," she said with a blush that gave Damien pause. Was he supposed to pretend that it didn't matter? *Did* it matter?

"He is the man whose place I took inside the tent?"

She reached back to pull on her bonnet. "Don't keep staring at him that way."

"Then it *is* him."

"What if it is?" she said, at once on the defensive. "It doesn't matter now, does it?"

"I'm not sure. You went to a great deal of trouble to persuade him that you belonged together."

"Well, you changed that, and it can't be undone."

Perhaps not. But there were enough obstacles in Damien's path that he didn't need the memory of a cricket player clouding a marriage that neither he nor Emily had planned.

So, while Damien remained confident that he would be his wife's first lover, he would have to wonder if she still had feelings for this man. How deep did her affection for him go? Damien wasn't an expert on the subject, but even he knew this was not how he wanted to start a marriage. Aside from the conspiracy and sexual compatibility, would they come to care for each other in time?

He had to admit that she wasn't unpleasant company. Through it all, she had managed to keep her wits about her for the most part.

They walked past the cricket match, Emily not looking back. Damien realized she was not in a talkative mood. "Do you mean that you staged a fortune-telling performance for that man and now you have no feeling for him at all?"

Emily stopped to stare up at him. "Well, yes. And no."

"What the devil does that mean?" he asked, annoyed by this fickle response, when his instincts should have appreciated how easily she had adjusted to her change of circumstances. Indeed, he wasn't certain whether her loyalty rested with him or the young man she had previously desired. Perhaps she was that uniquely dangerous sort of woman who saw foremost to herself.

"Are you going to insist I humiliate myself by telling you everything?"

He looked around. There were other families and couples watching them, waving and doffing hats as if they had known Damien from birth. "Yes," he said. "Tell me everything."

She sighed, walking a few steps ahead of him to the pond. "His name is Camden Jackson, and I've been waiting five years for him to notice me."

To notice her? Was the man oblivious? "Does he know that you feel this way?"

She halted in her steps to pull her skirts away from the duck that had waddled behind her from the pond. "I'll never know whether he knows or not. I had planned to read myself into his future at the party. The cards had been arranged so that I could predict our romance."

Another duck splashed toward them from the murky

water. Damien said, "Excuse me while I wipe a tear from my eye."

She blinked and looked up at him in such disbelief that he felt like a bastard. "Emily, I shouldn't have said that. I—"

She started to laugh. "Don't turn around too suddenly."

"Why? Is your beloved approaching?"

"No. Just a mother duckling and her babies. I wouldn't want you to step on them."

Chapter 26

*E*mily had never been interested in cricket, and she wasn't about to pretend enthusiasm for the game now. She was too conscious of Damien, of the silence between them. He had asked questions and endeavored to learn more about her. Wasn't it fair that she do the same?

"Have you notified anyone in your family that we are to be married, my lord?"

He hesitated. "I haven't been the best correspondent. I did write letters off and on."

He glanced at her. His blue eyes almost made her not care about his beginnings. "I have three younger brothers in England, numerous cousins, and a mother, a *duchesse*, who is living in France. I set out at an early age to conquer the world. I was in a private rivalry with my cousin Grayson, who is the fifth Marquess of Sedgecroft and as rich as Croesus."

"Oh," she said, smiling a little. "Did you achieve your goal?"

"Not quite. I was given an earldom as a reward for my dedication to the East India Company. I made and lost and remade a personal fortune. But did I accomplish what I set out to do? Not quite."

"Why not?" she teased, wanting more than a glimpse into his past.

"I hoped to impress my family. When my father died I inherited his viscountcy and made plans to secure my foreign investments and return home."

"Why didn't you?"

His mood seemed to darken. It reminded her of the dangerous sophistication that existed beneath his outward charm. "I was placed under arrest and imprisoned for three years."

"But you gained your freedom." She didn't know what else to say. Three years in a foreign prison? She couldn't imagine how he had come out not only sane and self-possessed but as a decent human being.

He smiled, and yet his eyes locked her out of his secrets. "I escaped. It is a story for a private moment. I cannot relate it and stand watch over you at the same time."

"You don't have to pretend that you're besotted with me," she said quietly.

"Why not? It makes more sense to those watching our courtship. It explains why I cannot wait to marry and whisk you away."

She pursed her lips. "But you aren't besotted with me."

"Are you besotted with me?" he asked, his smile sardonic and perhaps curious.

"Not yet," she admitted. "In my most truthful moments, I'm sorry that I ever met you. Can you in all honesty say that you are overenthused at the prospect of marrying me?"

His mouth firmed. "I'm not the sort of man who is enthusiastic about most of what matters in life. Gentlemen who are prone to an excess of emotion do not generally make good espionage agents."

Which led Emily to wonder whether good agents made doting husbands. She suspected not.

The moment the cricket match ended, Camden abandoned his team and dashed across the green to intercept Emily and Damien. Emily again felt the moodiness that emanated from Damien in the other man's presence and quickened her pace, doing her best to ignore the sweet lumphead she had been infatuated with for years. But Camden would not be ignored, even though a few days ago he hadn't regarded Emily as a female interesting enough to notice.

She wasn't sure he noticed her now as much as he did Damien. "My lord, Miss Rowland," he said breathlessly, bowing at Damien and flashing Emily a perfunctory smile. "I've heard the news of your engagement. I couldn't be happier for you both."

Damien stared through Camden as if he were a window looking into an empty room. "And you are—"

"Oh, sorry." Camden swiped his hand through his tousled hair. "Camden Jackson, my lord. One of Emily's oldest friends. We toddled together on this very common."

"Did you?" Damien said as if he were addressing the toddler Camden had once been. "How quaint. I don't believe my betrothed has mentioned you."

"No?" Camden looked so disappointed that Emily could have poked him with her parasol. This was the most attention he'd ever paid her, and even now he was more engrossed in making Damien's acquaintance than in her. She might well have been invisible.

It made her wonder why she had spent so much energy trying to impress the lout.

A thousand love potions would not change what Camden felt for her, which was a thousand times nothing.

The brooding aristocrat at her side might never fall in love with her, either. She couldn't forget that he saw her as an obligation in the short term. And she saw him as— Well, she hadn't decided what he was to her yet. She needed to know more about Damien before she passed judgment. But what she'd learned today about his past intrigued her. Standing next to Camden, the earl's self-possessed elegance put Camden's athletic vigor to shame.

It was impossible not to compare one man to the other. But, obviously, she'd best keep her comparisons to herself. Damien had admitted that he was competitive in business. It was rather intriguing to anticipate that he might also compete for her interest.

She couldn't understand why Camden was acting like an awkward schoolboy. Perhaps one day, with Miss Whitlock's tutoring, he would mature into a stronger man. Damien, on the other hand, was more than enough man for Emily, as dark and enigmatic as a demigod who had been sent to save her against her will.

He might not ever love her, but he had promised to take care of her. And if he was willing to be her guardian, she would learn how to be the wife he'd have chosen on his own. As soon as she understood what that was.

"Come, Emily," Damien murmured. "You've been standing in the sun too long without putting on your bonnet or using your parasol."

"What sun?" Camden said jokingly. "The sky is as black as a kettle."

Emily swallowed at the rather unpleasant smile that settled on Damien's face. "I don't want her to become overwarmed. That fair skin flushes so easily."

Emily's skin went straight from a blush to boiling red, and Camden blinked. Damien smiled again and started to stroll across the green.

"I'm sorry, Camden," Emily whispered. "He's quite protective of me."

Camden kept his eye on Damien's progress. "Possessive, too."

"I'd better go with him."

"Right. But I want to confess something because we probably won't ever have the chance to be alone again."

Emily hastily pulled up her bonnet. She hoped he wasn't going to admit that he'd loved her all along and hadn't realized it until her engagement was announced. She glanced around. Damien had turned back to them.

"I know that you and the earl had a liaison on the night of the party, Emily."

"No, you don't," she said, indignant and surprised.

"Yes, I do. There's no other reason that you weren't at Lucy's party. When your father burst into the ballroom, I knew he had good reason."

"Well, aren't you clever?"

"It's just that you're so sweet and honest, it had to take a persuasive man to make you disobey your father. I won't tell anyone. I'll keep your secret until I die."

"Thank you, Camden," Emily said, as Damien finally reached them.

"Just be careful," he said under his breath. "Men like that make their own rules where women are concerned."

*   *   *

Later that same night Damien escorted Emily to an intimate supper dance at Lord and Lady Fletcher's house. "I don't think this is a good idea," she said as the small carriage lumbered up the hillside road.

"Why not?"

For one thing, he looked like sin personified in the darkness, and they were alone. Michael was following on his horse. The baron had stayed home, confessing he needed a quiet evening to recover from all the excitement over Emily's engagement.

"Isn't it a gamble to return to the place where our troubles began?"

"It would be a gamble for Urania and Sir Angus to put in an appearance, certainly."

"I wish I had your courage."

"That will come in time. Just follow my lead."

She shook her head. She had a feeling that she'd be his follower long after tonight. In fact, soon after they arrived, she was so absorbed in his behavior that she forgot why she had been afraid. Several of Lord Fletcher's neighbors had been invited to the party, including a physician and his wife.

The lady examined Damien with long, oblique looks that perplexed Emily and that he seemed not to notice. But then, his negligent attitude covered nerves of iron. He hadn't once asked what Camden had said to her today. Or mentioned why he had been concerned about a farmer's cart.

"You're being stared at," she whispered as they sat waiting for the first course to arrive.

"So are you."

He might only be playing the part of the devoted fiancée, but he was so convincing that Emily could almost believe the attention he paid her was sincere.

"Be careful of that knife, Emily," he said as she sliced a piece of beefsteak.

"I will, my lord."

"And let it cool a bit. It is delicious, but sizzling hot. I wouldn't want you to burn your tongue."

"Thank you," Emily murmured, catching the glint of amusement in Lucy's eye.

"Would anyone like another glass of champagne?" Lady Fletcher asked.

Damien held up his hand. "None for me or my fiancée, please. We're reading poetry to each other when we return home."

"Poetry?" Lord Fletcher said, shaking his head. "Why don't you read a horrid novel? Nothing I like better than a scare before bed."

Emily shuddered. He should have been told what had happened in his tower.

"I want Emily's dreams to be sweet and restful," the earl stated, giving her a quick smile.

She stared at him in admiration. He was spellbinding in the lights of the girandoles placed around the dining hall. He looked younger without his beard. But his features still gave the impression of a man who understood his own power. And who understood women.

After dessert a quartet began to play in the ballroom. Out of habit Emily took her usual chair beside Lucy against the wall. The instant she settled in her seat, Damien strode up to her chair, bowed, and took her hand.

"One dance, at least?" he asked, as if she had to fit him into a yard-long dance card.

"Well—" She looked back at Lucy, but her friend had come to her feet at Michael's request.

"You're going to make everyone suspicious," she whispered as Damien took her gloved hand.

"Suspicious? Why? Because I can't bear to keep you out of my sight?"

"I've told you," she said softly. "You don't have to pretend when no one can hear us."

"Who said I'm pretending?"

The first strains of the country dance quivered in the air. A half-dozen dancers lined up in a set. Lucy and Emily grinned at each other. They had danced together in the ballroom nearly every week, driving the dancing master into a frenzy with their improvised steps and figures.

But tonight the master would have been gratified. Emily did not glide into a footman, and Lucy did not gallop across the floor like a runaway horse.

It was another night of make-believe, and Emily didn't care. Damien didn't glance at another woman; whether he had his eye out for spies was another matter. He stayed beside her except when the dance separated them. And before the band could begin a reel he reclaimed her hand and took her out onto the terrace, where a footman brought them lemonade.

Damien watched her as she endeavored to sip and not gulp down her drink. Away from the scrutiny of the others, she expected him to lose interest in her. But, to her surprise, the intense expression on his face indicated the reverse.

"That dress looks a little too enticing on you," he murmured, his eyes raking her up and down. "I've noticed a couple of gentlemen studying you behind your back."

She didn't believe him. "You look more handsome in

your tails and trousers than the ladies of Hatherwood deserve."

"But you can't see my curves and charming backside in these clothes."

Emily shook her head. "Would you like me to change?"

"No, I'd like to take you upstairs, where no one but me can see you."

Her heartbeat quickened. She finished her lemonade to hide her reaction. "Are you going to talk to me like that after we're married?"

He took her glass and handed it to a passing footman. "If it pleases you," he said, his eyes heating. His hand curled around her waist. "I assume that it does."

Emily had started to fall asleep against him in the carriage. At first he was tempted to let her rest. She had carried on beautifully tonight. He was not only impressed by her mettle, but he was also starting to enjoy her as a partner. But he couldn't allow her to become so important that he lost sight of his purpose.

Her muslin skirt had bunched up under her backside. He slipped his hand underneath to gently pull it down. She was curled up like a conch shell, and he thought it an apt metaphor for her character—strong on the outside, sensitive within.

As his fingers skimmed over her white silk stocking, he felt the softness of her upper thigh. The warmth above enticed him. He stroked his thumb between her folds in idle pleasure.

He should have known better than to touch her when they were alone.

He reached up with his other hand for the curtain. They would be married in two days. He could wait.

He *should* wait.

She made a sound in her throat. He pulled up her skirt and watched his fingers disappear inside her.

"What are you doing?" she whispered in a voice that said she knew but had to make a protest.

"Making us warm."

She kept her eyes closed as he continued to play with her. The slickness that coated his fingers, the shiver she gave, encouraged him to enjoy her at his whim. "The coachman must be cold, too," she murmured, a smile on her lips. "Are you going to do this to him?"

"Should I stop?" he asked, his fingers quickening, sinking deeper. "Say the word."

She moaned, her back arching. He loved every moment of her helpless arousal, even as his body hardened to a point close to pain. He loved looking at her as she submitted to his control, her skirt riding her hips, her skin soft and glowing. He almost came when she reached her peak. She was so beautiful lost in passion, his woman to tease and pleasure.

"There," he said as her trembling subsided, and the air in the carriage turned cool again. "I'll suffer in misery until I return to the inn. Perhaps I'll have another dream about you tonight. In case you're still concerned about him, the coachman can put on his muffler if he wants warmth."

Emily was fully awake by the time the carriage settled to a stop in front of her house. "Despite your teasing, I had a wonderful time tonight," she told Damien. "With the exception of the physician's wife looking at you as if you were on the menu."

"I didn't notice her."

"You're only saying that to make me feel better."

"I'd be an idiot to antagonize my bride-to-be." He cupped her chin in his hand. An involuntary shiver ran down her shoulders. He lowered his head, his mouth touching hers for a deep kiss. "It will be different after we're married. You'll wish, perhaps, for another person in the room to distract my notice then."

"Why?" she asked, guessing what he meant but wanting to hear him admit his desire.

"It's understood that in return for my name you'll give me the right to your body."

Her mouth stung where his lips had touched hers. "Couldn't we build a friendship first?"

"Of course we shall become friends. I don't wish to be my wife's enemy."

She waited for him to kiss her again. She even closed her eyes in anticipation, only to feel him draw away at the approach of footsteps in the drive. "That's your father," he murmured. "Tonight I'll hand you to back him. And the day after tomorrow, he will give you to me."

She hung back as the carriage door opened. She wasn't in the mood to talk to her father or Iris or *anyone*. She wanted to hurry upstairs to her room and sit alone in the dark before the indescribable magic of what Damien had done to her wore off. Was this exquisite intimacy what the future held? If this were only a prelude to other acts, what else would he demand of her?

She had a vague idea. She and Lucy had discussed such matters in depth. But in all of Emily's imaginings, there had never been a man like Damien, whose knowledge made her eager to understand the unspeakable mysteries of marriage.

*   *   *

Winthrop was waiting at the inn when Damien returned home from the party. "A day later and I would have been forced to send Mr. Rowland," he said to the valet. "There were no problems?"

"None." Winthrop opened his greatcoat to reveal an interlining of concealed pockets that contained documents allowing him passage into high places; the middle row held an arsenal of pistols and knives.

"Good God," Damien said. "I don't know how the horse can carry all that extra weight."

"Half of it is for Mr. Rowland."

"As I recall, Michael has a considerable talent with a knife. I witnessed him throw his blade and hit a target before anyone blinked an eye." He frowned. "What is that I see beneath that dueling pistol?"

"The marriage license."

Damien frowned. "Placed between your personal armory? I hope that is not another prophetic sign."

"Is your fiancée trained in weaponry, my lord?"

"I never thought to ask. I have felt no concealed weapons on her person the few times I've been close enough to notice."

Winthrop glanced away. "An oversight that you will no doubt correct in due time."

"Are you suggesting that I search my fiancée's person?"

Winthrop lifted his pistol case to the table. "It wouldn't hurt to take a detailed inventory."

"The ceremony will be held the day after tomorrow, Winthrop. Lady Fletcher and the baron have invited the entire village to witness the happy event. I do not anticipate having to disarm my bride at the altar. That pleasure has to wait for the wedding night."

Winthrop smiled as he examined his master's pistol. "But you *will* be armed during the ceremony?"

"With the anarchists unconcerned over who they must kill for their cause, I would be irresponsible if I had no means of protecting my bride."

Chapter 27

$\mathcal{T}$he dressmaker had managed to finish Emily's blue tissue wedding dress by the morning before the wedding. It was a simple gown, the only adornment a row of silver silk rosettes with seed pearls on the skirt's hem. She had never worn anything as fragile before. It draped her curves in a way that the earl would have to notice. Whatever happened in the future, she wanted on this one day to feel desirable. She wanted everyone in the village to watch her exchange vows with the earl and wonder how their awkward Emily had become a countess, when all signs had indicated that she would lead a lonely spinster's life.

She shopped that afternoon in the village for a small trousseau, all the while aware that the villagers who had been lukewarm toward her for years now went out of their way to acknowledge her.

"Everyone is staring at us," Iris said, at Emily's side.

"No," Emily said, smiling ruefully. "They're staring at *him*."

The earl had insisted he would accompany Emily on her most trivial errands. If she needed a new hairbrush, he stood by to offer his opinion.

By the end of the day she wanted to shake him. "I hope you don't intend to shadow me like this for the rest of my life."

"Like a thundercloud, sweetheart."

Oh. She knew she ought to scold him when he teased her. She ought to feel more anxiety as their wedding day approached. She ought to feel anything but the inexplicable anticipation that built inside her whenever she heard his gently mocking voice.

Lucy and her stepmother, Diana, brought their own three maids and a hairdresser to help Emily prepare for the ceremony, which would be held at Fletcher Manor. Iris gave an audible sigh of relief when the army of women arrived. The windy day would turn Emily's hair into a bird's nest if it was not properly secured, and Lady Fletcher had a talent with cosmetics that might prevent Emily from walking to the altar like a ghost risen from her eternal repose.

"She's as pale as a corpse," Lucy said over and over, pinching one of Emily's cheeks while Diana vigorously smoothed rouge across the other.

Her pallor was nothing to worry about, Emily thought. *Wait until the wedding night, when the earl demands repayment for his protection.* She would be blushing from head to toe as she kept her part of their arrangement.

Chapter 28

$\mathcal{D}$amien stood at her side in Lord Fletcher's chapel, the pews packed, onlookers crowding at the doors. People he'd never met smiled at him as if he were a favorite son. Some ladies wept, but Emily wasn't at all teary-eyed. Stoic, she repeated her vows in a steady voice that he found somewhat startling. *Who* was he marrying? Didn't she feel some uncertainty about the commitment they were embarking on?

She showed no signs of it. Perhaps she looked a little pale, but that blue gown accentuated a body that sent his pulses soaring. The scent of lilies twined in her hair wafted to him whenever she turned her head to give a wave at someone who called out a blessing.

Dear God. What was he going to do with her after the ceremony? Well, of course he knew what he would do tonight, and presumably for the next few weeks, but what would happen once they reached London and had to settle into a life together?

He would introduce her, as his wife, to the family who might not even recognize him. Would Emily be surprised to know that she was better acquainted with him than his own brothers were? She knew almost as much about him as did his valet. He was a solitary person and it was the way he had always lived his life. Now that must change.

He could just imagine how the conversation with his Boscastle relatives would go.

"How did the pair of you meet?"

"Well, I knew her brother."

"But *when* did you fall in love with her?"

"We exchanged many letters."

"That's rather dull for the start of a Boscastle seduction."

"I didn't seduce her," he would insist, although he doubted anyone would believe she had told his fortune and entangled their destinies.

This was only a role. She was playing her part, as he was his. He couldn't forget that Michael and Winthrop were both standing at the back of the chapel, armed beneath their jackets in case Ardbury or his journalist had made the connection between a gypsy girl and the serene, bright-haired bride who was calmly taking her vows.

Husband and wife.

He kissed her on the mouth. To his approval, she swayed and closed her eyes. He wanted to crush her in his arms. A group of young people, her friends, apparently, laughed. One shouted, "We never thought we'd live to see this day."

But her father did not smile. He stood back and watched in wistful silence. Perhaps he'd also thought the day would never come when his daughter would marry. Now she would be gone for good.

Damien had sworn before God that he would take care of her for the rest of his life. And yet he was taking her away from her family. From the village she had always known. From the cricket player whose love she had sought.

At the reception he drank champagne and played the attentive groom next to the bride, who laughed less and less as the day wore on. "This might be the last chance we have to celebrate together for some time," he said, pressing his face against her scented hair.

The blossoms had fallen off one by one. While he and Emily broke into two lines in the ballroom, the last lily slid down her back and into his hand. He tucked it into his vest pocket. Perhaps one day she would press it in a Bible as a keepsake.

The band launched into a country dance. Damien suppressed a groan. He had too much on his mind to prance about like a puppet. Protecting Emily from curious eyes. Escaping from Hatherwood. Their first night together as man and wife. He did not give a damn about dancing. He'd behaved himself long enough. Once they reached the castle there might not be many opportunities to sleep with Emily, uninterrupted by duty. Even their wedding reception would be cut short if they were to reach the next village by evening. He didn't want an exhausted bride in his wedding bed.

The ladies had assembled in one line. The gentlemen stood parallel in another. It reminded Damien of a firing squad, only now the weapons employed were come-hither smiles and graceful movements. Was Emily's smile for him or someone in the crowd?

She swung around before he could decide. His gaze dropped from her face. Had her sleeve slipped off her shoulder? There was no need for him to panic; there was no identifying mark marring her shoulder any longer. That didn't mean he wanted the world to admire her creamy skin. He grasped her hand so tightly that she gave a gasp.

"Mind the shoulder," he said under his breath.

And the lady on his left, who had taken hold of *his* hand said, "The soldier? Is that a variation of the dance?"

Emily crossed before him, whispering, "It's covered in lace."

He stared at her as she moved down the line. How was it that she seemed more beautiful by the moment?

"Excuse me, my lord," a vaguely familiar voice said a few inches below his shoulder. "May I claim the next dance with the countess?"

The countess? Damien felt a shock of realization. He had a countess now, a counterpart to share in all the intrigue and hopes he had kept hidden from the world. It struck him in that moment that he didn't feel like sharing her with anyone yet, even though he wasn't sure what he would do with a wife.

He saw Emily bite her lip to conceal a smile. He glanced around reluctantly to see Camden bowing at his back. Emily looked up at Damien, her eyes asking his permission. He felt a flare of . . . he didn't know what it was. Something dark, unpleasant. Uncivilized.

He wanted to refuse. They couldn't spare the time. They had to return to her house with her father. Damien had last-minute instructions for Michael. The excuses mounted in his mind, each one emptier than the last. He pressed his lips together. Let the little bugger skulk off. After all, it was Emily's infatuation with the nodcock that had thrown Damien's life off course.

"My lord?" Camden said uneasily as the band began another set.

Damien allowed his thoughts to wander. It was rather

insulting to realize that he was this boy's replacement, not that Emily had chosen Damien any more than he had chosen her. If he refused, Emily might conclude he was jealous when, of course, such an emotion was beneath Damien's dignity. But did he want to set a precedent? He and his wife might never see this bat player again.

"One dance," he said, and felt ridiculous, like King Arthur to Lancelot and Guinevere.

Emily's heart wasn't in dancing with Camden. She'd lost her place in line on purpose and contemplated dancing off the floor when Camden looked the other way. She was more concerned with Damien's apparent lack of interest in who partnered her than she was in a consolation dance with Camden. After Camden had approached the newly wedded couple, Damien had retreated from her without another word of complaint.

Did that mean he was relieved to be gone from her? She'd known his mind was a hundred miles away from the wedding. From her.

But she craved his attention for the afternoon. She wanted him to laugh and toast their marriage and make her feel the illusion of love for a few hours.

But, then, he had desperate matters on his mind. And soon she and Damien would leave here, and she would rely on him for everything.

"Emily, did you hear what I said?" Camden asked, startling her when he took her hand.

She saw Camden now as if he were the stranger that Damien had once been. How odd that she had envisioned this very moment down to the last detail—dancing with him at her wedding reception—except that all the details had changed. He wasn't her groom. She wasn't a bride bubbling over with uncontainable happiness. And there had not been a dark nobleman standing beneath the wall tapestry waiting for her, with his arms crossed over his chest.

The courtship was over. Their marriage was about to begin. She would be in her husband's bed before the moon rose over the village.

Chapter 29

$\mathcal{D}$amien had no idea how he managed to act appropriately detached at the wedding reception. He had been anything but unmoved by the sight of his bride in another man's arms.

By the time they reached the inn where they would spend their first night alone, his baser urges were escaping the polite veneer he had worn at the wedding. He wanted to have her, to show her that her place was with him.

He gathered her against him the instant they stood alone together in their chamber. The seed pearls on the hem of her bridal gown clicked lightly against his ankles as she shifted her weight. Damien's hand moved up the small of her back, drawing at her laces. "For your sake," he said, "I won't behave like an uncouth schoolboy in our bed."

She lifted her face to his. "No?"

She looked disappointed. The sweet weight of her body against his made his blood smolder. He was dying to undress her. "An uncouth man, yes," he said, tilting his head as his hand continued untying and unwrapping her wedding gown. Slowly. Deliberately. He would undo her undergarments next. His demons protested against his restraint. He ordered them back to hell and heard their mocking laughter.

"Damien," she whispered, her mouth so tempting, so close to his. "The innkeeper has set a dinner for us on the table."

"I noticed." Under the silver covers on the table waited the light meal of beetroot salad and roast pheasant that he had ordered. Damien, however, did not have an appetite for anything but his wife. He had been ravenous for her all day. "Are you hungry?" he asked her.

"Not at all."

"Good," he said, and then kissed her with a practiced languor that tested his will more than it did hers.

A game of passion well played did not always need a single winner, and they no longer needed to impress anyone.

"I know nothing about the art of love," she whispered as if she'd read his mind.

Her gown and undergarments fell away from her body at Damien's determined efforts to disrobe her. "Do what your instincts advise," he said in amusement. He lowered his gaze. He had every intention of taking his own advice. Eventually. But . . . had she stolen the air from his lungs? "What is the first thing you would like to do?"

Her voice had a husky sweetness that stirred up his demons again. "Put on a robe and run away."

"But you can't run away. Neither of us can. And honestly, Emily, do you really want to?"

"Ask me in the morning." She backed up a few steps toward the bed. "How long do I have to stand here in the nude?"

He studied the sculpture of her body, the soft breasts

and rose-brown tips, the flare of her hips, and the shadow at the apex of her thighs. He had not guessed how perfect she would be beneath her bridal gown. He had not guessed how badly he could want a woman who had confessed that her instinct was to run from him.

"It doesn't matter anymore how we came to this place. Today we were wed."

"To appease the world."

"It is a commitment, nevertheless," he said, his eyes raking her again with unmistakable intent. "In a few minutes we will take another irrevocable step."

Her lips parted, but she said nothing. He would be patient, even though his body demanded instant gratification, a rough taking to calm his blood.

He drew a breath, swore to himself he would not overwhelm her. She was vulnerable, yes, uncertain what he would do to her. But in a heartbeat his need had weakened him. Even worse, he felt a reluctant fondness for her that couldn't be dismissed as the result of circumstance. Was it possible that their marriage was meant to be?

Aside for her one deception, and he really hadn't been her intended victim, she had been honest with him. She had agreed to his demands with good sense.

He hoped she would be in a good mood in the morning. He glanced back to make sure he had locked the door.

During the time he turned around, she'd found the dressing robe that Winthrop had laid out across the bed, thoughtful fool that he was. Emily was lifting the black silk to her shoulders when Damien reached out and took it from her hands. She retreated into the bed curtains. He followed until she had no recourse but to stand her ground or drop onto the mattress.

She stood.

There would be no pretense of modesty in his marriage.

"You have beautiful hair," he said, taking another tentative step toward her. "Why don't you pull it loose?"

She raised her hand, tugging at combs that fell to her feet. The gesture drew his eyes to her breasts, and his body reacted in a primal manner. Outwardly composed, he removed his dark coat and his neckcloth and placed them on an empty card table.

"There," she said, shaking her head. "Is that what you wanted?"

In the next moment he was standing in front of her. She gasped, pulling her hair over her breasts.

He went down on one knee, sliding his hands up from the back of her thighs to her bottom. She bent to put her hand on his shoulder, an artless move. He stroked his fingers down the cleft of her rump. He pressed his cheek to her soft tuft of hair beneath her belly. He could have died with want for this woman.

"I have no idea what you are doing on the floor, Damien, but if you release me I will assuredly join you. I'm having a problem standing on my own. I would prefer the—"

"Bed." He rose, grasping her by the wrists. "Or would you like me to kiss you until we are both incapable of making a conscious decision as to our destination?"

He ran his hand up her inner arm, curled it around her nape, waiting for her response. She had closed her eyes. Was she shaking because she was eager for her initiation? Aroused? Apprehensive? "One day," he said, "you will be bold enough to ask for what you want."

"I doubt I'll ever be as bold as you."

He smoothed his other hand down her neck to the peak of her breast, rolling the tip between his forefinger and thumb. "Does this please you? Is my touch too hard, too light? Tell me what excites you. I can be as good or bad in your bed as you like."

She bit her lip, answering him with silence. He dipped his head to circle his tongue around one elongated nipple. She bowed at the waist, lost her balance. He steadied her with one arm, and with the other lowered her to the bed. Her hair fanned out across the coverlet. She looked like an offering — pure, corruptible — and, better yet, she looked willing to be his wife in every sense of the word.

"I need air," she whispered, closing her eyes.

"I think you need a kiss, and after that a long night of lovemaking."

She laughed. Thankfully, he didn't need to persuade her. She was only too grateful to oblige his whims. At least so far. "What if I admit I'm already exhausted and wish to sleep for a few hours?"

One corner of his mouth lifted in a decadent smile. "You won't know what it is to be tired until we're both unable to move. Why don't you kiss me and reconsider?"

"A kiss? Why not?" She rose a few inches from the bed and offered him her mouth. The moment she did he teased her with slow, light brushes of his lips against hers and then rolled onto his back. "You are indecent at heart, husband or not," she said in breathless resentment. She drew the edge of the sheet over her breasts, as if that would stop him. "And you have the advantage of being properly dressed."

"I might be indecent to the core." He lifted his hand to unfasten his waistcoat and wool trousers. "But," he added, "you still have the advantage, believe me."

Emily sank back against the pillows while he pulled his shirt over his head. "Nudity is supposed to make us even? I've never felt more susceptible in my life." She chanced a look at his erection as he threw his clothes onto a chair.

Her gaze followed the hard lines and dark hollows of his body. How well made her husband was. The candlelight cast his figure in bronze as he was revealed to her. He seemed to be more lean muscle than anything else. Strong. Firm. Lovely. She smiled inwardly at the thought. A lovely, indecent lover.

So this was the card that had been dealt her. *Passion.*

Wasn't he what she had asked for? It wasn't love. Was it all he wanted? Did the thought even enter his mind? Not at a time like this.

He lowered himself over her, bracing his weight on one arm. She felt his other hand skimming her inner thigh, reaching her wet cleft and caressing her there with feather-soft strokes of his knuckles. The steady friction made her flesh swell and ache for the ending that he withheld from her. Heat pulsed inside her, where she needed to feel all of him. Yet she didn't know what to ask for or whether she could wait before pleading for some relief.

"This is nice," he whispered as he pressed a finger inside her. "Tight. I'll try to stretch you a little before I put my cock inside you."

Her cheeks felt hot from the words he said. Her body was his playground, and he knew that sucking at her breasts while forcing another finger into her body would madden her. He knew that the sensations bombarding her would strip her of her reason. She wanted him. Inside her. Touching her everywhere. Her body grew taut with the sensual tension that she could not endure much longer.

"Why are you torturing me?" she whispered restlessly.

"Torture? I'm just making sure you have enough room to take me without hurting you too much."

She caught her lip in her teeth and stared down at the knob of his shaft. She watched his other hand reach down to spread her sex completely open. Damien stopped moving. Her eyes lifted to his to acknowledge the invitation.

"Please," she whispered, her hips moving, her breathing uneven. "I want you inside me."

He slid down her body without warning, holding her thighs apart with his hands. For a moment Emily thought he was backing onto the floor. But then his head lowered between her legs. In shock and bliss she felt his mouth settle on the bud of her sex. He suckled hard, his tongue flicking below as his hands pinned her hips to keep her from lifting off the bed.

What degradation. How could she have anticipated the pressure that built in her lower body, that made her writhe against his face? The feelings he unleashed were too intense. She whispered, "Stop. I need to breathe. Stop for a minute. Give me time to think."

He didn't stop. "I can't," he explained as his fingers pushed deep inside her, and his mouth ate and teased her without the smallest show of mercy.

"You don't understand. It's more than I expected. I didn't know it would feel like this."

"You haven't felt anything yet."

"How can you say that?"

He raised his head briefly to stare into her eyes. "You haven't felt me inside you."

"You—" Her voice broke on a groan. He was breathing hard, too, but at least he could breathe.

"Hmm? What was that? I couldn't quite make it out."

She fought her impending release even as she shook in need. She was his wife. It was his right to unravel her. And the day would come, she vowed, that she would do the same to him.

Innumerable knots tightened in her belly. Despite her apprehension, she was desperate for him. Her body knew, lifting, moving, opening to take the length of him.

"It will be good," he promised, and the knots inside her broke, the pleasure of her release beautiful, unbearable, a rush of sensation that left her shivering and so mindless she didn't realize that he was between her thighs. In a haze she heard him whisper to her to put her legs over his shoulders. She obeyed. An instant later she felt the fullness of him forcing inside her, and she was his.

"Look at me," he said with an urgency that she would not have understood an hour ago. She looked up at his face as he caught her wrists in his hand and strained into her. His body went still before he whispered her name. He pressed deeper and deeper. He moved faster, harder, until he thrust a final time, and he was hers.

He shuddered, exhaled, and buried his face in her hair. She didn't move. Her body might have resisted at first; it was embarrassing, unfamiliar, but he fit perfectly inside her like the missing piece of a puzzle.

She liked the feel of Damien's body imprisoning hers. Could she be dreaming? She felt as if she were half-awake and yet drifting in a dream. Would she ever become as uninhibited as her husband? She couldn't deny that what they'd just done had felt natural.

Would he view her differently from here on? Would they mate again before the morning? She wondered whether he'd mind if she squeezed out from beneath him to wash herself in the dark before he stirred again. She wanted to brush her hair. She also yearned to touch his body and learn every inch of him.

She wasn't quite ready to disturb this unexpected intimacy or to arouse all that dormant sexuality. She felt altogether possessed, taken. Ploughed. That was the vulgar term the village boys used to describe the deed. It made a woman sound like a field.

Could she have conceived Damien's child after their first lovemaking? She didn't doubt his virility. How many times had she heard Iris warn the younger maids? *"It is entirely possible for a man to put a bun in your oven the first time he tries. Many a girl loses her maidenhood only to realize a month later that she's to become a mother."*

At least Damien had married her before *ploughing*—she smiled at the word—her.

"Emily," he said, his voice slurred with sleep. "Stop doing that."

"Stop doing what?" she whispered.

"Stop smiling and playing with your hair like a siren. You're asking for trouble if you don't." He rolled onto his shoulder, staring down at her face. "What is it?"

"I didn't realize I was smiling."

He raised his brow. "I shall take it as a compliment." He studied her face and the shape of her against the sheets. "I only have to look at you like that and I'm hard. Are you too sore?"

"Are you wanting to plough me again?" she asked quietly.

"Am I—" He laughed. "Yes. I am." He ran his hand

down her breasts to her belly and then between her damp thighs. "Do you mind if I don't wash our scent away yet? I find it pleasant."

"Like an animal," she whispered, trying not to laugh.

"Yes." He hesitated. "What a shame you are still too tender to ride me." He brushed away the hair that hid her breasts from his view. Emily felt shivers deep in her own stomach as he bent his head to kiss each sensitive peak in turn.

"Ride you?" she whispered.

He glanced up, his eyes rueful. "Not yet. I have to remember that you are to be tenderly used our first few times in bed. I am long estranged from innocence. You make me forget that fact."

"You make me forget a great deal myself."

"I'm struggling," he said, sliding his knee between her thighs, "to keep my depravity under control for as long as I can."

"If what happened in bed is an example of what you consider self-control, I am in more trouble than I thought." She went quiet for a few moments, working up her courage to whisper, "Damien? Have you done this many times before—ploughed other women?"

"If you use that word again, I will start to think of myself as an ox. I don't know how many times, to be truthful. Not as many as you appear to think."

"Tell me again how you became wealthy."

He smiled. "I wanted fortune more than anything. I worked hard. I fought. I invested, until one day I realized I was nothing but a marauder with fine ancestry. I suppose I was as interested in plundering as well as ploughing at the time."

"Isn't that what most gentlemen are like?"

"Yes. But I grew tired of it. So did the woman I was going to marry."

Emily's eyes widened. In a neutral voice she asked, "You were engaged?"

"Until I lost everything. She married another man."

"Oh. How very cruel of her."

"It was kindness, in retrospect. It allowed me the freedom to do what mattered the most."

Emily desperately longed to know everything about the woman who had first captured his heart. "Do you still love her?"

"Let me put it this way. I'd sooner kiss the innkeeper's arse than kiss her again."

She sighed. "Romantic sentiment just rolls off your tongue, doesn't it?"

He stared down at her with a darkly unapologetic smile. "Do you want a poet or a protector?"

There, that was blunt. Well, at least she recognized it as honest. "I'll take a protector for now. If we live to a good old age, then we can write poems to each other." Emily knew he was tired, but he seemed to be in a mood that was receptive to her questions. "What did you do before I met you?"

"My past in foreign service is hard to explain to a young woman who has never left England," he said. "Several years ago at the urging of my cousin, Heath, I was asked to find out once and for all the fate of Heath's youngest brother Brandon, and Brandon's friend Samuel. The family had been led to believe they'd been murdered in Nepal."

"And they hadn't?"

"I pursued false leads until at last, in prison, a guard's daughter gave me reason to hope that they had survived.

It was an Englishman, Samuel's uncle, who had ordered their execution. Their bodies had never been recovered."

Emily was silent.

"All I discovered was one mystery leading to another until ultimately the end of the search led me back to England. I thought I would put my financial affairs in order, meeting up with old friends and family, when I was asked to become involved in crushing the conspiracy, which meant assuming a false identity."

"Of course you accepted."

"Yes."

"Are you one of those men who need action and purpose all the time?"

"Emily, go to sleep."

She closed her eyes. But now Damien was awake and full of his own questions. Would his wife prove to be another mystery he'd spend the rest of his life trying to solve?

He looked down to see that she had drifted off to sleep in his arms.

Was it possible that a woman, like a flower, could physically blossom before one's eyes with the right exposure? He was far from a poet. But he had to admit that Emily had either brought out his vulnerabilities or her hidden talents.

Now he had to wonder who had pulled the wool over whose eyes and who, when every last layer had been bared, they would become.

Chapter 30

It was early morning when Emily finally woke and opened the bed curtains. A light breeze stole through the window Damien had cracked open. He was sitting at the table before a brace of pistols and a breakfast tray. Emily sat up, grateful for the food and the consideration he had shown by drawing the curtains around the bed before their breakfast had been delivered. How had she slept so soundly?

"Good morning," she said, poking her head through the curtains. "I hope you don't have an immediate reason for putting those pistols out on the table."

He looked up, his hard face so handsome in the half-light that she sighed with longing. He had already shaved, she realized. His linen shirt and black pantaloons made her embarrassed that she had slept so deeply in her disheveled nudity.

"How do you feel?" he asked, as she swept her hair off her face.

Wicked. Wonderful. Uncertain. "Well enough," she said, blushing at her thoughts.

"No physical complaints?"

"Nothing that I care to discuss." She bit her lip as he

rose from the table and approached the bed. "Are we staying in this room all day?"

"I regret not." He pushed aside the curtains and sat down on the bed beside her.

A moment later his hand swept down her back to her bare hip. She was in the same predicament as the night before, if only a little better prepared. He cradled her face in his other hand for a kiss that she hoped was a prelude of pleasures to come.

"I don't think my heart can withstand this, Damien."

"Neither can mine. But it's a decent way to die."

His tongue penetrated her mouth. She lifted herself to meet him, but he pushed her farther down onto the bed. Still kissing her, he cupped the fullness of her breast in his palm. The instant dampness she felt between her thighs disconcerted her. She had turned into a wanton in one night.

As if he sensed her readiness, he stroked his hand along her outer thigh and into the warmth between her legs. She turned her head, needing to catch her breath, needing him even more. Tremors ran through her not only at the intimacy of his touch, but also at her desire for it. She felt tender inside, and yet her body's moisture eased the burn, the intrusion of his fingers to prepare her for their coupling. She started to hide her face in the pillow. She heard him unfasten the flap of his trousers. She wanted to plead for him to stop, or to move faster, or maybe to slow the rush of blood through her veins.

"Damien," she said, daring a look at the starkly handsome face of her husband as he stood poised, his shaft in hand, ready to enter her. "Aren't you even going to remove your boots?"

"Yes. No." He threw back his head. "Will you forgive me if I don't?"

"I think boots might leave marks on the bedding."

"Emily, please. This is not something you're supposed to think about. At least not when I'm ready to burst." He inhaled. His eyes locked with hers. "Tell me if this is too soon. Tell me that I am causing you discomfort. But do not expect me to care that my boots might damage the blessed sheets. I can afford to replace them. Do you want me or not?"

She glanced down from his face to his flat stomach and full erection, and nodded before she closed her eyes. There was no point in denying with words what her carnal self had so unashamedly admitted.

"Thank you." His raw voice quickened her pulse. The bed clothes slithered to the floor. "Place your legs around me, Emily."

His sexual power pulled her from the mist that permeated her thoughts. She had unlocked her knees and lifted her legs to grip his buttocks when she felt his deep thrust inside her.

"Sweetness," he whispered in a low voice, sheathing himself in her depths.

His untamed sexuality made her shiver, made her feel a little wild. She raised her bottom from the bed to take as much of him inside her as she could. He kissed her again, groaning into her mouth, and gave her more than she expected. She swallowed a cry. It hurt a little, but her body wanted more. Her body needed every inch of him.

"God," he muttered, withdrawing only to surge back inside her.

Sensation took over. She put one hand over her face, certain he would pummel her through the mattress. She would beg him in silence for more and more until she broke into pieces.

"I'm going to fill you with come," he said above her, his voice deep, distant.

She spiraled out of control. She grasped his wrist with her other hand, whether holding on to him or holding herself back, she was at a loss to know.

He was still buried inside her when Emily worked up the nerve to open her eyes. He offered her a smile that filled her with sweet humiliation, as though to say he knew he'd unhinged her and would do so whenever he pleased.

She met his stare. "You don't have to gloat."

"A gentleman doesn't gloat."

She laughed in reluctance. "But he does rob a lady of her reason?"

"Yes. Of course. It's only fair when she has disarmed him of his wits. I'm sorry to tell you that now we must get dressed. I've lost track of time since yesterday afternoon."

Emily sighed as he withdrew from her and refastened his trousers. How easy it was for a man to take his pleasure and return to the ordinary world. But had he implied that *she* had been responsible for their mutual loss of control? If he needed time to adjust to her innocence, then surely she could reciprocate and make accommodations for his impropriety.

She put on her robe and went to the washstand, grateful to see soap and fresh water for her toilet. Her hair needed brushing, and she was wishing for her maid when Damien cleared his throat.

"You might want to move a bit faster than usual," he said. "I've invited your brother, your maid, and Winthrop to take luncheon with us before we set out on the road."

Chapter 31

An hour later Lord Shalcross and his wife sat down to an early luncheon with Michael, Iris, and Winthrop in Damien's private room.

"I have decided upon a plan for the five of us during the night," he said as soon as everyone was seated.

This announcement did not appear to surprise anyone at the table, with the exception of Emily. When and where had her husband devised this plan? He had been more than attentive to her in their bridal bed. She couldn't have put two words together during the attention he paid to her. He must have been plotting over breakfast while she slept.

"It is a simple plan of action," he began, "but its simplicity does not make it any less dangerous. We all know Michael is an experienced horseman. He also has an ability to live on his own resources if necessary."

Emily glanced at her brother's grinning face. "What are you asking him to do?"

"To ride to as many of the villages where revolts are to take place as he can and sound a warning."

"He could get killed," Emily exclaimed.

"It's better than dying of boredom," Michael replied.

"Why should anyone take a rascal's word on a matter so grave?" she asked.

Damien glanced at Michael. "He'll carry papers from the Home Office. By virtue of a signature and royal seal, he'll be fed, his horse will be exchanged for another, and he'll be praised for his intervention. It's not as if he's the only former soldier who is supporting England."

Emily frowned. She had a feeling that this had been prearranged long before breakfast. "What about Iris and Winthrop?" she asked, noting Damien looked uncomfortable at the question.

"Iris and Winthrop have a different assignment."

"Assignment?" Emily said, her voice rising. "Does Iris know about this?"

Iris paled. "This is the first I've heard of it, and I'm hoping I misunderstood what his lordship just said. You aren't asking me to be a spy, are you? Because, honestly, I don't even know how to use a pair of field glasses."

"What do you expect her to do?" Emily demanded. It was one thing to have married Damien in the name of duty. She was not convinced that her timid maid needed to be sacrificed as well.

"Iris and Winthrop are to be employed as temporary servants at Viscount Deptford's party," Damien said. "They'll hold positions beneath their current ones. As guests, you and I can only witness so much. They can be the eyes and ears inside the castle."

"It won't appear suspicious, the pair of them suddenly in service at the castle?" Emily said.

Damien shook his head. "It's not uncommon to hire temporary help when one is hosting a large affair."

Iris gave Emily a helpless look.

"I don't know if I approve of this, my lord," Emily

said. "You'll have to give us more details before we agree."

To be involved in an espionage plot to protect her country was an honor to which, honestly, Iris Brookshire had never aspired. What lady's maid had the time to indulge in political intrigue when her mistress had just become a countess? What sensible woman would choose the uncertainty of spying over the security of domestic service? Still, Iris understood the hierarchy of obligation. Never mind what happened in London; it was her primary obligation to help her mistress establish a house worthy of her title and wealth.

That the unremarkable Miss Rowland, despite her efforts, had not hooked Mr. Jackson as a husband but instead had landed an earl of infamous lineage was a coup that would be lauded in domestic gossip for years to come. Iris now worked for a countess who would start her own aristocratic dynasty. It was a privilege to serve as a lady's maid in a prestigious house.

Iris, had not, however, envisioned herself becoming an espionage agent alongside a conceited-looking valet as a condition of her promotion. "I do not know the first thing about being a spy," she protested again to Emily and the earl over her cake plate.

"You're an expert at it," Michael said as he poured her a splash of brandy. "Think of all the schemes you and Emily have enacted over the past five years."

Iris made a face as her first sip of brandy went down. "All those schemes failed, by the way."

"The last one didn't," Michael said pragmatically, popping a sliver of cake into his mouth. He swallowed before adding, "Emily has leg-shackled a husband."

"Must you use that vulgar expression?" Emily said, frowning at him.

"Shalcross doesn't mind," Michael said.

Damien stared at his brandy. "Yes, I do. I prefer to think that she will be shackled to me, if there is any shackling to be done."

"That is completely off the subject," Emily murmured into her glass. "I don't like the idea of my maid exposing herself to danger with only your valet to guard her. That is not to demean you, Winthrop."

"I'm not keen on the idea myself," Michael admitted, with a quick look at Iris.

She did not return his look. There was another benefit to Emily having married an aristocrat who'd live far from Hatherwood. Iris could hope she might find her own husband one day in the earl's employment.

"Of all the plots we pulled off," she said aloud, "I never imagined I'd be involved in treason. My French is barely passable."

She noticed Winthrop put his hand to his mouth as if covering a smile. *Smug thing.* "We are not at war with France anymore, Miss Brookshire. You won't be required to speak that language during our work together. Although, if it makes you feel more at ease, I can provide you with a list of common phrases to memorize."

He had cunning eyes behind those spectacles, she realized, shrewd and an inscrutable shade of brown. He appeared to think so highly of himself that Iris decided she would not get along with him at all. Not a humble bone in either his or the earl's lithesome bodies. "I'm sure I won't need a list of common words, sir," she said. "Simple phrases I know well enough."

"You misunderstand me, miss." he said, setting down

his drink. "I have no doubt you are more than competent to pass as a chambermaid. After all, you serve in a higher role as lady's maid and confidante."

She glanced away, catching Michael's eye. The big cad was grinning, as if he knew Winthrop was overstepping his bounds. She supposed, however, the valet had meant to mollify her by his last statement. It was a polite attempt to smooth her feathers. She would accept it for now, to show her manners, but she had a sense the pair of them would not see eye to eye on other issues.

At least it would separate her from Mr. Rowland. He'd be looking for a wife of his own soon enough, and Iris did not have the heart to witness that courtship. He would not have to go to outrageous lengths to attract a young lady. The village girls always knew when Michael had come home. His wandering challenged them.

"You shall have to travel as man and wife," the earl said unexpectedly.

"Man and wife?" Iris and Winthrop said in horrified synchrony.

"Well, you do not remotely resemble each other. It would be difficult to deceive anyone into thinking you're brother and sister," the earl said, sipping his Madeira.

"This is going to be awkward," Iris said, "living and travel arrangements, I mean." Her voice quivered. "I do have standards to maintain."

"You don't have to worry about Winthrop," the earl assured her. "He is a professional. He will find a way to convince everyone that you are living in connubial bliss together without taking the smallest liberty."

Iris stared across the table. "I'm not sure I can do a believable job of this. It isn't in me."

"Oh, Iris," Emily said. "You've done more unconventional things for me."

"That was different."

"How?" Emily asked with a faint smile.

"*You* were the one whose reputation was at risk. Now I shall be the lone agent."

Winthrop stared at her. "I will be your partner, Miss Brookshire. You can trust me all the way."

"I trust him," Damien added in his valet's defense.

Emily lifted her brow. "All the way?"

"Well, yes. You and I are trusting each other all the way, aren't we?"

"That is not the same thing," Michael observed. "You and Emily are actually married. Trust is implicit in a marriage. It is not in a deception."

Winthrop rose from his chair. "I would like to speak with Miss Brookshire in private about our mission. It's essential to show her the layout of the castle, the guest list, and to warn her of the dangers we might encounter. While the viscount's demise might be the primary intention, the rebels will presumably not hesitate to eliminate any obstacle that threatens the plot. We need an agent who understands discretion. Miss Brookshire, I think you are ideal for the job."

Chapter 32

Two days had passed since Iris's interview with the earl. Now she found herself traveling with his valet in a public coach. As if they had known each other for years.

She dreamt of a warm bath, a clean bed, and privacy. During her years of service as a lady's maid, she had grown spoiled. She'd eaten good meals, worn Emily's cast-offs, and had no cause to travel farther than to Lord Fletcher's estate. Most assuredly she was not forced to share a carriage with ill-mannered passengers who broke wind, gossiped about their family to strangers, and trod on her toes.

Winthrop did not appear pleased with their class of company, either. But he managed to be polite when a dowager asked him to hold her hat with ostrich plumes that poked his nose. And he kept his patience with the little girl who kept pulling a thread in his jacket until the cuff came unhemmed.

"I can stitch that up easily," Iris said softly, not wanting to make a fuss.

"So can I, my pet."

My pet? She thought he was being snide, a young man

talking about sewing and using an endearment in the same breath. But once inside their room at the inn, he took out a needle and thread, repaired his cuff, and asked immediately what she would like for supper.

"I think, sir, that before we settle on our food we should come to agreement about our sleeping arrangements."

"I told you not to worry. Your virtue will not be compromised by my doing."

Iris closed her traveling bag. "What does that mean? That you think I might lose my wits and compromise myself?"

He gave one of his sly smiles. "I'd never suggest such a thing. Not that it hasn't happened before, you understand. But you can trust me to stand strong."

"How self-sacrificing of you. Can I also trust you to sleep outside the door?"

"Oh no. That would look peculiar. I shall sleep behind the dressing screen. There shall be no temptation for either of us that way."

Iris nodded, undecided whether he had dealt her an insult or a compliment. Was he hinting that he found her a bit attractive? Attractive enough to mention temptation. As for her, she found him an impossible man to fathom. All this intrigue and then stitching up his cuff as if he'd graduated from a lady's academy.

"How did you learn to sew like that?" she asked, still standing in the middle of the room.

"What do you mean?" He pulled off his spectacles. She stared into his eyes in surprise. He became a different man without those glasses. He seemed younger, unguarded. Not unpleasant to behold at all.

"I was only curious how you learned to sew that well. Like a tailor. Was that your previous occupation?"

Perhaps he or his father had worked on Bond Street, fashioning jackets for gentlemen. Such experience would be an asset to a valet. That would explain why Winthrop and the earl always appeared elegantly dressed. It was in the detail. Coat buttons aligned like rows of little soldiers. A pristine neckcloth handled as delicately as a christening gown. Oh, what a skill, all right. To be able to alter one's identity with a needle and thread as deftly as Lady Fletcher did with her cosmetics.

"No," he said, laughing as if she'd embarrassed him with her observation. "I was never a tailor, miss."

"I should be proud to admit if I were—"

"An army surgeon," he said.

Iris lowered her bag to the floor. "Oh."

"Let me get that," he said, hurrying toward her. "Why don't you sit by the window? Keep an eye on who's about."

A surgeon? What a dreadful spy she made. Those strong hands had sawed off bones on battlefields. Fancy her picturing him in a shop. "I can't do this," she said, moving to the chair. "I'll be hopeless."

"Why is that?" he asked over his shoulder.

"I was convinced that you had worked on Bond Street. It appears I have a better imagination than I do instincts."

He hefted her trunk to the table. "What on earth have you packed in there?"

"Everything. A lady's maid has to be prepared."

He sat down at the other end of the small table, withdrawing his handkerchief to sweep off a thin layer of dust. "'Everything,' meaning?"

She swallowed and stared at his glasses. "Most of my personal belongings. Books, mainly. The accessories I have used for masquerades."

"Genuine costume balls or your mistress's escapades?"

She bristled. "I beg your pardon."

He leaned across the table and studied her so intently she felt as if he were dismantling her piece by piece. "I should be begging your forgiveness, miss . . . Iris. We must practice using each other's first names. And you are right to be offended. What the countess did for previous entertainment is only his lordship's business."

She gave him a glance that said she agreed. He was smiling at her now, but in a confidential manner. Iris gathered her wits. Surgeon and spy he might be to her virgin maid, but she had not survived a childhood of cruel abuse from relatives without developing her own strategies to survive. She would make that much clear. The last time she had been physically assaulted was the day she'd come to realize she had to depend on herself.

"Surely, sir, we don't need to play man and wife when we are alone together?" She dropped her voice, jerking her head meaningfully toward the door. "Or do you think someone's listening?"

"They aren't going to learn much if they are," he said in a stage whisper. "We are an ordinary husband and wife traveling to fill our new positions. You're fortunate there was no sketch made of you to be nailed on tavern doors."

"Lady Shalcross is fortunate that she was in disguise," Iris said worriedly. "It's her safety that concerns me."

"His lordship will watch out for her, Iris. The viscount is the intended victim. Keep your head."

"I don't intend to lose my head."

"That's the spirit."

"Are we really going to sleep in the same room together?"

He unbuttoned his waistcoat. "Three nights until we reach the castle."

Iris looked at him in chagrin as he removed his coat. "And what of our arrangements once we are there?"

"The arrangements have already been made. We have a room in the servants' quarters that gives us immediate access to the private stairs to the upper floors."

"One room?"

He hung his coat over his chair and reached for her hand. "It will only be an act, Iris. We are to do a job."

Knowing that didn't help the tingling nerves that jumped from her wrist up her arm as his hand touched hers. She recalled his nimble fingers plying a needle. His steady eyes unsteadying her, perceiving things about her that she knew could not be proper. The valet to an earl and spy. *He can have his pick of any maid he wanted, and some ladies, too,* she thought.

"Are you proficient in the use of any weapon?" he asked her out of the blue.

She blushed. Here she sat imagining he had seduced her with his stare when his mind had moved on to practical, if disturbing, matters.

"The pistol?" he asked, nodding in approval before she had even answered him.

"No. Daggers."

He slid his hand from hers. She felt another forbidding tingle; this time it was because *she* had startled him, and neither he nor his master seemed the type of man easy to unsettle.

"You're talking about a knife as in chopping carrots or onions," he said. "For a minute there you gave me a fright. Imagine a dagger in your delicate hands."

"A lady's maid does not chop vegetables," she replied, smiling at his confusion. "I meant what I said. I am proficient in the art of throwing knives and using a dagger, although I've never had cause to injure anyone. Neither has my mistress, but she's a better throw than me."

He nodded in obvious condescension. "Village sport, I assume. It's unusual that ladies are allowed to participate."

"Oh, I'm not talking about throwing a dart," she said, letting a patronizing note sneak into her voice. "I have a few skills of my own, sir. Mr. Rowland taught us to throw using an apple on his head as a target."

Chapter 33

$\mathcal{D}$amien woke Emily early the next morning by reaching under the pillow and withdrawing a long white rectangle imprinted with an illustration. "My card!" she said, astonished enough by his discovery to forget her nakedness. She sat straight up to confiscate it from his hand. "I thought I had that hidden. Are you playing tricks on me, Damien?"

He narrowed his eyes in speculation. "Passion? I presume this was meant to crop up in number seven's reading. Is it a keepsake for you of what should have been?" He lifted his brow in speculation.

"Is this your way of forcing me to make a false confession? You know how susceptible I am when I'm half-asleep." She was susceptible to him at other times, too, but this was *not* a welcome awakening. How could that card have reappeared under her pillow by itself?

"Am I going to find a cricket bat in your trunk?"

"If you continue to be unpleasant, I might wish I'd brought one."

He retreated from the bed, tossing the card across the table. "I suggest you get rid of this before anyone else sees it and makes a connection between a certain countess and a larcenous fortune-teller."

She reached for the dressing robe twisted around the bedpost. He did not make an effort to avert his gaze as she turned to draw on the wrapper.

"I didn't make a fuss like this when you told me you wanted to marry another woman."

"What I told you was that I'd sooner kiss the innkeeper's arse than kiss her at the altar. She belongs to the past. And so should these cards."

"I'll admit they've been a nuisance. I know they could be dangerous in the wrong hands. But those cards brought us together."

She turned again, finding him directly behind her. "Pardon me if I don't appreciate your hidden reminder of another man."

"You're wrong," she said softly. "I don't feel anything for Camden."

"That's not what you wrote in the letter you planned to give him at Lucy's party."

She stared into his eyes. "You lied to me. You promised me you burned the letter before you could be tempted to read it! Oh, Damien, you are a—"

"I didn't read it," he said, looking contrite. "I started to, but at the time I didn't realize how important a part you and Camden would play in my life."

"Camden isn't a part of our lives."

And, yes, she had kept the card, as if it would help her to keep Damien. It reminded her of his heroic intervention in the tower. And what she wished they would come to feel for each other in time.

Passion.

And love.

And a marriage not in name only. She had grown more confident since their wedding. She wanted a true marriage at any cost.

The middle-aged merchant pushed a path through the passengers boarding the stage, jostling Iris from her pre-occupied worry and up against a little boy. "Move, move, move," the merchant said, giving her another jab with his elbow. "Woolgathering women and children cannot be allowed to hold up the line. Some of us have business to conduct."

Iris was debating whether to answer or overlook this rudeness when, to her relief, Winthrop appeared. She didn't know where he had come from, but he took her hand and pulled Iris back into her place.

Iris would have protested this physical display, but she could not find the words to express her gratification. Who would have thought that the earl's valet had such a sense of himself? A presence, that's what Winthrop had. Even the merchant seemed disinclined to argue his own superiority. Built on the slight side and bespectacled, Winthrop could hold his own.

"Do get inside the coach," he said with a practicality that ended her musings. "I shall be watching him to make sure he does not insult you again. Besides, we'll reach the castle before evening. You won't have to put up with bad-mannered travelers after that."

No, Iris thought. *Only secret assassins and traitors who think it their duty to destroy the fabric of all I hold dear. What about my mistress?* she wondered. *Is the earl kind to her? Had Emily managed to conduct herself like a proper young lady?*

Winthrop nudged her arm. "I've received some good news," he said quietly.

"Oh?"

"The others are doing well."

"Even—"

He frowned. "Mr. Rowland has made remarkable progress, if that's who's on your mind."

Iris pressed her lips together and turned to the window. She felt guilty that her first thought had not been about Michael. What had happened to her? What would happen to all of them in the end?

Damien walked Emily halfway to the carriage, insisting that she wait inside while he settled the bill. She complied without argument. She was dying for a chance to eat the bacon and scones she had wrapped in a cloth and tucked inside her reticule. Damien had purchased a bottle of wine for the journey. Emily had never indulged in spirits before supper. But after the way Damien had indulged himself in her last night, she realized she would have to adjust to his worldly tastes or fall by the wayside.

Such a sacrifice, she thought, hiding a smile. Not to worry that her mortal life was in danger. Damien made her die a little every time he took her to bed.

She did not intend to become a wallflower wife, even if one glass of wine would go to her head, and she would surrender her dignity at his demand. She would respect her rank as the Countess of Shalcross and hope to leave her rustic habits behind. The prospect made her wistful for Michael and her father, who would be lonely without his children, for all his complaints. Emily couldn't believe how much *she* missed her beloved Iris, who had not asked for any of this and was likely at this moment cursing Emily for dragging her into this life-or-death intrigue.

"My lady? A moment, please."

Emily turned at the carriage step to the mop-capped young woman who had addressed her. Damien had warned her not to look anyone in the eye or engage in a conversation during which she might be recognized. He wanted her to conduct herself in an aloof manner—except when they were alone, and his sensuality knew no limits.

"My lady, pardon me, but I believe you dropped this."

Emily's heart pounded as she glanced down at the card the girl held half-concealed in her apron folds. Good heavens, it was an unholy thing. Had it grown wings that it could appear to her detriment again? To think she had kept the card as a rueful memento of how she had met her husband, who assumed it was a token of her lost love. One day she might admit the truth to Damien, but not until she felt confident he would not mock her.

"You may toss it in the rubbish," she said quickly. "It isn't mine."

"Are you sure, my lady?" The maid studied her in anxious silence.

"Yes, I am quite sure."

"But I saw it fall from your person. I swear I did. The gypsy peddlers sell such items to ladies who are newly married and seeking secret methods to ensure—"

"Then perhaps my maid bought and tucked it away where I did not notice it. More likely it belongs to another passenger. Card games are played for entertainment here at the Sign of the Raven, aren't they?"

"Not with cards like this. It looks a little naughty, don't you think?"

Emily refused to look at either the card or the woman

holding it. "I don't think about things like that, and neither should you."

"If your maid bought it," the girl chattered on, "I hope she didn't pay overmuch for the thing. It gives me a queer feeling. I hesitated to pick it up."

Emily wished that she hadn't. The card must have become caught in the mantle she had thrown over her arm during Damien's rush to travel in good light. "Dispose of it, please. My husband will not want it in my possession."

Which was an apt word to describe what had happened to her since the night the Earl of Entitlement had disrupted the dullness of her life. She felt another pang of homesickness, of nostalgia for the hapless romantic she had been and was still, sadly, at heart.

"You're sure you want me to get rid of it?" the maid asked again. "It might have—"

"Oh, just give it to me," Emily said, tugging it from the maid's hand. "I will pass it along to someone who appreciates it."

Late evening had fallen by the time they reached the next inn. Damien and Emily took supper in their room, washed, and went straight to bed. It was a chilly night, despite the fire in the grate. Emily had inched closer to her husband, not only to absorb his heat, but because the heavy anchor of his arm around her waist made her feel safe. She was drifting off with her chin on his chest, lulled by his slowing heartbeat. His was a strong pulse, steadier than hers. Now, suddenly the rhythm of his pulse changed. Her breath hitched as he opened his eyes and stared at her.

His face looked angular and alert in the dark. A shiver ran over her skin. "Damien," she whispered, "weren't you invited to a game of cards in the colonel's private—"

He raised one arm from beneath the sheets, his hand brushing her breast, and put his finger to her mouth. "Ssh. Not a word." He pulled her against his chest. "The door," he said under his breath.

The door?

She peered over his sinewy arm to the doorknob. Had it just turned? How could he have been disturbed by such an indistinct sound when he was falling asleep? All she had heard was his heartbeat.

Before she could put together another rational thought, he grasped her by the waist and rolled them to the edge of the bed and onto the floor in a tangle of bedding. His body broke the impact of her descent. Then he was on his feet, grasping a sheet to knot around his hips. She was left to huddle under the blanket that he dropped for her.

The doorknob turned again. This time she heard it, too. It seemed, impossibly, that Damien had disappeared. His shadow on the wall vanished from her view. He could not have melted into the furnishings. Was there a secret exit from the room? Would he leave her alone on the floor? She strained her neck to see around the bed.

Heavens, he was crawling half-naked to the side of the door, the sheet spread beneath his body, presumably to protect him from splinters. What a sight. Those chiseled muscles moving with sinuous grace, his lean torso and hips twisting with a purpose that reminded her of his agility in bed.

He turned his head. She swallowed a gasp. The knife clamped between his teeth prevented him from uttering the warning that glittered in his eyes. She drew back beside the bed, listening. Now she could hear the thudding of her own heart. If whoever had turned that doorknob managed to gain entry, he would not encounter an empty room or even a sleeping couple, but an angry, naked, knife-armed man who clearly did not take well to an intrusion of his privacy.

The door creaked as if the person on the other side had decided to force entry. Were two intruders trying to break inside? A maid would have knocked or used her set of keys. Of course, it could be a drunken guest who'd mistaken Damien's room for his. It happened often at house parties and crowded inns. Sometimes a room was left unlocked for a liaison.

But it could also be that one of the conspirators had recognized Emily, despite all the efforts Damien had taken to protect her. She looked up at the glass and saw his bare body crouched beside the door.

She couldn't cower naked on the floor, hiding uselessly, acting as helpless as a pudding while he fought to protect her. She stretched her arm to the hearth and reached backward for the handle of the brass shovel. It burned a little from being left close to the fire.

But she ground her teeth, grasped the handle, and prepared to jump up the instant that the door burst open.

It never did.

There was another furtive rattle at the knob, followed by receding footsteps and then quiet. Damien and Emily rose in unison. He blinked when he saw her, hair streaming over her bare breasts and hips, a coal shovel held above her head, her belly smudged with soot.

"Good God," he said, removing the knife from his teeth. "I have never seen such a sight in my life."

He stared. He couldn't help himself. If Aphrodite had launched an attack against Hephaestus when she was banished to Hades as his bride, she would have paled in comparison to Emily. The fire blazing at her back, the deep shadows of the evening, did nothing to dispel the image. "I assure you, Emily, that your state of undress would do far more to distract an intruder than a hearth utensil." The moment would be forever emblazoned on his mind. She was a goddess who deserved his worship.

She lowered the shovel. "I was not about to hide under the bed while you were set upon by assailants."

"Assailant," he said in a clipped voice, searching for her robe. He resented the bastard for terrifying her. "I heard only one pair of boots at the door."

"Perhaps it was the colonel coming to invite you again to cards. Perhaps he'd had a few too many and—"

"Those were not the boots he was wearing," he said as he came up beside her. He helped her into her silky Chinese robe. His gaze lowered on her breasts before she covered them from view. "Maybe we should dress at night and stay dressed for the remainder of the journey. I don't want any other man seeing you like that. Whether he is a friend or enemy."

She stared at his back as he walked to the dressing screen, his disregard for propriety as fascinating to her as ever. "The thought occurs to me that I don't wish to share you with other women, either," she said, the admission startling her perhaps more than it did him.

"What?" He pulled his shirt from the screen and faced her, unconcerned by his blatant state of undress. "What women?"

"I know you wanted to marry another woman. I thought I wanted another man." She took a breath. "But we were wed so quickly there wasn't time to discuss whether you will take a lover during our marriage. I know it's done. I detest the practice. Infidelity destroys a woman's heart." And even though her mother had not deliberately betrayed her father, she had broken his heart.

He put on a fresh shirt, regarding her in irritation. "I have more than enough on my hands, what with preventing an assassination and protecting you, than to even consider taking a lover," he said. "Do you intend to take one, detesting the practice aside?" he asked, pulling on his trousers.

"Excuse me?"

He advanced in her direction, not put off when she dropped onto the bed and settled against the mound of covers in the middle as if claiming sanctuary. He merely moved to the bottom of the bed, resting his shoulder against the post as if to suggest there was no escape.

"Someone might have just made an attempt on our lives. And you're worried about a woman who doesn't even exist?"

"Is passion ever rational?" she asked philosophically.

"You were madly in love with another man when I met you. What reason would I have to believe your feelings for this young man have changed?"

"Well, I'm married to you, for one thing."

"All you know about me is what I've told you. Quite honestly I know a little more than nothing about you. Never in a century would I have pictured myself with a wife so desperate for marriage that she resorted to using a love potion to ensnare her victim, and then bungled the job with snail poison. At least you could have bewitched the right man."

She shoved the bed covers between his legs. "Is that right? I've paid the consequences for what I did."

He pulled away the covers she had thrown at him,

lowering his head to hers. "You'll be paying those consequences for a long time."

She raised her chin. "So will you."

"I'll survive." He glanced down at the crumpled bedding. "I might even thrive. Don't go back to sleep. I'll have hot water sent up for a bath. You have left soot marks on the bedding. I have never seen such a mess."

She frowned. "Where you going?"

The playful edge faded from his voice. "Just down the hall into the middle of the stairs."

"Do you think we were followed here?"

"I wouldn't be surprised that your theory about a fellow traveler seeking company is correct. Don't bother getting dressed. It would please me to watch you in your bath."

She blushed. "You want to—"

"I want to see your body wet." He swept his gaze over her. "And I would like to wash you. You may do the same to me."

She nodded. "If you like."

"Hand me my jacket, please," he said quietly. "And here, take this."

Emily numbly passed him the jacket on the chair beside the bed. "What do you want me to do with this?" she asked, staring at the pistol he had laid carefully at her side.

"Do not unlock the door for anyone else. If it is forced open, take aim and, if necessary, fire. I will be within earshot. Do try not to shoot me."

"What if it's the chambermaid making sure this room meets your precise standards?"

"Standards?" he said in exasperation, balancing his hip on the bedpost to put on his boots.

"The fresh towels for one thing and the bathwater for another. Then there is the wine and the sheets that are to be freshly washed, pressed, and folded between dried herbs."

"You need not make me sound like a cosseted dowager, Urania. I asked for those accommodations to make your life as pleasant as it can be for a bride dragged from her wedding bed and involuntarily enlisted in covert affairs."

She softened. "Damien, I'm trying my best to understand. Only last month I was playing whist with my neighbors and wishing I were a married woman whose only concern was to please my husband and host parties for strangers to enhance his reputation. Now I am married to a stranger who is entrusting me with a gun and referring to me as Urania when he knows perfectly well that is not my name."

He straightened. "Why is it that women wait until the worst time to hold a serious conversation?"

"With you it's always the worst time. There isn't a minute when we can feel truly safe."

He gave her a grim look. "I can't deny that."

"I'm sorry I said it."

He smiled. "What a beautiful mess you are with your tousled hair and smudge marks on your skin. Are you still sorry that I walked into your tent?"

"Do I act like a woman with regrets?" She smiled up at him. "Are you sorry?"

He glanced away. "I'll only be sorry if anything happens to you because I intruded in your life."

Chapter 34

*J*ris had quickly adapted to the life of a chamber-maid in the castle. In fact, from the hour of her arrival she had found so many flaws in her fellow servants' efficiency that she had no time to worry whether a radical was standing in her shadow.

It was good practice, she decided, for her future in a noble household. Considering this as her training for a glorious future rather than thinking of herself as an inept spy made it easier to forget her fears.

Unfortunately Viscount Deptford gave his bodyguards no little grief in their efforts to shadow him. He refused to adhere to a routine. He resented following rules. An eccentric known to raid the kitchen for a midnight collation, he often sat up talking to the scullery maids until the sun rose.

The guests had retired to their beds after a brain-numbing performance of the French satire *Tartuffe* when Iris felt Winthrop slip from her side as she pretended to sleep. She had given up any hope of maintaining a decent decorum between them and had insisted they share the bed in their stone-floored room.

It would have been cruel to assign him to a chair or a

cot. Heaven knew he hadn't touched her when they were in bed together. Not a brush of a bare toe to her ankle. She wondered what was wrong with her that she had caught herself more than once hoping for a kiss. She would have to rebuff him, of course. She was a lady's maid, not a ladybird.

Iris appreciated that he had kept his promise to show her respect. But she did begin to question whether his coolness had less to do with duty than it did with the fact that he found her unappealing.

She also wondered where he had snuck off to this early in the morning. She'd noticed after the play that he had his eye on another housemaid, who grated on Iris's nerves. The minx had made an excuse about checking an upstairs chimney during the last act. When a few minutes later Iris had followed, she had spied the snippy maid looking outside the door of the room Winthrop had entered.

"Let the needle puller have his maid," she muttered, scooting across his bare place in the bed. Iris would make a cup of tea and maybe indulge in a little flirtation herself with the castle's rheumy-eyed butler, if the man were about at this hour.

She tightened the sash of her robe and wended her way through the warren of the castle kitchens. She wasn't surprised to discover the fires and ovens lit, the chef overseeing the production of meat and fruit pies on numerous tables while scullions scrubbed great black pots for gravy and delectable sauces.

She peered at the menu on the table:

Braised Beef
Roast Leg of Lamb and Pheasant

Salmon in Lemon Sauce
Buttered Peas

None of this surprised her. She was not even alarmed
when the kitchen hedgehog brushed around her feet.
Winthrop had explained that the nocturnal creature was
kept to eat any beetles that might crawl onto a platter.
Winthrop, however, was nowhere in sight.

Before anyone could notice her, she turned on her
heel and climbed the kitchen steps back to the servants'
quarters. And walked straight into Winthrop's wiry frame.

"What are you doing out of our room?" he said.

"I had a feeling that something was wrong."

He paused. "There has been an incident. An uniden-
tified person shot at the viscount as he rode off with his
hunting party."

Iris felt a sudden need to drop into a chair.

"Is he dead?"

"He is distraught but not otherwise harmed. The shot
missed. It is still dark. It could have been an accidental
discharge, but I doubt it."

Iris blinked, aware of light footsteps in the hall.
"Hunting mishaps are common, aren't they?"

"Yes. But until I am convinced it was an accident, it is
prudent for him to retreat for a time. At last he believes
that his life is in jeopardy."

He stilled at the rustle of linen behind him. Iris looked
past him to the young chambermaid who had material-
ized from the gloom of the hall.

"What is the matter?" the girl asked in a tentative
voice. "Did I see Lord Deptford leaving in his coach? I
thought he'd gone hunting with the other guests."

"Go about your duties," Iris said, vexed at the girl

without justification. Or perhaps it was because Winthrop had fallen silent to stare at her. Didn't he pride himself on being the consummate professional? Hadn't he enough to do without ogling the housemaid? Worse, it seemed to Iris that the impertinent girl was staring right back at him. It wasn't that Iris gave a fig. But if she had to pretend to be Winthrop's wife, he must pretend to behave like a proper husband. Even though their "marriage" was a sham, Iris would not tolerate a philandering mate. It went against the grain.

She waited to question Winthrop until the maid excused herself to polish the ancestral coats of armor displayed in the entry hall. "Wouldn't a guest have admitted his gun went off by mistake?"

"Aristocrats and their followers are prideful people, Iris. It is not in their nature to apologize easily. They consider themselves above the law, my employer being the exception."

"Pride seems to be a failing in all classes." She released a sigh. "You do not suspect anyone in the castle?"

"I do not care for Mr. Batleigh of York. He excused himself early from the performance."

"I can't say I blame him for that. I only peeked in on the first act and noticed more than one guest dozing off."

"I shall keep a closer watch on him nonetheless. And I insist you do not go to his chamber should he summon you."

"I thought my job was to investigate the guests."

"Investigate, no. Observe, yes. I forbid you to put your life or your virtue in peril."

Her knees felt as shaky as a jelly trifle. He *forbade* her. "I suppose you will launch a personal investigation into the maids who are recently employed at the castle?"

"What you mean by that?" he demanded, catching her by the elbow before she could elude him.

Iris shook off his hand. "Nothing. One of those observations I have been asked to make, that's all. You carry on your work, sir. As I shall do mine."

"I have to inform the earl of this incident immediately. I might be gone a few hours while I locate one of our contacts in the castle."

"Do not worry about me, Winthrop. There is little danger that anything will happen during your absence. I will keep an eye on Mr. Batleigh from a safe distance. And when you return, you can resume eyeing the maids again."

Before Emily, the most twisted machinations of mankind had seemed so simple, and now, as she stretched across him to stare out the carriage window, Damien realized that her slightest move could undermine him. It had become more difficult by the day to deny her anything.

He wanted to please her. He had dragged her into this mess. She deserved what little happiness he could give her.

"Damien," she said, shaking him from his slouched position. "Isn't that a country fair?"

"What of it?" he asked grumpily, aware of nothing but her silk-clad curves pressing into his vital organs.

"I've never been to a genuine fair."

His eyes closed. "Unless you have an immediate wish to buy a cow or catch a pig by the tail, there's no reason we can't go at another time."

She sighed. "Fine. I suppose you're right. It is frivolous to ask."

Damien and Emily had traveled during the early-morning hours, when the busy traffic made highway robbery less likely to occur. Winthrop had drawn a precise map and timetable for his master to observe, and Damien had followed his instructions so well that he was ahead of schedule.

That didn't mean he could fiddle while Rome burned. If anything happened to Viscount Deptford before Damien reached the castle as promised, he would be at fault. It wouldn't matter how many maidens he had saved or married along the way. A man's assassination would be on his conscience. It wouldn't matter even if all his efforts to save Deptford failed. He had given his word that he would help guard the man.

"Then that's settled," he said, smoothing his hand down her back.

"Yes, Damien."

Dammit.

For a man accustomed to wearing a disguise, it was frightening to realize he no longer recognized himself. He reached around her and rapped on the roof for the driver to stop.

Emily slid out of his lap. "What are you doing?"

"I don't know."

She smiled. The siren knew she had won.

A half hour later they were eating gingerbread and watching a wheelbarrow race. They drew attention, too, an aristocrat and his enchanting wife. "I think we need to leave," he said, brushing some crumbs off his coat.

He turned, glancing idly at a puppeteer's cart, and his heart took a plunge. Several notices had been nailed to the back of the cart, but there was only one that caught Damien's eye. He pulled Emily by the hand. "Turn around. Walk toward our carriage. Don't look at anyone. If you must nod and act preoccupied."

"What is it?" she said as he swiftly helped her up the carriage steps. "Did you see one of the rebels?"

"No. But there's a sketch of you posted on the Punch and Judy cart."

She paled, but to her credit did not look back. "Does that mean we've been followed?"

"Not necessarily." He hesitated. Their frivolous hour had been ruined. "It does mean that Ardbury is intent on catching you."

"This is far afield, isn't it?"

"He *won't* find you."

"How do you know?"

"Because he is being hunted down himself by men more dedicated than he realizes even exist."

Chapter 35

*D*amien hurried Emily through the common room of the next inn on their journey. Travelers drank and diced while barmaids and waiters bustled about to satisfy the usual clientele. Smoke and the scent of meat roasting over a spit thickened the air. Emily kept her attention on the stairs at the end of the hall. Damien used his body as a barrier against the stares that she drew from the customers dining in the public area.

"Did a flame jump the fireplace, gentlemen?" one youth asked, craning his neck to watch Emily's progress. "I swear it has suddenly become a bonfire in here."

One of his friends, appraising Damien in a glance, cuffed the youth on the head and urged him back against his chair.

"All my life," Emily muttered, dragging Damien by the hand, "I have been an object of controversy because of my hair. One would think that the young gent had never seen a red-haired woman in his life."

Damien hesitated, as if he were debating whether to acknowledge the affront to Emily or not. "One would think that the sapskull had a desire to see the end of his life. I ought to teach him some manners."

Emily half turned, realizing when she looked up at his stony face that he was serious. "We are not to draw notice to ourselves," she said, tugging harder at his hand. "Perhaps I should wear a hat with a veil in future."

"Perhaps." He divided his attention between her and the room below as they climbed the staircase.

Soon all she could hear was the occasional laugh or clunk of a mug.

"I thought you had to go to desperate measures to attract notice from other men."

"I did." She halted on the first landing, feeling his eyes cut through her. "You, of all people, bore witness to my desperation."

He turned, his hand grasping hers. "Have you ever traveled outside Hatherwood before?"

"No."

He took the lead, drawing her from the landing to the next flight of stairs. The tumult below receded as they climbed. She saw the innkeeper open a door at the end of the hall. A moment later she was pulled into a candlelit room redolent of beeswax and rosemary. She took a breath.

Damien bolted the door and led her across the room as if he owned it. Perhaps he did. Who else in the world commanded the best chamber that an inn had to offer? Only a prince or nobleman. She would have thought she was dreaming, except for the soft thud of their two bodies on a bed whose solid rosewood frame absorbed the impact.

"You are worse than wicked," she murmured between kisses and awkward pauses when he unfastened one or another part of her traveling dress. He pulled the bed curtains closed as an afterthought. She rescued the tapes of her skirt from his impatient tugs.

"You are never to attract the attention of another man in my presence." He kissed and tenderly bit a trail down her throat to her swollen breasts. "Or outside my presence, either."

She managed to answer between the gasps she would have preferred to quell. His hands caressed the curves of her hips. She closed her eyes to concentrate on maintaining a modicum of control. But when he parted her thighs, spreading her sex lips wide, she surrendered her dignity and wound her fingers through his hair. "I've never had a comment made like that about me before—only in jest."

He laid his face against her bare thigh. She heard him inhale. The lulling pitch of his voice liquefied her bones. "In jest? No. An offer rudely made, yes. But you *do* understand that you're a beautiful woman?"

"You can't expect me to honestly believe that."

She lifted her head to look at his face. The serious expression in his eyes made her feel dissolute. He knew how to entice a woman when he wanted pleasure, but even so his words pleased her. No one had ever told her she was beautiful before. Not even Iris or Lucy—or had they? Had she refused to believe them? If she had the ability to move from this bed, she might have gone to the mirror to see whether she had undergone a remarkable change.

Then again, what did a mirror's reflection matter? She felt beautiful in his eyes. A woman could live in bliss when a man as magnetic as Damien found her desirable.

"I expect you to believe everything I tell you, Emily," he said. "I'm not known to waste words."

Nor time and opportunity. He had been stroking the bud of her cleft with an absorption that brought her to the edge twice before he pulled off his trousers and pressed himself inside her. Aching and damp, her body accepted his slow invasion; then she moved against him before she could curb the impulse. She couldn't take enough of him inside her. Her muscles tensed but she still needed more of him.

His soft laughter resounded in the silence that enclosed them. "You have an appetite for passion. You'll learn to like everything I do to you."

"How do you know?" she whispered, breathless, waiting for him to keep his promise.

He angled his head to hers and licked slowly at her mouth. "Your body tells me."

Infuriating man. He raised his hips and withdrew from her as if to show her what the punishment for resistance would be. "Darling," he added. "It's useless. Enjoy yourself. Let me enjoy you. I've played enough love games that I should know."

"But I caught you without even trying," she whispered, her voice wicked and victorious even if she was shocked to hear herself admit what she hadn't realized until this moment.

His eyes locked with hers, and he went so still that she could only hold her breath and await his next move. His smile warned her, heightening the suspense until she shifted slightly, to end the anticipation or perhaps to provoke him.

"Is that a confession?" he asked softly.

"I have little experience to confess compared to yours." He pressed inside her and began to move again. He filled her with a sharp pleasure that she felt to her spine. Her hips moved in the ritual that he had taught her. "You're playing a game with me."

"Yes."

"That isn't fair."

"Fair doesn't matter. You belong to me." He bent his head and kissed her so deeply that she forgot what she had just said. She raised her hand to his wrist and slid her fingers up his arm to his shoulder, his neck. When he ended the kiss she was desperate, tempted to tell him that he had proved he could control her if he chose. He thrust faster now, deeper. He thrust until the echo of his mocking voice faded in her mind.

Fair doesn't matter. You belong to me.

They had only three days together before they reached the castle. So far on this journey Emily had learned a new lesson from her husband every night. At this rate she would soon be able to apply her knowledge to show him what *she* decided was fair. As long as they remained safe. He had been afraid for her today. Their honeymoon would have been bliss if not for the menace that shadowed their every move.

Chapter 36

They spent the next-to-last day of their journey at a charming galleried inn with dormer windows and a courtyard separate from the public stages. Emily stared out the window as the coach rolled beneath a stone arcade. Who would have known that the aristocracy could command a private entrance? Who could have guessed that *she* would marry a man whose name opened doors into private worlds that others only dreamed about?

She was so impressed that for the first time during her travels she did not jump at the blare of a horn as a smaller conveyance rattled into the common yard. She was even more pleased by the amenities offered by the high-priced inn. Below the sign hung another which said:

FINE WINES
PRIVATE DINING
HOT, COLD, STEAM BATHS

"A steam bath?" she murmured as Damien helped her down the carriage steps. "Doesn't that sound like heaven?"

"We don't have the time for that," he said before she

could plead a case for her aching body. And then, as if he regretted his abrupt reply, he added, "When the anarchists are thwarted I'll buy you a house with its own steam bath."

"Do we have time at least for luncheon?"

He watched a pair of footmen unload their luggage from the carriage. "I suppose we could manage a short meal. We might take it in a private dining room other than our own. It wouldn't hurt for me to study the other passengers, in the event one is a potential assassin."

"There's the romantic in you coming out again."

He smiled. "There will be time for romance once we settle into our own home."

Our own home.

Did this mean they would live together after the charade ended? Would he leave her there alone while he went off on other adventures? Dare she ask his plans? But even Damien could not know whether the Crown's mission to stamp out the conspiracy would work. The only thing she could do was to drop hints here and there during his receptive moments. She remembered that he owned property in London. But he'd made the offer to buy a house. The idea of establishing a household together had to have crossed his mind.

He might have said it only to placate her. She would dream of a home with him all the same.

Shortly after they returned to their chamber and Damien made a thorough search to determine that no one was lying in wait, he realized that Emily's quest for social affairs was perfectly natural and would have to wait until they moved about freely.

They had by mutual accord lain upon the bed. Damien

had started to remove his afternoon attire. He needed to think, to plan ahead, review the faces of strangers he had seen in the courtyard. He needed to recall behaviors that might have passed for ordinary but seemed suspicious in retrospect. He and his wife were not the only agents in England to employ a disguise.

"You look so intense," Emily whispered.

"Something isn't right. Something in the back of my mind tells me I've missed the obvious."

She snuggled against his side. "Perhaps you should sleep on it."

He closed his eyes again. "I think I shall."

No sooner had she leaned over to take the newspaper he'd been perusing than she bolted upright in the bed. "What, in heaven's name, is that racket? Is there a riot in progress below our room?"

Receiving no immediate answer from the male nodding off beside her, she grasped him by the collar of his shirt. "Damien, it sounds as if the inn has been invaded by soldiers."

He opened his eyes, scrutinized her face, then reached up his hand and pulled her down hard against his chest. "If you want me again, there is no need to scream it to the world. Whisper in my ear the next time you need me. God forbid I should mistake you for an assailant. Ignore the noise. It's nothing."

For a moment she forgot what noise he meant because his firm muscles were so distracting. Then riotous thumping resounded again to shake the timbers of the inn. Oddly enough, Damien did not seem concerned by the disturbance. He sighed and closed his eyes again.

"Damien!"

He cracked open one eye. "What is it now?"

"Our bed is shaking, in case you hadn't noticed," she whispered, wondering what was wrong with the man that he could sleep with the floor shaking as if an army had occupied the rooms below. Was there a riot in progress? Would troops storm their chamber at any moment?

He lifted his head. "Why are you still awake?"

"How can anyone sleep through that noise from below! It sounds as if a farmer has driven a herd of cattle into the common room. You *have* to hear it."

"Hear— Oh, that noise. I wondered what the blazes you were talking about. I should have warned you in advance."

He dropped his head back on the pillow. "This is one of the finest inns in the country."

"With cattle allowed inside?"

"That isn't a herd of cattle, Emily. It is a dance being held in the assembly room below. It abuts the public house."

She turned to him, her prior embarrassment replaced by sheer delight. "It's a dance? This isn't a tease? Truly?"

"Yes. It's not unusual in the better hostels. Let me take off those slippers, sweetheart. We don't want to tear holes in the sheets with those heels."

She buried her slippered feet under the covers. "A genuine dance? At an inn? What a wonderful notion."

"I wouldn't call it that. The assembly is likely comprised of only a handful of well-paying guests and the local gentry. These tend to be small events. Certainly not a grand affair."

"But it's a *dance*."

"If you tell me that you have never attended one, I know you're fibbing. We danced at our wedding and at Lord Fletcher's party."

"But everyone who danced at the wedding had an obligation to please the bride."

He stared into her face. "I danced with you. At the reception and at Lord Fletcher's party."

"Because it would have looked peculiar otherwise. And, yes, of course, I've attended balls. But no one except Michael and Lucy ever danced with me, and then only out of pity."

"You can't wait until we reach London?" he asked in a disgruntled voice. "Or the castle? There will be fancy balls at the viscount's party. I would think that a castle dance would be more romantic than the stomp-about beneath our bed."

"But, Damien," she said in an appealing voice, "I won't have your attention once we reach the castle. You will be keeping watch for rebels."

"I will be keeping watch over you as well."

"That is exactly my point. We shan't be able to lower our guard to enjoy ourselves in front of the other guests."

"There will be nights alone to enjoy each other, Emily."

"That's fine, Damien. You're right, of course."

"It could be dangerous. After seeing that sketch of you, I'd prefer not to mingle in public unless we have to. Besides, I'm in no mood to watch other men dance with you, radicals or not. For all we know, Lord Ardbury has figured out the true identities of the gypsy girl and Scottish man who disappeared from Hatherwood on the same night."

She picked up the newspaper that had fallen between them. "I understand," she murmured, sitting up straight to catch the light. "I wasn't thinking."

"It isn't a question of dancing. By next week, when Sir

Angus doesn't appear with either a gypsy girl or the gold he promised to deliver, Lord Ardbury might have us on our toes, whether we like it or not."

"Yes." She squinted to read the paper's small print. "I couldn't agree more."

"Although you deserve one night to pretend we are any other newlywed couple," he admitted.

"Except that we aren't." She put the paper down on the coverlet. "What were you reading about before you dozed off?"

"Reading?" He frowned. "I was looking at properties for sale. There's one in particular that sounds suitable for us." He lifted the newspaper to the light and read, "'A Most desirable Mansion, consisting of a coaching house, pavilion, and farmhouses on three thousand acres of fertile land.'"

"You aren't serious?"

"If it doesn't have a steam bath, we'll build one."

"I meant all that land."

"Well, we'd be our own village. Little Shalcross? Emilywood?"

Emily shook her head, her lips twitching.

"We won't buy the first hovel we see."

She started to laugh. He rolled over onto his stomach, her unshaven, shameless, and adorable husband. "What are you staring at?" she whispered.

"Your breasts. They look like billowy clouds from this angle."

"Full of romantic sentiment as usual."

"I'm sorry." He turned onto his back and slid to the floor to recheck the keyhole. When he returned to the bed she leapt up and threw her arms around his neck, pulling his head to hers. "I need another kiss before I go to sleep," she whispered, straining upward to press her mouth to his. "And *I'm* sorry that I caused you and our country so much trouble."

The strains of a Scottish sword dance reached them from the assembly room. The floor shuddered from the repercussion of footwork. Emily's heart was beating a tattoo. She tumbled onto the bed, laughing helplessly at Damien's efforts to undress and kiss her at the same time.

It was the most beautiful evening she had ever spent. And all because her decadent husband had taken the time to start looking for their home.

By the grace of God the dance below finally came to an end. Damien hadn't been able to sleep again after Emily had demanded his attention. *This routine is getting too comfortable,* he thought. He liked falling asleep with her in his arms. He enjoyed sharing ideas with her on the style of house or villa they would buy. It was a relief to plan a peaceful future.

He wanted her voice to be the last thing he heard before he dropped into a sleep populated by the horrors of his past imprisonment. His soul had grown weary of his cynicism and search for material riches. To view the world through Emily's eyes had restored his hope. It was impossible to hold anyone as sweet and strong as his wife without feeling his usual darkness lift. She shed light on the melancholy he had learned to live with.

Ambition might have corroded his spirit. But he wished that he could become the man he presented to the world—a newly wedded groom escorting his bride to a party in a castle instead of one entangled in a game of death and betrayal.

Trouble. Deceit. Desire. In that moment he cared for nothing except the woman whose kisses transformed him into an inferno of need for her.

At least he and Emily had two nights of intimacy left before reality intruded. He planned to use that time well. Or so he had decided when only an hour later a coded message arrived by private courier from Winthrop.

An attempt had been made on the viscount's life. Lord Deptford had gone into temporary seclusion in a countryside cottage and was ready to cooperate with the Crown. He had asked to be placed in Damien's custody.

Chapter 37

The castle stood gray and majestic on the horizon when Damien's carriage trundled off the main road. For almost two miles the coachman had traveled a bumpy track enclosed on either side by sessile oaks. Emily vented a sigh of relief when at last they came to a halt. In the midst of a clearing sat a quaint half-timbered cottage that she adored on sight. Behind it a stream bubbled over a bed of sun-dappled stones.

"It's perfect," she said to Damien who, ever the romantic, responded, "Deptford uses it as a retreat when he suffers an attack of gout and needs to soak his sore foot in the stream. The water is damn near freezing, from what I understand."

"What an enchanting image. I vow that one day you should sit down and record all the romance in your soul for the world to savor. I was about to discard all my clothing and splash about like a water nymph."

His smile promised a sweet revenge. "I must have forgotten to mention it in the excitement since our first encounter, but you are forbidden to splash or frolic in the presence of anyone but me."

"The same goes for you," she said as she stepped

down from the carriage, only to notice that it wasn't Damien's footman who had opened the door but another man with a flintlock musket on his shoulder.

She hung back until she noticed Damien nodding at the behemoth stranger. "It's all right, Emily. He is a footman. One of us."

"Does he know that?" she whispered, noting that the musket did not waver even after Damien's nod of greeting.

"He knows. He's only making sure that no one followed us off the road."

Emily offered the enormous footman a smile, which he returned with a broad grin. Relieved that he was a friendly giant, she followed Damien to the cottage door. Another footman answered the earl's quiet knock and escorted her and Damien to a small musty parlor. There two men sat playing cards at a lamplit game table. The closely drawn curtains allowed no other light into the room.

The elder of the players half rose from his chair to acknowledge Damien. His unkempt gray hair and long lawn shirt made Emily think of an old buccaneer. His leathery face crinkled as he spoke to Damien. "I was a fool not to take your advice, Shalcross. I trust you did not meet our enemies on your travels here. I appreciate the inconvenience I've caused you. I know you were not supposed to arrive until the party formally began."

"I might have suggested you hide out here if you'd trusted me," Damien said. "I would even have arrived earlier, but then I had a lady to court and a wedding to attend. Lord Deptford, this is Emily Rowland Boscastle, my wife."

"Lady Shalcross," the viscount said, his eyes bright with mischief. "I am honored to make your acquaintance. But if you will pardon me for asking, how did a woman who looks like an angel end up with your devil of a husband?"

Emily realized that the viscount was full of flattery, but she welcomed the compliment all the same. And Damien? She waited in suspense for his answer.

"An angel she is indeed," he said, and caught her wrist to hold her at his side. "It is a wonder that her wings stopped fluttering long enough for me to lead her to the altar."

The viscount looked from Damien to Emily in amusement. "Did you have to chase her there?"

"Well, it was a—"

"—whirlwind courtship," Emily said, sparing Damien an explanation that might embarrass either of them. "We didn't know each other except through letters before the wedding. I'm afraid we are both guilty of misrepresentation."

"Well, 'marry in haste, repent at leisure.' You must have fallen head over heels, Shalcross, that you couldn't wait to marry her until the conspiracy was crushed. But, then, I suppose you could not bear to be parted from each other. I notice your hand is wrapped like a padlock over her wrist. Are you still afraid that she'll run away?"

"I wouldn't dream of it," Emily said.

The viscount nodded in approval. "Good. Because your husband tried to warn me repeatedly that my life is at risk, and if the conspirators guessed his identity, then you might become their enemy by association. Now, please let us sit for tea so that I can make amends for not cooperating as I should have done."

Damien took Emily to a wood-framed settle that had been drawn far from the window. It wasn't her place to explain that this marriage was anything but a love match. Except on her part. She was afraid to admit to her husband that he had stolen her heart. She hoped only that he would protect it as he did her physical person. But it was nothing she would undo—he was everything a man should be and more. Honorable, heroic. As seductive as sin.

She sat, drawn back to the moment by the sound of his voice. He had diverted the conversation to the original purpose of this meeting.

"What happened during the hunting party?"

Viscount Deptford took the chair opposite the settle. "We had only set out when I reached the border of the woods and heard what I thought to be thunder."

"You heard a loud noise," Damien said, listening intently.

"I did not react at first. The dogs set up a furious barking. The stream running over the rocks made conversation impossible. Naturally none of the gentlemen were about to let a little rain ruin their sport. As we charged on through the woods I heard again what sounded like a deafening thunderclap above the trees. This time I realized it was not a storm."

"How did you know?" Damien asked.

"There was another shot. I was pushed off my horse by Hamm before I could warn the others."

"You were hunting for— Did you say it was ham?" Emily asked, trying to picture this.

"It wasn't a ham," Damien said. "It was Hamm, my cousin Lord Heath's footman and bodyguard from London. That was who met us outside with the musket."

The viscount snorted, motioning to the other card player, who might have been the butler, to leave the parlor. "Bodyguard? The man is huge enough to shelter a small house. I was certain he had dislocated my shoulder when he pushed me down. Still, I wouldn't be alive today without his intervention."

Damien frowned, deep in thought. "And you have no idea who shot at you?"

The viscount glanced at Emily in concern. "Is this subject upsetting your wife? She's quiet all of a sudden."

"Are you all right, Emily?" Damien asked, turning to study her face.

She was touched by the worry in his eyes, but also surprised by it. Still, she refused to distract him from what must be done. He would puzzle this out until he identified the culprit. Fussing over her every moment would not help the cause.

"Yes." she said. "I'm fine. But if this person has not been caught, who is to stop him from trying again?"

"I am," Damien said, affirming what she had feared.

She lowered her gaze to hide her anxiety at his admission. She had known Damien would be gambling with his life, but now that the time for sacrifice came near she was not at all as complacent about it as she'd hoped to be. Yet he needed her to have faith in him. He needed her to believe he would win against his enemies. And she did. She believed in him with all her heart. But she didn't want to consider what the cost would be. "Might this person still be at the castle?" she asked as an afterthought.

"Yes," Damien and the viscount said simultaneously.

"It couldn't have been an accident?" she asked in hesitation.

"One shot after another?" Damien shook his head. "No."

"I wanted to believe that, too, Lady Shalcross," the

viscount said. "But it was no accident that put two pistol balls in the game wagon that traveled behind me. To be honest, I was convinced the threat to my life was an exaggeration. I no longer feel that way."

"It was never the Crown's intention that you serve as a decoy," Damien said.

"It is damned insanity," the viscount said with a gruff laugh. "But your life is in danger, too, I fear. You're standing in the way of unprincipled men."

"I'm hardly alone," Damien said.

Emily felt her heart beating faster.

Both men lived in a world of plots and betrayals, a world she hadn't really believed existed. Now it was her utmost hope that she and Damien could settle down in a village of farmhouses. She doubted, however, that when the time came, Damien would be content to trade his dangerous pursuits for domesticity.

How irrevocably he had changed her life. What if Camden had admitted in the fortune-telling tent that he loved her? What if he'd confessed that he was going to propose to her that night and hadn't been able to find her at the party?

She might have shed her disguise on the spot and revealed herself to him. He might have fainted. He might have had second thoughts about marrying a woman who employed such devious tactics to wangle a proposal.

He had been her hero, the boy who had saved her a half-dozen or so wasp stings that she would have gladly suffered for his love. The most exciting event in his mind had been playing ghosts with his grandmother. She would have been invisible if Camden had chosen her. Invisible and buried in a small village's society.

Damien, in comparison, had changed course to protect Emily from political zealots. She didn't know him well enough to hazard a guess as to what he considered had been the highlight of his life. She was fairly certain that it had nothing to do with his grandmother.

But she could state with confidence that he had been the most exciting thing that had happened in her previously tepid existence.

Damien's regrets about dragging Emily into his battle seemed to mount by the day. It had been one thing to promise her protection while they traveled together. It was another to take her to a castle where she might be caught in the conspiracy's crossfire. Then again, he'd had little time to make other arrangements. What else could he have done with her?

She wouldn't have been safe at Hatherwood. Nor could she have galloped off with Michael on his mission. Damien had done what he'd had to do. He shook off these thoughts and stretched out his legs, wondering how he had been excluded from Emily's conversation with the viscount. Then he realized that she had drawn the eccentric old man out of his shell because it was easy to talk to Emily about anything. Treasonous plots, family affairs, and the astrolabe that she had noticed on the viscount's whatnot table. She showed interest in the small matters that Damien took for granted.

The last woman in his life wouldn't have known what an astrolabe was if one had hit her on the ear. She would have gone into hysterics if he'd even mentioned an assassination. Emily didn't have to feign interest to be agreeable. She had a mind of her own, a mind receptive to knowledge.

If Damien weren't careful, he might come to need her.

And that was a possibility he had never considered. He had never needed anyone. He could not allow himself to be at her mercy. He glanced up to discover the viscount asking Emily if she had chosen a permanent home yet and discussing Damien's preferences as if he were not there. He cleared his throat. They appeared not to hear him. In fact, the pair of them had started to laugh. He could have been sitting in the next room.

"Excuse me," he said lightly. "If I am to be the subject of your hilarity, I insist that you let me in on the joke."

Emily straightened in her chair like a chastised schoolgirl.

The viscount made no effort whatsoever to hide his mirth. "Sorry, Shalcross," he said unsympathetically. "It's just that your wife and I both realized we had met you when you were Sir Angus Morpeth. No disrespect intended, but you are half the man you used to be."

Another laugh escaped Emily. "Thank goodness for that," she said, braving a look at Damien.

The viscount chortled. "He looks a damn sight better than he did with all that red moss hanging from his chin."

Damien refused to smile. "What a couple of ingrates you are. Poor Sir Angus left this world having done what he could to protect you, and this is the thanks you show him?"

Emily attempted to look mournful. "If you like, we could hold a memorial service for Sir Angus. I'm sure we'd have to invite the sheep whose fleece he sells."

The viscount slapped his knee and burst into unrestrained laughter. Damien folded his arms across his stomach and stared at Emily, who belatedly added, "I'm afraid that I'm also guilty of misrepresentation. Damien did not know me well before our marriage."

His eyes narrowed. "It would seem that I do not know you now."

"All women are unfathomable, Shalcross," the viscount said, as if he were Emily's defender. "We shall never uncover their secrets, and that is how it should be. A woman is like a book, revealing herself one page at a time."

Damien said nothing for several moments. He felt like the biggest spoilsport in all England. "Do either of you know what it feels like to wear iron padding? Or to grow a beard and dye it red every day?"

Emily opened her mouth to answer and then apparently reconsidered and subsided into silence.

"I'd no idea the subject touched a nerve, Shalcross," the viscount said. "I've worn uncomfortable costumes to a masquerade."

"Not for five weeks straight," Damien said, his irritation eroding at the guilty look on his wife's face. "Oh, bugger it all. Wearing disguises is essential in my work. Laugh if you like. I felt damn ridiculous in that costume, if you must know."

"I thought you looked rather handsome," Emily said in an overt effort to placate him.

"It was a convincing disguise," the viscount added. "I'd no idea that Sir Angus was a fictitious character when we first met."

Damien looked away from Emily to the window. "This isn't the time to let personal issues distract us from our goal. I regret that it took an attempt on your life to make you realize that we are up against men dedicated to committing monstrous deeds. But I have to wonder why you didn't believe those who warned you. Nor do I understand why you withheld evidence against the ring when your own existence was at stake."

A shroud of heavy silence fell. The viscount seemed to age a decade as Damien awaited his answer. Emily looked down at her lap.

"My only son is one of the conspirators," the viscount said at last. "To give evidence is to sign his death warrant. But I can no longer protect him or hope he will see the error of his ways. I can't allow him to harm others for whatever warped reasons he believes are justification for his grudge against all authority."

Damien shook his head. Of all the scenarios he had considered to explain the viscount's resistance, this had never crossed his mind. Would Damien have gone to such lengths to conceal his own son's crimes? He could not know. He prayed that he would never face such a test. Still, his child could be forming inside Emily as he contemplated the strength of family ties. Would he as a father put country before flesh and blood? How long had the viscount carried the secret?

He said, "I didn't realize what personal sacrifice you would have to make by agreeing to cooperate with the Crown."

"He will be hanged as a traitor."

"Perhaps not," Damien said. "If he has not committed prior crimes and can be stopped before he causes harm, there is still hope for his redemption."

Chapter 38

*I*t looked like a fairy-tale castle from the carriage window, but who knew what evil lurked within its walls? Damien had warned Emily time and time again that she was not to trust anyone at the party. He was afraid for her, he had said. But what of his safety? Did he believe himself untouchable because he stood for what was right? Keeping her at his side might protect her, but it also made him vulnerable.

The carriage climbed a rutted dirt road; closer and closer the castle loomed. A bank of clouds drifted across the sky. The sun that had illuminated the castle ramparts vanished. In its place shadows gathered, silver-mauve and unwelcoming.

"I don't like it," she thought aloud. "It looks cold and has an aura of death about it."

Damien's deep voice teased her. "Is that your private opinion as a countess or as a fortune-teller sharing one of her prophecies?"

She turned from the window to find Damien studying her intently. How he flustered her. She wished she could read his mind. Was he remembering his domination of her during the night? How elemental he could be at times, and she no better. She had denied him nothing. Something had changed between them since their visit to the cottage. Even while she had conversed with the viscount, she'd felt Damien scrutinizing her. And then, afterward, during the final leg of the ride to the castle, he had withdrawn from her.

She could not help thinking that she had displeased him. Had she seemed gauche and awkward in his view?

"Emily."

She blinked.

"This is no time to go into a trance," he said, frowning at her. "From the minute we cross the castle drawbridge, you are to be on your guard. Doubtless many violent acts have been committed here in the past."

"Am I allowed to talk to anyone, or shall I just stand at your side like a trained monkey?"

"Obviously you will have to talk to the other guests. Perhaps you'll be able to draw useful information from them. But do not put yourself in a precarious situation from which I might not be able to help you."

"I have no intention of climbing the castle tower, Damien. I am not the dunderhead I was when we met."

"I've gathered that."

She settled back against the squabs. "What if something happens to you?"

"There are four other agents assigned to the castle, including Winthrop. I will not formally introduce you to them, but I shall indicate who they are upon our arrival." He wavered. "And, above all, else do not stray off with any attentive young men."

She sat up straighter. "Do you honestly believe I would take a chance of being alone with a member of the conspiracy?"

"To be truthful, Emily, I was referring to a member of the male sex in general."

He was in a passionate mood when they settled in their bedchamber early that evening. He kissed Emily three times after they excused themselves from the tennis match in progress on the lawn. He would have kissed her up the staircase and through the door had another couple not trailed a few steps behind.

Inside their chamber, she surrendered as Damien's touch shed her clothes like autumn leaves.

He gathered her into his arms without a hint of gentleness and drew her closer until she could feel the length of him, his need. And while he kissed her, she unbuttoned his jacket and slipped her hand inside his waistband. He grew hard and thick in her hand as she stroked the head of his penis. With a groan of frustration he broke the kiss to remove his clothes, allowing her a few moments to catch her breath.

But his eyes held her a helpless captive. No sooner was he undressed than he pulled her across the room to a yellow brocade couch and said, "Let us finish what we started. I do hate to leave matters undone. Do you mind if we don't use the bed? This couch appears sturdy enough for what I have in mind."

"It's fine with me, Damien. Why don't you lie back and let me have a turn for once?"

He laughed. "This sounds promising. Please be my guest."

It was not in Damien's character to submit to either pleasure or pain. He preferred to be the one in power. But this was a novel experience, his wife attempting to seduce him. Surely what she had in mind was more interesting than anarchists.

He laid back his head to watch her through hooded eyes. She had gone down on her knees while he sprawled back against the couch.

When her fingers skimmed his belly, he released his breath.

"Do you need my guidance?" he asked in a silky voice.

"Yes," she whispered, her fingers brushing his rampant erection. "Isn't this how it's done?"

He groaned. "That depends on what you mean to do."

"May I kiss you there?"

"How do you know about this act?"

She smiled demurely. "Diana had a book that Lucy and I used to sneak into her room to read."

"You should have both been sent to boarding school," he said, not managing to sound at all sincere.

"The book had pictures." She lowered her head. "The man wasn't as big as you."

"Dear God."

"Well, you did it to me. Do you want me to stop?"

"Don't you dare."

He stared down at her face, her mouth hesitantly closing around the head of his prick. The suction of her lush red lips, so delicate, so uncertain, filled him with a fierce arousal. He called upon his willpower to keep from shoving his shaft into her mouth. But as he eased through her teeth, he felt her suckle him harder. He pushed deeper before he could restrain the urge. And she took as much of him as she could, her tongue slowly encircling the stiff muscle from knob to base.

He reached down blindly for her shoulder, certain he

would come in her throat if she did not release him from her amateur seduction. Not that there was anything amateur about her instincts. This was pure female intuition. Her sweet attempt to suck his rod was an exquisite surprise. Clearly she wanted to please him. And she had more than succeeded. She drove him right to the edge. Her tongue flicked up and down, around the swollen base of his erection. Her hair fell like silk against his belly and he pushed it to the side. He wanted to watch her mouth swallow him. He could grow too attached to a wife who amused him outside the bedroom but who made him feel like a beggar in his bed.

"Is this the right way, Damien?" she whispered. "Shall we continue in the bed? They were in a bed in Diana's book."

"This is fine. I couldn't move if I wanted to."

Her lips formed a seal around him, then slid up and down his straining length. He could not bear it. His groin tightened with every teasing lash of her tongue. He closed his eyes, his body still and at her mercy before he surrendered to the strongest climax he had ever known. When moments later she crawled up beside him, he could barely move to embrace her.

"Did I do it properly?" she whispered.

He stroked her hair. She was lying awkwardly between the cushions and his lower body. "I am almost too replete and grateful to answer." He exhaled. "I don't think I have ever appreciated the value of books as much as I do at this moment."

And her, he thought. What an amazing woman was his wife.

Chapter 39

By the end of their second afternoon in the castle, Damien had formed an impression of four out of the viscount's thirteen guests. The remaining nine he met during a midnight supper. Five others were expected to arrive the following day.

The viscount insisted that every lady and gentleman invited to the party was well-known to him. This did not mean that Damien could dismiss them as suspects. Deptford's admission about his son proved that an enemy could exist in one's own family.

The castle steward assured Damien in private that letters of character for the old staff and temporary hires had undergone thorough scrutiny.

Only seven guests had participated in the hunting party. Those who remained behind included three middle-aged gentlewomen, an architect, a retired professor, and a young wastrel lord whose wit was his only salvation. The fact that they declined to participate in the hunt did not rule them out as suspicious persons.

Damien decided that his prime subjects were the architect, Sir Norman Finch, and Lord Benham, the amusing young aristocrat, who flanked Emily on either side at the supper. He had no actual reason to suspect the two men, aside from the fact that they were flirting with a lady whose husband sat across the table, glaring daggers at them to no avail.

Worse, Emily indulged their interest with a few shy comments and a smile Damien thought was entirely too enchanting. Finally he caught her eye and frowned his displeasure at this flirtation across the table.

To his astonishment she frowned back at him and returned her attention to Sir Norman.

Damien was not amused. In fact, he was contemplating how he would interrupt their conversation without creating a disturbance when a footman appeared with a bottle that he waved in Damien's face.

"May I, my lord?"

Damien did not look up at Winthrop. "Yes, please. I would also like a bottle brought to my room tonight."

"As you wish, my lord."

"And please ask a chambermaid to deliver another set of towels and see to my wife's comfort."

"At which hour should we arrive?" Winthrop asked, pouring the wine into a glass with the steadiest hand Damien had seen.

"Three o'clock would be convenient," Damien replied, then added, "It appears that Sir Norman also needs his glass refilled. Do be careful not to spill any wine on his fine blue coat. And do me a favor. My second trunk has not yet been delivered to my room. Find it as soon as possible."

Chapter 40

$\mathcal{D}$amien sprawled back against the sofa in his shirt and breeches, his gaze following Emily around the room as she prepared for bed. "I don't know why you had to glower at him all evening, Damien. It was not at all subtle. I thought we had agreed we would not draw undue notice to ourselves."

"I had agreed to act like a husband, Emily, and as such I did not appreciate the way he monopolized your attention."

She removed her remaining stocking and pulled at the ties of her petticoat. Damien stared at her bare rump, forcing himself to remain on the sofa. "What did he talk to you about, anyway?"

"Architecture. He went on and on about flying buttresses and how castle kitchens should be remodeled for efficiency so that the food is not served stone-cold, as it was in days past."

"Did you think he was attractive?"

She looked at him over her shoulder, the smile on her full-lipped mouth threatening his concentration. "You're jealous."

"Perhaps," he said, his voice cool, his blood the opposite.

"You have no reason to be," she said with a provocative smile.

His anger faded. His arousal did not. He forced himself to remember what they had been discussing. "I find it strange that he has made a tour of the kitchens, don't you?"

"Not necessarily. He's an architect. Perhaps he can't help forming a professional opinion of the castle. I assume he would be well compensated if the viscount decided he wanted a structural change."

"I don't trust any man who inspects a kitchen unless it is his place of employment. I also distrust a man who devotes all his attention to my wife while I am present. It makes me wonder what he would dare behind my back."

"Well, I don't think you need worry on that account," Emily said. "I do believe that when Winthrop spilled the wine in the man's lap, it cooled his ardor."

"Are you blaming *me* for Winthrop's awkwardness?"

She cast him a cynical look. "Do you deny that he acted on your advice?"

"What is my confession worth to you?"

"Damien, really. You are an outrageous man. Do you truly expect to trade sexual favors for the truth?"

"I expect sexual favors from you because you are my wife. The truth is another matter."

"You would lie to your wife?"

He laughed. "I would elude an answer that might upset you. But lie? No."

She struggled with the first hook of her corset until he stood and crossed the floor to complete the task. "I miss having a maid."

He nuzzled her neck. "I miss having a valet to shave me, too, but at the moment I'm glad that neither one of them are here. Hold still a minute while I get this last hook."

"The hooks always resist. I despise wearing a corset, if you must know."

"It gave you a décolletage tonight to make a man swoon. Brace your hands on the bedpost. I'm having a spot of trouble."

"Is it that hook?"

"No, it's getting out of my trousers and drawers using only my left hand."

She obeyed, knowing from her experience with this man that he would not brook a refusal. She sighed at the delicate strokes of his knuckles between her shoulders and then the hollow of her spine. He could entice her to the edge of the world. How wretched to know he could so easily arouse in her this maddening desire.

He said in a low voice, "This is what happens, Emily, when you flaunt your beautiful body in front of me."

She clung to the bedpost with her back to Damien, bound not by chains but by her own need. He closed his hands around her hips, drawing her into the heat and hard contours of his lower body. Slowly he rubbed his erection between the crease of her bottom, and to her mortification she braced herself, spreading her legs wider in shameless anticipation.

"I was jealous, Emily," he said as he slipped one hand around her belly. "I was jealous enough to forget that I have a job to do."

"You're insane if you think I'd ever be unfaithful with another man."

His teeth grazed her shoulder. His hand found one

plump breast and squeezed her nipple into aching hardness. "That seems to be the trouble. I'm not able to think when we are together. That's a disability in my profession."

She pressed her forehead to the bedpost. "I guarantee that you are better able to make sense of your thoughts than I can at this moment."

He realized now that he had lost the battle to remain emotionally disengaged in his marriage. His wife trusted him. Perhaps if she had known him only a year ago she would have done anything to escape him. He had returned to England disillusioned by the sins he had witnessed and committed in other lands. Empty. Hollow. A shell that had survived for what purpose, he had not understood until now.

He might have seduced her body, but she had stolen and restored what had been left of his soul. And now he feared he could not live without her. He needed the passion she engaged in him and the sweetness of her submission.

He could feel her invitation, the dampness of her on his cock when she opened herself to him. As her bottom brushed against his groin, his entire body tightened in desperation he could not restrain. He wanted to feel every forbidden crevice of her body. To conquer and caress.

"Damien," she whispered, releasing one of her hands from the bedpost. "Why are you teasing me so?"

"I want you to beg for it," he replied, the hoarseness of his voice betraying his own excitement. He taunted her with shallow thrusts into her sheath. His senses took delight in the helpless shivers that coursed through her.

"Hurry," she whispered faintly, her other hand dropping to her side. "It's late."

"What a shame I asked Winthrop and Iris to our room tonight."

She turned and placed her arm around his neck. "According to the clock on the mantel, we still have half an hour."

"Thirty minutes?" He took her hand and she led him back through the bedchamber to the sofa. She reclined before him, the candlelight illuminating her soft curves and inviting flesh. He needed no other enticement. He bent over her, kissing her into a daze as his hands caressed her creamy breasts and belly.

She was *his*. His wife. He lost track of time when they were together, whether it was during sex or sitting in an uncomfortable carriage. At times she soothed him. At others she heated his blood and he knew she was the only woman who could put out the fire before it consumed him. But when they made love, it was as if nothing else existed.

$\mathcal{I}$ris sat across from Winthrop at the tea table in their room. He brought a pot of chocolate and two mugs for them to share every night before they retired. Iris didn't have the heart to tell him that chocolate before bed caused indigestion. Besides, they would be staying up into the wee hours for a reunion with the master and mistress. Iris was almost afraid to hear what trials Emily had undergone since marrying the earl.

Iris realized that her life would never again be the same as it had been in Hatherwood. She had been introduced to espionage, an activity that in Iris's mind had seemed more adventurous than the reality of spying on houseguests at a party.

She hadn't solved any mysteries or gathered any information that would assist the Crown. She *had* discovered that at least one of the guests, a married gentleman, intended to have a secret affair with his brother's wife. If that was the type of sordid knowledge one gained while spying, Iris wanted nothing to do with it.

"Drink your chocolate, Iris," Winthrop said sternly. "You missed supper again tonight. I don't know how you exist on the little you eat."

"I exist on nerves," she said. "Perhaps you are comfortable living under the same roof as an assassin, but I am not."

"You've been very brave from the start," he said. "I don't know many women who would keep their wits about them in this situation."

She felt a flush of pleasure. "If you'd been maid to my mistress and survived her escapades, you would have learned to keep your wits about you, too." She put her hand to her mouth, realizing this was the first she had ever spoken ill to him of Emily.

"I didn't mean that as it sounded."

He nodded in understanding. "The earl is not the easiest person to serve. He's dragged me through the pits of hell in his travels. The places we have been. You would be shocked, Iris, straight down to your stockings, if you ever saw the deplorable prisons and hovels where his lordship and I stayed. I won't tell you the details."

"Please don't."

"Do you know what a scorpion is?"

She grimaced. "They're awful things that don't live in England."

He nodded again. "They're used for torture in some foreign prisons. Come on, have a mug of chocolate. You've gone pale on me."

She sipped the chocolate he poured into her mug. Indigestion would keep her up all night. That and the image of scorpions he'd put in her head. She was looking forward to the hour when she would be reunited with her mistress. Perhaps Emily would surprise her and have scads of little stories to share about her first impressions of life as a countess. Nothing remotely exciting had happened to Iris. Except for Winthrop, and she couldn't admit she thought him dashing.

"I'll be glad when the conspirators are caught and we can resume our ordinary lives," she said, while Winthrop drank his chocolate. "I wonder where his lordship will settle when this is over."

"London, as far as I know." He took off his spectacles and reached his arms over his head.

Iris stared at him. She didn't know how well he could see without his glasses. She didn't know whether being forced to live with him under false pretenses had warped her opinions. But tonight she finally admitted to herself that he was the most attractive man she had ever known. And it wasn't only his boyish face or reedy form that made him appealing.

It was his imperturbable dignity that she had come to admire. He still ordered her about. His insistence on placing their shoes in a certain order by the door still annoyed her as her need to arrange bottles by their size did him.

But he had brought her chocolate to drink because he was concerned about her health. Iris could kiss him for that. In fact, Iris would kiss him right now if she could invent a plausible reason for doing so.

"What is it?" he asked, lowering his arms. "Do I have chocolate on my mouth? A tear in my shirt?"

Now, she thought.

This is the time. Scoot the chair closer to wipe the nonexistent smudge from his lips, and let him take the initiative from there.

"Let me look," she said, leaning forward.

He sat still, his eyes searching her face. "It would be wise of you not to come any closer, Iris. I should not tell you this, but I have been struggling against temptation since we argued with each other in Hatherwood."

She felt a spark of hope. "And what have you been tempted to do?"

"All manner of wicked acts."

"With— Me?"

"With you, inside you, behind you, all—all over you."

"Sir."

"Disgraceful, I know."

"I never would have guessed," she said, primly lowering her gaze in case her delight was obvious. "You have hidden your feelings well indeed."

And with his next words, he extinguished her hope like a candle flame. "You can rest assured that I will continue to subdue my urges, Iris. The chances are that we will have to live in the same residence, serving the master and mistress. I would not disrespect you or our positions by behaving in anything but a straightforward manner."

"Oh," was all she managed to say.

"We have fifteen minutes left until our interview with the master and mistress. I promised Hamm that I would stand the morning watch over the viscount so that he could take a meal in the kitchen. He will be close enough to you in case of trouble."

"That is thoughtful of you, sir."

He reached for his spectacles and stood. "Try not to engage his interest while I am gone."

"Engage Hamm's— What do you think I am?" she asked indignantly.

"A temptress in a maid's clothing. It takes a disciplined man to resist a woman with your qualities."

Then he was gone to fetch a bottle for the earl, leaving Iris to wonder what qualities in her character had provoked his welcome confession.

They washed and dressed each other between kisses and bouts of laughter. Damien opened the armoire in his dressing closet to discover that instead of his tailored attire hung a wardrobe of dresses that could belong only to a dowager.

"Damn me," he called in the direction of Emily's dressing room. "The footmen must have mixed up my missing trunk with some beldame's at the party. I don't think any of these will suit me, do you?"

Emily appeared at the door of her dressing closet. "Your trunk is in here, sitting right next to mine. It doesn't look as if it has been opened."

"I hope not. Winthrop was supposed to be on the lookout for our luggage."

"Is there anything inside it that you do not want others to see?"

He proceeded to the closet, holding the ruffled ball gown he had removed from his armoire. "Is the lock still intact?"

Emily stepped aside to allow him into the closet. "It looks to be. I hope you aren't considering another disguise, Damien. That bodice will never fit around your chest. You could never pass as a woman. Your shoulders would be a giveaway."

He glanced up wryly. "I hesitate to admit this, Emily, but I have passed as one before. I do not, however, have any intention of doing so again. It was a frightening experience. My legs do not look well in stockings. Gowns just aren't made for my proportions."

"I can imagine."

"It is true, though, that a shawl can conceal any number of physical flaws, my shoulders being one of them."

"I do not consider your shoulders to be flawed," Emily said. "Merely broad. The rest of you is undeniably masculine, too. I would not believe you were a woman for an instant."

His stare pierced her composure. Had she just confessed that she had found his body to be the epitome of male beauty? "You would be surprised to see what changes Winthrop can affect with a bag of hairpieces and cheek plumpers."

He knelt then to examine the padlocked trunk and extracted the key from his pocket. Swiftly his hands delved through the first layer of clothing to the leather bottom.

Emily was curious now to see what he had brought to the party. Clothes or weapons? A love letter or two from the last woman in his past? Or were there private documents that would implicate him as an agent?

He closed the lid and stood, looking into her eyes. "Nothing appears to be missing."

"None of your papers?"

"I keep those with me at all times." His gaze caught hers, as if suddenly she were the only thing that mattered.

Emily stared down at him in pensive silence until a discreet knock sounded at the outer door. She turned reflexively, noting from the corner of her eye that he had slipped his hand into the pocket of his waistcoat. Clearly he'd found whatever he feared had been stolen. And it was not anything he wished to share with his wife.

"That has to be Winthrop and Iris. Shall I answer?"

He closed the lid of the trunk and stood, his gaze

skirting hers. "I'll let them in." He pulled from his shoulder the pink dress that he'd apparently forgotten in his haste to learn whether any of his belongings had been searched. "There is probably a lady in this castle right now accusing a servant of stealing her clothes."

Chapter 42

*E*mily could not contain her joy at being reunited with her maid. "Oh, Iris, I have missed you more than you can ever know."

Iris's eyes misted up as Emily drew her into the spacious dressing closet. They sat down at the same moment on the chaise lounge. "I have so much to tell you, except that certain details have to be omitted because they are too private. All I can admit is that I never want to be without you again."

"Well, I have plenty to tell you, too, miss—I mean, my lady." Iris swiped her knuckles under her eye to catch a tear. "The things that Winthrop has said to me—"

Emily felt her blood chill. "Has he insulted you in any manner? Tell me, and I will insist that my husband punish the varlet."

"Valet," Iris said absently.

"Varlet. Valet. If he has dishonored you, there is no point in making a distinction."

Iris sniffed. "But he hasn't dishonored me. He ignored me during the journey here until I convinced myself I was unworthy of even a kiss. I have never felt so lacking in my life. And then to have the nerve to call me a—a—"

"The prissy upstart," Emily said feelingly. "How dare he offend you by—by doing exactly what, Iris? I'm not certain I understand what you're trying to say."

"He called me a temptress," Iris blurted out. "A *temptress*."

Emily blinked, too stunned to respond.

Iris nodded vigorously. "Yes. You heard me. I did not misspeak. He accused me of leading him into temptation. He said that I made him forget why he had come to the castle in the first place. He accused me of muddling his brains."

Emily hesitated. "Did you?"

"Only in my thoughts. But that doesn't count, does it?"

"It might if he could read minds."

"I must say that you aren't being helpful at all. Oh, I should have kept this to myself."

Emily took Iris's hand. "You were right to tell me. I'll take the matter to my husband and insist he put Winthrop in his place."

Iris looked horrified. "You can't do that."

"Well, why not?"

"It might jeopardize our investigation. It would be disloyal of me as a citizen to allow my feelings to interfere with justice."

"Perhaps you could work with Hamm instead."

"You mean the bean-stalk giant?"

"He's intimidating at first impression, but it's rather reassuring to know he's on our side."

"You've forgotten one thing, my lady. Winthrop and I are supposed to be man and wife for the duration of the assignment. If I left him for another footman, the guests might not notice, but the domestic staff would. I'd lose their respect, if not my position. And where would I stay until the earl is ready to leave the castle? I have to abide by the rules if I don't want to cause a stir."

"I see your point, Iris." In fact, Emily saw more than her maid had intended to reveal. Iris had fallen for the earl's valet, and Winthrop, from the sound of it, had been fighting against the same affliction. It was a blessing in disguise, really. She had finally moved past her feelings toward Michael. Emily's brother would never have married Iris, if he married anyone at all.

"And what should I do about it?" Iris asked.

Emily frowned as though giving the matter grave thought. "I suspect that my husband would urge you to carry on as usual until after his assignment is over."

"So you are advising me to continue living with Winthrop as his wife?"

"I'm afraid that all of us have been forced to make sacrifices," Emily said, although so far the rewards of marriage had surpassed whatever she had sacrificed.

"But what am I to do if Winthrop accuses me of being a temptress again?"

"The way I see it, Iris, is that you can insist you have no feelings for him and that he must put you out of his mind, or—" She paused to reconsider her advice.

"Or what?"

"Or you could turn into a temptress and call his bluff."

Iris's cheeks turned pink. "Never did I expect to hear that sort of advice from you. I couldn't be a temptress if I tried. Could you?"

"Neither of us ever thought I would marry," Emily said carefully. "Now I have a little more experience to offer than when we lived in Hatherwood."

"It hasn't even been a month," Iris retorted. "I don't see how you could have gained enough experience to consider yourself the Encyclopedia of Love and Marriage."

"Let us just say that my husband is an intense tutor and I have been a rapt student."

"But you are married. I am not."

"And we both know *why* he married me. Only time will tell how strong our union will become. If it lasts at all."

"Do you want it to last?" Iris inquired after a pause.

"Oh, yes. Very much so."

Iris gave a nod of approval. "To be honest, I never cared much for Mr. Jackson. He was a fine cricketer, but he always seemed to be—I don't know—more a boy than a man."

"I assure you, my husband is mature in all the ways that matter."

"So is Winthrop," Iris said. "You'd never know it to look at him."

"I take it that you look at him often."

"Perhaps."

They lapsed into silence. Emily detected the murmur of male voices coming from Damien's dressing room. She decided it would be wiser to steer her conversation with Iris toward more neutral ground. "I heard that there has already been one attempt on the viscount's life."

The ploy worked. Iris gave one final sniff and lifted her head, returning to her standard form. "He was shot at twice as he was going off to hunt. The castle steward ordered a search of the castle and grounds for evidence, but neither the culprit nor the weapon used was found. I've got an idea who the suspect is, though."

Emily leaned in closer. "Who?"

"It might sound far-fetched, but I have an uncanny

feeling it's one of the housemaids hired for the party. I've caught her at least twice under questionable circumstances."

Emily mulled over this information. With Iris so upset, now wasn't the time to remind her that she'd also had an "uncanny feeling" that Camden would propose to Emily on the night of Lord Fletcher's party. "What precisely did you catch her doing?" she asked.

"She was giving Winthrop the eye."

"As in handing him the spectacles he misplaced?"

Iris scowled. "The eye, Emily. The *eye*. The look that a female gives a man to indicate she is open to flirtation."

"And on this basis you are convinced that she is a paid assassin?"

"It's hard to explain."

"It's harder to understand," Emily said bluntly. "What does Winthrop think of your theory?"

"He disagrees with it, naturally. For all I know, he's flattered by her attention. The other odd thing is that I've seen her sneaking up to the guest rooms late at night. Sometimes she is carrying a tray or a crystal decanter."

"Have you reported her to the housekeeper?"

Iris shook her head. "Winthrop is adamant that we not bring undue attention to ourselves. He has another suspect in mind."

"Do you know who it is?"

Iris made a face. "Yes. It's an architect named Sir Norman Finch, and he's probably the most pleasant guest at the party. If you and I had not been buried all our lives in Hatherwood, we might have heard of him. He's designed cathedrals and town houses in London and Brighton. He tips well, too."

"I met him at supper tonight," Emily said, reviewing

the conversation in her mind. "I thought he was perfectly charming, but he did go on about flying buttresses and— I *do* remember hearing Lord Fletcher mentioning his name before. He is respected in his field."

Iris turned unexpectedly to examine Emily's hair and wrinkled evening gown. "I can see that you have suffered without my assistance. Why are you wearing your hair in that unflattering knot?"

Emily tried to think of an excuse for her unkempt appearance. Lady's maid or not, Iris did not need to know that Emily had been cavorting on the sofa with Damien a short while ago, or that she was fortunate she'd managed to put on her clothes at all, let alone worry about her coiffure before Iris arrived.

Damien felt on edge whenever Emily was not in his sight. Obviously he could not sit at her side while she and the other ladies at the party took afternoon tea and discussed the latest French fashions. Nor could she join him and the other male guests in an after-dinner smoke and game of billiards. Yet his instincts said that the viscount would be at his most vulnerable to attack during those times that the guests were engrossed in an amusement.

How, when, *would* the assailant strike again? He pondered these questions late into the night, only to hear Emily sigh in her sleep or to feel her roll against him, seeking his comfort. He'd put his arm around her and his thoughts would scatter. Time and time again he forced himself to review the guests he had met, their mannerisms and possible motives for murdering an eccentric old man.

Could the motive be money? Loyalty or the absence of it could be bought. Lord Ardbury had the riches to purchase an assassin. Could the Crown buy information from one of the rebels? Was one of the guests a gambler mired in debt?

The first person who came to mind was the young wastrel lord who had been seated across from Damien at the table. He might be desperate for cash. Then there was that architect who had with his eyes devoured Emily as if she were the dessert course.

The suspect did not have to be a man. A married woman named Mrs. Batleigh had smiled at him invitingly more than one since his arrival. Her husband had appeared to be more interested in one of the other ladies present than in his wife's potential infidelity. For all Damien knew, the couple swapped bed partners at every affair they attended.

And the domestic staff, especially the temporary servants, should not be excused from suspicion simply because they carried letters of reference. Signatures could be forged.

He would have to wait again to ask Winthrop and then Hamm their opinions on the matter. Winthrop had a talent for detail. Hamm had the experience of working for Damien's cousin in London, Lieutenant Colonel Lord Heath Boscastle. As a footman to a high-ranking agent, Hamm would undoubtedly have noticed anything that merited investigation. The men would put their heads together. Perhaps the castle steward had a few suggestions to share.

At any rate the assailant would presumably have to make a move in the next three days, when riots had been planned to break out across England. Would he choose poison, another shooting, a shove down the stairs to take the viscount's life? That was unlikely to occur when the viscount had a bodyguard with him at all times.

But as Damien had learned, even a guard could be distracted from duty.

Chapter 43

*D*amien and Winthrop had retreated to the master's dressing closet. It was a sizable room with two matching armchairs. The door stood practically open so that Damien could look into the adjoining suite. "It's good to see you, Winthrop. I have missed your management." Which wasn't quite the truth. Damien had been too engrossed in his wife to care much whether his boots could use an extra blackening or that he had worn the same neckcloth for two social functions in a row.

Winthrop glanced around the closet in disapproval. His critical gaze came to rest upon the gray jacket that hung from the wall peg. Damien had worn it earlier in the day.

"Good gracious," Winthrop said, taking off his spectacles to examine the lenses. "Either I need new glasses or that is animal fur on your jacket, my lord. Did you wrestle a wild boar on your way here?"

Damien glanced up at the jacket. "Nothing quite that dramatic. The viscount's pugs escaped the kennels this afternoon and decided to invade our picnic. I captured one of the little porkers, but another made off with the roast beef. Then a third charged and knocked over the Chablis. He drank it, too."

"It sounds as if you are enjoying the party, my lord."

"Did I say that, Winthrop?"

"Not in so many words. But you had a smile on your face as you were describing the incident."

"Are you insinuating that by assisting in the capture of three runaway pups I have forgotten the reason I came to the castle?"

"My lord," Winthrop said, looking affronted. "I would never doubt your strategy. You would not attend as frivolous an affair as a picnic unless you had an ulterior motive."

Damien glanced through the door into the connecting room. Trust Winthrop to perceive that Damien's motivation for going on the picnic was not only to catch a murderer, but also to spend time with Emily.

He frowned, catching Winthrop in the act of reaching under the chair for one of Damien's gloves. "Organizing my wardrobe can wait another day, Winthrop. What personal observations have you made at the party that might be of help in catching our prey?"

"It is difficult to cull a suspect from the guests who have arrived," Winthrop said. "I dislike the majority of them."

Which did not surprise Damien in the least. Winthrop disapproved of humanity as a whole. "Well, which of them do you dislike the most?"

"This assignment would have been easier if I did not have to worry about Miss Brookshire."

Damien stared at the second glove Winthrop had recovered from beneath the cushion of his chair. "Surely you have not been holding her hand the entire time."

"I have observed the strictest protocol in her presence," Winthrop said.

"I haven't accused you of doing otherwise." Damien rubbed the vein that had started to pulse in his temple. "Has *she* accused you of impropriety?"

"Not yet."

"If you admit to being lax in your observations because you are fighting an attraction to my wife's maid, I shall, well, I shall smack you with one of those gloves."

"I never said anything of the sort." Winthrop swallowed. "But I will not lie. It is no easy thing for a man to live night and day with a comely woman and not feel a stirring of desire, no matter how disciplined he is. This was not our original plan. I've had difficulty adjusting."

Damien understood too well the truth of that statement. If he had not been able to sleep with Emily, he would have soon become a raving lunatic. But had Winthrop just described Emily's maid—that tall, fair, and complaining woman—as comely? In fact, had Winthrop ever allowed any person or thing to stir his desires before?

"This is a serious matter," Damien said. "It is unfair to keep you from doing your job. I should never have suggested that the pair of you join forces in the first place. I will think of a solution during the night."

"No." Winthrop adamantly shook his head. "I accepted this assignment, and I will not allow it to be compromised by a personal conflict. After all, this is not going to be a permanent situation."

Damien shrugged. "I'm afraid it might. It appears that my wife is as dependent on her maid as I am on you. All four of us will live together in my future residence. The relationship between my top-ranking valet and her ladyship's maid will set the standards for the rest of the staff. You will have to make the best of it."

"Then you have made the decision to settle down, m lord?" Winthrop asked, craftily turning the conversatio back to Damien's life.

"I can decide nothing until the conspiracy is broken, Damien replied. "Now, putting our disconcerting desire aside, I insist you describe your general impressions o every guest you have met so far as well as any suspiciou behaviors that you have noted."

Winthrop sighed as if it were a relief to return to suc a mundane subject as murder. "Let us start with Lor Benham. He has already racked up considerable debt a the gaming tables. The viscount has quietly informed th croupier that all his losses will be covered."

"What in God's name for?" Damien wondered aloud

"I have gathered from the butler that Lord Benham reminds the viscount of his own estranged son. Benham who has been disowned by his own family, is only too happy to take advantage of this unofficial adoption."

"Hell's bells," Damien said. "That sounds more like the plot of a penny dreadful than of a deadly conspir acy."

"There is more."

"Go on."

"A Mrs. Gladwick is having a tryst tonight with Mr Batleigh of York."

"Then I assume they are not planning an assassina tion. What of their respective spouses?"

"You would have to question Miss Brookshire on the subject. I only keep up on gossip as it pertains to the conspiracy."

Damien sat up to open the door all the way. "Then le us all four discuss our impressions and devise a plan fo the remainder of the party."

But privately Damien doubted that putting their heads together would be of any help. It was unpardonable, really, to think that he and Winthrop might bungle this operation to protect two young women they had known for such a short time.

On Saturday morning there was a rowing contest on the lake for the gentlemen. The first to reach the ruined pavilion at the end of the left bank would win the competition. Ladies lined up along both shores, waving colorful banners to cheer on their favorite for the race. Below them at the water's edge stood footmen offering towels and refreshments to any participant who found the race too strenuous or who slipped into the mud.

Before any other guest had the chance, Damien announced he would partner with Viscount Deptford. As he climbed into the small boat, he scanned the faces of those standing on the shore. Winthrop stood prepared to take action if necessary. Iris was holding over Emily's head a parasol that obscured her face from view.

He scanned the guests on the shore again.

Several were missing.

Some might have chosen to lie abed. Especially those who had stayed up most of the night.

After all, not every guest enjoyed athletics or standing in the mud. There were no prizes awarded to mere spectators.

The castle steward appeared at the end of a small dock. He held a gun above his head and fired into the air. A few craft surged ahead. Two paddled into each other, which in turn blocked the progress of the other competitors.

Damien plied the oars steadily down the middle of

the lake, his gaze moving from left to right. The viscoun
gave rowing a decent try; he was more agile than hi
gaunt appearance suggested, but it had just occurred t
Damien that they were a pair of sitting ducks. He hadn'
noticed the density of the trees above the shore unti
now.

"Allow me to row, sir," Damien said, his shoulder
bunching as he leaned into the oar. "In fact, why don'
you slide down a little lower on the seat?"

"Slide—" Deptford glanced through the hills above
the left bank. "Do you think that someone is lying in
wait for me?"

Damien recognized a footman walking through the
hillside foliage. "It's always best to be prepared. If you
are having second thoughts about this, I'll row us straigh
back to shore."

"But what will everyone think?"

"I don't know," Damien said. "And I don't damn wel
care. I'll explain that I've got a cramp from something I
ate at breakfast. Or I'll make up a story about being at
tacked by pirates at sea, which is true, by—"

The pistol shot hit the stern where only a momen
before the viscount had been seated, plying his oar with
surprising vigor for a man his age. At the gun blast, he
had thrown himself at Damien's feet, knocking an oar
from his hand.

"Stay there," Damien said, pulling off one boot at a
time. "If the boat capsizes, swim underwater as best you
can to the right shore. In fact, do it now."

"But what about you?"

"It didn't hit me."

"A miss is as good as a mile," the viscount muttered.

Damien sprang from his crouched knees and dove

into the lake, the boat tipping sideways at the sudden shift of weight. He was vaguely aware of shouting and activity on the right bank. But Damien did not look back. He cut through the water without taking a breath and clambered up the embankment as a final shot, this time aimed at him, exploded from the pavilion.

The guests stared in disbelief as the viscount swam underwater across the lake and then rose from a screen of duckweed and water grasses. Was this part of a staged event? Had the master of ceremonies fired prematurely to declare a contest winner? Even the other competitors seemed unsure of what to do, their small flotilla sitting idly in the middle of the lake. What had happened to the earl? Had he been shot? If so, why had he clambered up the left shore?

Emily knew instantly that this was no staged performance. Her gaze followed Damien until he surged to his feet on the opposite shore. An instant later he ran up the embankment in the direction of the ruined pavilion, and she lost sight of him.

A firm hand gripped hers. "Come with me," Winthrop said. "His lordship gave me specific instructions to hide you and Iris in the event of an emergency. You are not to remain in view."

Emily shook her head in panic. "But he's alone with an assassin. Won't his gun be useless if it's wet? That means he's unarmed."

Winthrop pulled her and Iris through the center of the dispersing group. The consensus of opinion seemed to be that someone had played a prank during the competition and that whoever it was should be ashamed of his childish joke. Or perhaps it was a poacher. Everyone knew how brash they had become. The castle steward had wrapped the viscount in a warm blanket and urged the other guests to follow him inside for fine French brandy and trifle. It would all be sorted out. No one was hurt. That was all that mattered. Accidents happened. An Englishman did not allow a gunshot or two to discourage him.

Winthrop hurried Emily and Iris upstairs to the earl's suite and made them swear they would stay put until he returned.

"You can't leave him there to fight alone," Emily protested, running to the window to stare across the lake. It was useless. She couldn't see a thing. "What are you going to do?"

Winthrop released a sigh. "Clean up after him, as usual."

Damien had climbed the hill above the pavilion and crouched in the thorny vines that covered the crumbling stone columns. He half slid down the hillside toward the ruins, undetected until the assailant turned, his gun leveled at Damien's face.

"Lord Shalcross," Mr. Batleigh said with a mocking bow. "Your heroics have ruined my afternoon, although I have to confess that the thought of comforting your wife after your demise gives me a great deal of pleasure. I—"

Damien lunged at him from the thicket, the momentum of his attack bringing both men down. Damien rolled on reflex to the dominant position, his weight imprisoning the other man. Batleigh raised his gun to fire. Damien caught his wrist and banged it repeatedly against the warped flooring until the weapon skittered across the pavilion into a pile of bracken fern.

"Shoot an innocent old man for money, would you?" Damien asked through his teeth. "You worthless little shit. Are there any others like you here?"

Batleigh pushed upward with all his might, managing to dislodge Damien long enough to break free. He surged to his feet, and Damien rose in the next second to block his path to the fallen gun.

Batleigh looked stunned, broken.

"Mention my wife and expect that I will allow it?" Damien went on.

He walked Batleigh backward into one of the pavilion's columns. A branch cracked in the thicket above. He glanced up, wondering whether he was about to encounter a friend or another attacker. Batleigh took the opportunity to strike again. He threw a poorly aimed punch. Damien ducked, grasping Batleigh by the lapels of his jacket and pinning him to one of the crumbling columns.

"You don't know who you're up against," Batleigh said, breathing hard, blood trickling down his chin.

"Where is his son?"

"I don't know what you're talking about."

Damien laughed. "Do you know how a traitor is treated before his execution?"

"The same way I'll treat your wife when I get her alone."

Damien drove his fist into Batleigh's nose and punched him in the stomach with the other. Batleigh shook his head as if he could not see clearly. It was a sham, and Damien knew it.

When Batleigh charged him in a final act of desperation, Damien merely stepped aside and let the raging bastard crash into the giant of a man who had been crouching in wait outside the pavilion.

Even if Batleigh managed to escape Hamm's hold, he

would not elude the castle steward and half-dozen footmen who had assembled on the hill above the lake to deliver him to the local authorities. Damien did not doubt for a minute that Batleigh, under duress, would identify the radicals who had hired him.

He didn't linger to watch the rest of the scene unfold. He had other obligations to fulfill. Despite the success he had achieved today, Damien did not look forward to the explanations the other guests would demand of him. He had a wife who would need reassurance that all was well, although Damien would no longer deceive himself on that account. He had come to need Emily more than she did him. And after he had reassured her he was fine, he had to console the valet, who would wring his hands when he saw the condition of Damien's clothes.

Iris had to give the devil his due. Winthrop excelled at his job, and a good part of his work included throwing people off his master's trail. Iris knew efficiency when she saw it. How often had she covered for her mistress's mistakes? Who in this self-serving world appreciated a servant who risked all and received precious little in return?

Winthrop had only to drop a few words here and there to a gossip-prone guest or servant, stir up an ash or two of trouble as it were, and the rest took care of itself.

By early evening the story circulating around the castle was that a poacher had been shooting at hares when the viscount's boat had sailed past the pavilion. The elderly fellow had never meant to injure anyone, neither today nor on the morning of the hunting party. He had been living like a hermit in the ruins of the pavilion for three years, by his own estimation. He'd surrendered his gun in exchange for a fishing pole without complaint.

The gamekeeper was still deciding whether to press charges or to chase the vagrant off into the woods, where he would become the responsibility of another parish. The whole incident had so upset Mr. Batleigh that he'd taken leave of the party.

This enormous fib generated several political debates at the dinner table. What right did a vagrant have to possess a gun and live off the viscount's hunting preserve? Did the aristocracy not have an obligation to the poor?

Was the poacher a malignant person or one incapable of caring for himself? Surely because a man could not afford a meal did not give him the right to threaten others. Arguments smoldered in the air and erupted over a person who did not exist. Some of the guests split into two self-righteous camps, each to the other refusing compromise. By the end of the first course Winthrop confided to Iris that this time he might have gone too far.

But Iris did not agree and told him as much as they passed in the hall to the kitchen. "Well done, Winthrop," she said.

And to her utter delight, he removed his spectacles, pulled her into his arms, and kissed her without once looking around for witnesses to this deed.

Chapter 44

After a leisurely breakfast the following day, the guests returned to their rooms to change their clothing for an al fresco luncheon on the lawn. Damien insisted that Emily looked fine as she was; he was certainly not going to bother changing to impress a group of people he was unlikely to meet again. Still, he agreed to indulge Emily, and waited at the bottom of the stairs for her to enact a ritual that he told her in no uncertain terms was unnecessary. But he supposed he had a little time on his hands now. His job was almost done.

As she hurried up the stairs, her skirt in hand, she was overtaken by a housemaid so engrossed in running an errand that she bumped Emily into the railing. "Sorry, my lady," she said without a glance in Emily's direction.

Emily was about to gently reprimand the maid when a familiar face at the top of the stairs drew her attention.

"Oh!" she said warmly to Iris. "What perfect timing," she whispered as the maid scurried away. "Will you arrange my hair for the luncheon?"

Iris appeared to be in anything but an accommodating mood. She glared at the careless housemaid, who had disappeared into another guest's room without knocking. "Did you see that? Did you see the sly look on her face? Did she not give you a sense of something evil?"

Emily frowned. "Was that the maid you were talking about last night?"

"The one and only. Something's not right about her. I told you, didn't I? I told Winthrop. But does anyone ever listen?"

"I think I might have seen her before," Emily said, resting against the staircase railing. "Her voice sounded familiar. Still, for the life of me I can't remember where I would have met her."

She stared over the balustrade at Damien, who took only one look at her face before he realized that something was wrong. "In the last room to the left," she said as he ran up the stairs toward her. "It's the housemaid that has behaved suspiciously."

He turned into the hall, Emily and Iris trailing at his heels. "The housemaid?" he asked. "What housemaid?"

"The one Iris distrusts."

Damien pivoted. "Am I chasing her down for any particular reason?"

"There's something off about her," Iris stated. "She's always listening when I talk to Winthrop."

Damien shrugged. "Winthrop never mentioned her."

"I have an odd feeling about her, too," Emily said.

"I have odd feelings about people all the time," Damien admitted. "But it usually takes more than a feeling for me to chase them into an unknown person's room. What exactly do you expect to say to her?"

"Ask her what she is doing upstairs when she has been assigned to the yellow-drawing room on the first floor," Iris said. And at Damien's perplexed look she added, "What if she is part of the conspiracy? Wouldn't a female assassin be the last person you would suspect as a conspirator?"

Damien looked pointedly at his wife. "As a married man I have made it a rule to never underestimate a member of the opposite sex."

Emily smiled at him.

"However," he continued, "this sounds like a situation that should best be left to the butler."

"He's taking Winthrop's side," Iris said to Emily.

Emily stared down the hall, shaking her head. "It can't be. I have seen her before, Damien. And I remember where. She was working at the Sign of the Raven when we stayed there only days ago. Can it be coincidence that she is here?"

He muttered an unintelligible curse. "There's only one way to find out."

As he entered the room, the housemaid swung around from the bed, took one look at Damien, then launched into a tearful confession.

"I admit everything. I am as guilty as the person who paid me. I knew what I was doing was wrong when I offered my services. My dad knows I became involved in their arrangement. He wanted me to do it."

Damien rubbed his face. How had this girl deceived Winthrop? She was a woeful amateur, and her voice made his head split.

"Iris," he said, "stand outside in case Mrs. Gladwick returns before we are finished." He turned back to the housemaid. "How did you become involved in the conspiracy?"

The girl gave him a blank look. "What conspiracy? Oh, you mean the 'arrangement'?"

"No," he said firmly. "I mean the conspiracy against the Crown."

"In this castle?" she asked, her shock palpable. "Don't tell me I've been taking tips from traitors this whole time. I'll give back every tuppence that I've saved for Sunday night gambling."

"Who hired you?" Damien demanded, wondering which of the conspirators had been impressed by this feather-brained female.

"The castle steward," she said. "I worked the harvest feast in the Christmas ball last year. I made enough to buy me mum the green cloak she'd been wanting. But she won't be happy if she finds out about this."

"Nor will the castle steward."

"Mr. James? Oh, he wouldn't mind. It only bothers him when a cuckolded husband finds out and insists on defending his honor with a duel. You should know what I'm talking about."

Damien glanced at Emily, who half covered her face with her hand. "Why do I have the sense that she and I aren't talking about the same thing?"

"I am employed at the Raven," the girl said with a nervous giggle. "My father said that hard work would pay off in the end, but I don't see that it's made a difference. The rich still treat servants like filth."

Emily lowered her hand. "You were the maid who approached me with the tarot card outside my husband's carriage. You do admit that, too?"

"Why wouldn't I?" the girl asked in confusion. "I was only trying to be helpful."

"Then why didn't you acknowledge me a few minutes ago when we passed on the stairs?"

"I didn't want to get you into trouble with his lordship. I knew he was watching, and you told me that your husband would be upset if he thought you had consulted the gypsies about your love affair."

"I said nothing of a love affair," Emily said indignantly.

"Not in so many words," the girl replied. "But the card you dropped said 'passion.' For all I knew you had another lover or had bought a spell to make your husband love you forever. Desperate women often resort to magic to hold a man's heart."

Damien walked to the door, shaking his head, and motioned for Emily and the maid to take their leave. Once the maid slipped into the hall, she wasted no time disappearing down the stairs.

"Well," Iris said, her hands on her hips. "Was I right or wrong?"

Damien glanced around the room. "You were right to alert me, Iris," he said guardedly.

"She's a little liar," Iris said, her face reddening.

"Yes. She is. Why don't you go with Emily while I think this over?"

He walked from the room in silence, watching Emily and Iris disappear into his chamber. Footsteps on the staircase diverted his attention. He turned to see Winthrop below him, his face dark with concern.

"What is it?" Damien demanded.

"It's Batleigh, my lord. I don't know how it happened, but apparently he tried to escape, and one of the viscount's guards shot him to death on the way to gaol. We'll never know now if he was working alone."

"How convenient," Damien said.

"I thought the same thing myself," Winthrop said. "He was never questioned or allowed a defense."

"He almost killed me," Damien said.

"Yes," Winthrop said, clearly shaken. "And I suppose you think it was an accident?"

Damien arched his brow. "Don't you?"

"No, my lord," Winthrop said. "I do not."

Damien was in a fretful mood while he and Emily dressed for the operetta that would be held in the great hall. He slouched against the door, his gloves in hand, his long black coat slung over his arm. Emily had come to the conclusion that this was how her husband dealt with a crisis: withdrawing into himself. She, on the other hand, could not stop chattering when she was upset.

Conversation, even one-sided, seemed preferable to his frequent bouts of silence in which, for all she knew, he was wondering whether another assassin would strike tonight and how he would thwart him if he did. She didn't know how much longer she could live like this, pretending to be a bride who had no worries in the world, except that someone had tried to kill her husband today. What difference did it make if Damien had not been the intended target?

"Are you worried that there will be another assault tonight?" she finally asked him.

"How do you think it would happen?" he asked, looking her up and down.

"He could be stabbed while the audience is engrossed with the action on stage. He could conceivably be shot during the aria, if the perpetrator enters and escapes through one of the screen doors."

"There are four guards disguised as footmen in the castle."

Emily turned to him, no longer able to hide her distress. "Counting Winthrop and Hamm?"

He nodded. "We are still all at some risk. Winthrop will have his eye on Iris the entire night, as I will on you."

"You cannot keep watch over me and the viscount at the same time. At least not properly. Your commitment is to him."

He placed his arm around her waist and drew her to him. Her violet satin skirt rustled in the momentary silence. "With apologies to the Crown, my wife comes before all else."

"Damien, you don't mean that, and I would not expect you to put me first."

"Pray God, then, that my loyalty is not put to the test."

Her emotions blocked the flow of rational thought in her mind. As touched as she was by his courage, she could not contain her concern. If she had ever doubted the dark motives of his enemies, she did not now. She wondered how her husband had ever been able to trust anyone after overcoming evils that she would never understand. And she wondered if it was possible he meant what he had said, that he cared for her and placed her above his profession. She grasped his hand, wishing that she could protect him for once.

Chapter 45

$\mathcal{D}$amien fell asleep within minutes of undressing and sprawling across the bed. He had not relaxed for a minute during the operetta. Now Emily sat beside him, studying his hard features and the sculpted perfection of his shoulders and upper torso. "I love you," she whispered, leaning down to kiss his cheek before she slid away from him to the floor. She slipped on the nightshirt he rarely wore and carefully drew the coverlet over his intimate parts.

For a moment he stirred and she waited for him to awaken. But he slept on while she surveyed the appalling state of their bedchamber. As quietly as she could, she hung his still-damp clothes on the linen press by the fire. She draped her discarded garments over the dressing screen. She placed his boots by the armoire and retrieved his gloves from under the table; then she spotted his waistcoat, fallen from a chair in the corner. The man truly did need a valet.

She reached down. It was the vest he had worn the night he searched his trunk and removed from it the paper he had not wanted her to see. It was none of her business. For all she knew it contained a cryptic message from the Home Office.

Whatever the mysterious article was, it had mattered enough to Damien that he'd removed it from the trunk. Then again, if this was a missive that contained any Crown secrets, he surely would not be so careless as to leave it where his wife would come across it and be tempted to take a peek at the thing.

Perhaps he was testing her integrity. Perhaps it was a letter from an old lover.

Perhaps Emily would be better off not knowing what his secret was. Except that not knowing would nag at her for ever after, and she might never have this chance again.

He might be furious at her invasion of privacy . . unless she didn't tell him, in which case she would be the one hiding a secret, and that might be worse.

She reached inside the pocket of his waistcoat and withdrew from it a slightly wrinkled card that read—

" '*Mariage,*' " he said over her shoulder, his warm body pressed to hers.

She turned, holding the card to her heart, uncertain whether she could trust what she saw in his eyes. "You kept it," she said in wonder. "I thought it might be a love letter."

"Oh, it is," he replied. "The woman who possessed it stole my affection from the moment we met."

She swallowed.

"She was an impostor," he said, plucking the card from her hand and dropping it on the table.

"Was she?"

"She had set a lure for another man. Fool that I was, I walked straight into it and took his place."

"What a shame."

"It was shock, you see. I thought I was to wed a sultry,

raven-haired fortune-teller who would make my life a living hell."

"And?" she whispered.

He shrugged his bare shoulder. "I ended up marrying an entirely different woman."

"Is she sultry?"

His mouth curved in a smile. "Like the last burning coal in a tavern fire on a winter's eve. She draws a man to her warmth."

"Do you prefer her raven hair to mine?"

He lifted a strand of her hair and let it fall to her breast. "There's fire in your hair, too. That might mean you are dangerous."

She placed her hand around his neck and drew his head to hers. "You do know that I have no talent for fortune-telling whatsoever? Will that be a mark against me?"

His eyes kindled. "It might have been a point in your favor if I'd planned to spend the rest of my life at the horse races. As luck would have it, I'm not much of a gambler."

"But you do take chances with your life."

He shrugged again. "Until now it's been mine alone to risk."

She drew a deep breath, the heat in his eyes stealing through her. "And—"

He waited, bending his head as though every word that she uttered enthralled him. The sensuality on his face made her falter, forget what she had wanted to say. "And what?" he coaxed.

"And you still desired this other woman, despite your certainty that she would make your life a living hell?"

His fingers traced the curve of her cheek, her chin, then stroked lower through the nightshirt with unmerciful skill. "On that account," he murmured, "I might have been mistaken. We'll never know, will we?"

His fingers glided over her swollen breasts. Arousal pulsed through her every vein. "Why not?" she asked, her breath constricted in her throat.

"For one thing," he answered, shifting his weight so that his hard body held her captive against the wall, "the fortune-teller disappeared the night we met, and so what influence she would have had on my life will remain a mystery. "And—"

"But you wonder—"

"For another, she loved another man."

She shook her head in denial. "That is untrue. The cricket player was an infatuation. There is only one man who could compete with you. He is—" She paused as he lifted the nightshirt to her waist.

"He is?" he prompted, guiding the head of his shaft between her thighs. "Tell me his name, and I will demand satisfaction."

She smiled, closing her eyes to concentrate on their coupling. Slowly he pressed through her plump folds, giving her only an inch at a time. "Sir Angus Morpeth of Aberdeen," she whispered. "Sometimes I dream of him."

"Doing what precisely?"

She moved her hips to allow him deeper penetration. "This."

Chapter 46

The earl and Emily departed early the next morning for London. It was given to Winthrop and Iris to pack what their employers had left of their belongings and then follow in a lighter carriage.

As usual the valet and lady's maid worked in silence, dedicated to the pursuit of leaving the earl and countess's suite in such pristine condition that the next guest to enter would never guess at the connubial games played by the previous occupants.

"Well, that's it," Winthrop announced, closing the door of the empty armoire. "The place looks better than it did before the party, if I do say so myself."

"Not quite yet," Iris murmured, her gaze averted as she marched past him to straighten a pillow on the bed. "There. Now, do not close the door on our way out or you will only dislodge dust motes."

He stepped in front of her before she reached the door. "There is no need to pretend any longer, Iris."

"Pretend what?" she asked in hesitation.

"Look me in the eye."

"No, I'd rather not."

"Why not?"

"Because there is no further reason to pretend, and I am not certain that I wish for you to know my true feelings. Furthermore, I cannot forgive the pain you caused me the day you called me a temptress."

"It was an unseemly word to use."

"It was a wonderful word," she said, forgetting she had forbidden herself to look into his eyes.

"A wonderful word? And you cannot forgive me for it? Or was it because I kissed you?"

"I cannot forgive you because you acted as though that kiss had never happened, Winthrop," she burst out, causing him to step back in self-defense. "You gave me reason to believe that you found me desirable, only to recoil from my presence from that moment since."

"But I thought I had offended you, overstepped my bounds."

"We have been posing as man and wife for the good of all England, sir. Do you think I am so accomplished at trickery that I could play this part without . . . without . . ."

Her voice trailed off into a sigh. She turned, lowering her gaze, only to feel his hand upon her shoulder.

"Temptress," he said loudly and deliberately.

She whirled around, raising her hand to his face. "I will not live in the same house with you again, even if it means I might end up living on the streets."

He closed his hand around her wrist, drawing her toward him. "I understand. When we reach London we will immediately announce our engagement. There will be no more pretending between us, Iris. The next time we share a bed I will not be lying beside you as stiff as a corpse. I will be your husband in every sense of the word, and I hope you understand what I mean."

Chapter 47

$\mathscr{T}$he Earl of Shalcross and his wife received a rousing welcome in London from Damien's aristocratic Boscastle cousins. One might gather that royalty had arrived, from the succession of routs and glamorous soirées hosted in their honor by Grayson Boscastle, family patriarch and Marquess of Sedgecroft. When Damien had last seen his brothers, the young men had been boisterous wildlings. He was amused to find that the three of them, Colin, Sebastien, and Gabriel, were now tamed, outwardly at least, by wives of their own.

There were new family members to meet, including a cluster of energetic children who behaved only when Weed, the senior footman to the marquess, threatened some form of ghastly punishment such as practicing at the pianoforte or memorizing a page from the *Odyssey*, to be recited before company.

Damien vowed to himself that he would never again lose contact with the people he loved. He might have to spend weeks catching up on everyone's life and explaining what he had done during his absence. But there *was* time, and somehow Emily—his bride, his bridge between the future and the past—balanced it all out.

He could sleep with Emily at his side every night and hold her in his arms every morning, even if his relatives abducted her during the day for shopping jaunts and social visits to introduce the young countess around town. London wanted to know everything about the earl and his wife. Where had they come from? There must be a scandal somewhere in their background. All too soon Winthrop and Iris started to grumble about the number of invitations to plays and parties that awaited an answer.

And Damien let them grumble, knowing that in the end the invitations would be answered and it would not matter. All that mattered was that Emily was safe from harm and the conspiracy was unraveling.

The most important meeting on his mind was a private one between Damien and his cousin Heath. Damien had news of his personal mission to impart, and whether Heath chose to share this information with the rest of the family would be Heath's decision to make.

They discussed the conspiracy first in the office of Heath's St. James's Street town house. "With Ardbury dead, there might appear to be a lull in activity," Heath said, his lean face reflective. "There will be others to fill his void."

Damien blinked. "Ardbury is dead? When and where did this occur?"

"A half mile from Maidstone. Or so the report goes. I believe he was shot in a tavern by a drunk while you were at the castle."

"No one told me."

"I had a message sent to you as soon as I found out," Heath said.

"Then the message was lost or intercepted."

A silence grew then, a pause between two men who had each survived torture at an enemy's hand. "I suppose it isn't important now," Heath said at length. "There have been no reports of riots or disturbances in the towns that were marked by the rebels. Your brother-in-law must have traveled like Hermes."

"Viscount Deptford's son," Damien said, sitting forward. "Was he one of the rebels arrested?"

"I have not seen his name mentioned once," Heath said slowly. "In fact, I wasn't aware he had a son. I thought he had a daughter. I am usually not wrong about such details. Perhaps I've been sitting behind this desk too long. This is a surprise to me."

Damien frowned. "I hope the son has come to his senses and will spare his father further grief."

"And as to grief," Heath said, looking into Damien's eyes, "I need you to confirm in person what you wrote in your last letter. Is it true? Is it possible that my brother Brandon is still alive?"

"I know only this," Damien said. "A mercenary was hired in Nepal by Colonel Sir Edgar Williams to kill your brother and his companion, Samuel Breckland. Two bodies dressed in company uniform were found in a ravine. They had been attacked by wild dogs, and there the story should end, but it does not."

"Explain," Heath said, his voice hopeful and weary at the same time.

"The man who claims he killed them later confessed that he was unsure they had died. A year later he denied having anything at all to do with their disappearance." Damien loosened his neckcloth. "Excuse me. It seems I can never talk of this without feeling the need for fresh air. I've lost too many friends to pretend I am not affected."

Heath got up from his desk and went to a lacquered cabinet for a decanter of brandy and two glasses. "I do not drink," he said. "But tonight will be an exception. I know the despair of a man who is in prison with no hope of release. After I was captured and tortured during the war, it changed me."

"Not for the worse," Damien said, watching Heath pour the brandy with a trembling hand. "You have not let what you suffered break you."

"Trust me, there have been times. If not for my wife and family—well, I have traveled to those lonely reaches more than once to investigate Brandon's death. But this was your world. You had inside knowledge of matters that even the Alien Office is not privy to."

"If you're speaking of the corruption within the East India Company, I did indeed learn of their practices. I don't doubt that many of my riches were ill gained. I prefer now to deal directly with the foreign merchants for fair trading."

"My brother could be alive." Heath handed Damien his glass. "I am gladdened beyond what I can show."

"Legend has it that a blue-eyed soldier and his friend escaped the hellhole of a hillside prison after living there for years. They made it out with the help of a sympathetic guard whose sister had fallen in love with your brother."

The clock in the outer hall chimed the hour. "How did you escape?" Heath asked, his face, his voice composed.

"The guard's sister said that my eyes reminded her of another Englishman who had been captured and consigned to the prison pit. I promised her and the guard a reward if they freed me. They might have been able to feign ignorance of an escape the first time. But they would not get away with it again."

"They agreed?"

Damien nodded. "And I kept my end of the bargain. From that point forward, after years wasted, I had to pick up Brandon's trail. It is nearly impossible to trace a man who does not want to be found in those hills. I hired a guide whose knowledge of the area was invaluable."

Heath shook his head. "But he did not ask anyone for help. He didn't send a message home."

"Perhaps he had a good reason," Damien said. "All I know is that he, another man, and a child bought passage to England and boarded the ship together. I did not see your brother, but there is good reason to believe he has survived his trials."

"I am in your debt, Damien. You have given us hope. There is no greater gift."

"It's good to be back in England. I don't think I shall ever leave again. There is no finer place for a man to raise a family."

It was during an afternoon tea in her honor that Emily met the other ladies of the family. Jane, the marchioness, presided over the gathering with humor and aplomb, introducing Emily to three duchesses, a viscountess named Chloe, and a half-dozen others. One lady, Jocelyn, had recently given birth to twin boys.

Emily felt lost at first. She couldn't possibly remember all their names and corresponding titles. Every one of them surpassed her in sophistication and confidence. She would have been completely overcome with envy had she not discovered she wasn't the only red-haired lady in the family. That made her feel a little less conspicuous.

After three cups of brandy-laced tea, she felt accepted, in a place where she belonged. These ladies did not put on airs. They talked all at once, flitting from one topic to another. She could not possibly follow the flow of conversation. A footman brought another tea urn and bottle of brandy into the drawing room.

Jane and her sister-in-law, Chloe, poured tea and passed around a plate of iced biscuits. Jane drank another cup of tea but refused the brandy, confessing to Emily that she was carrying her second child, and spirits made her queasy.

"Now tell us how you met your husband, dearest," Jane said as she settled back in her chair. "Few of us seem to have met our mates in the normal manner. Was yours an ordinary romance?"

Emily forced a smile, freezing at the innocuous question. Every lady present conducted herself with ease and elegance. How could she admit the dire act she had committed in order to catch a man different from the one she had married? A man who had surpassed her naïve dreams in every way possible.

She was too embarrassed to reveal the truth. And yet she could not bring herself to lie, not to these women who had openly embraced her as one of their own. They knew nothing about her. If Damien hadn't exaggerated, he was even more of an enigma to his family. She felt the need to protect him as he had her.

She placed her cup on the table, straightened her shoulders, and opened her mouth only to shake her head in apology. "Perhaps one day I shall be able to discuss it."

Every lady in the room looked at her in sudden interest, in sympathy, perhaps. Or was that her imagination? In any event she had only whetted their appetite for the entire story.

"It is perfectly all right," Jane said, holding up her hand to still the last murmurs that had followed Emily's announcement. "We have all been in your shoes."

"I doubt it," Emily said, looking down at Jane's exquisite tapestry slippers.

"Confession is good for the soul, Emily," Chloe said, motioning to the footman who had been standing so quietly in the corner that Emily only now noticed his presence. "I would like another splash of brandy, please. Ladies, I think our countess needs a little encouragement. Let me go first."

Chloe cleared her throat. "I met my husband after he had crawled through my window and dropped half-dead in my trunk of undergarments. I hid him in my closet. One might say I had a love affair with a ghost. The world believed he was dead. He proved otherwise to me in private."

Emily reached for her tea. She was feeling better by the minute.

"I sabotaged my marriage to one of Grayson's cousins and ended up marrying Grayson instead," Jane said with an airy wave of her hand.

"I shot my husband because I thought he was a fox," Julia, Lord Heath's wife said. "One would think he'd be furious, but he took it rather well."

Emily finished her tea and took a breath. She was no longer afraid for her life, and for all she knew, Damien had already told his brothers and cousins how he and Emily had met.

"We will never tell," Jane said, and every head in the room, possibly even the footman's, bobbed in agreement. Emily broke down.

"I was posing as a gypsy fortune-teller at a friend's party when Damien walked into my tent. It's rather complicated after that, and he was in disguise for other reasons that I shall omit. But we were caught out by my father, and the rest I shall leave to your imaginations."

The room was quiet for only a moment before every one started talking at once again, but it was Jane's voice that predominated.

"How perfect," Jane said with a radiant smile. "We're holding a costume ball almost two weeks from now, and I was wondering what I could do to entertain the ladies. The gentlemen will have their fencing displays. It would be so much fun if you would be a fortune-teller for a few hours, Emily. You will be the most popular person at the party—I know it. And if we charge for your predictions the proceeds will go to charity. Will you agree to do it? It would make me so happy."

Chapter 48

A masquerade ball in a Park Lane mansion. Emily would have loved to invite her father and brother, and Lucy and Lady Fletcher, too. Everyone back home would tease her about her costume, although considering how it had all worked out, she had no regrets about that evening. How could she regret anything that had brought her and Damien together?

Tonight was only for fun, to enjoy rather than to entrap. A small tent emblazoned with mystical symbols had been constructed on the terrace. A huge line had formed outside, but thank heavens she wouldn't be reading palms alone. Chloe, Viscountess Stratfield, and Jocelyn, Lord Devon Boscastle's wife, had volunteered to take over whenever Emily grew tired. Chloe had sneaked a list of invited guests and a few tidbits of personal information for Emily to use as a tease.

But Emily didn't feel as awkward in her costume as she did when she dressed in satin and jewels. She vowed to predict only happiness for the guests who flocked to her tent. It wouldn't be hard, when her own life had turned out to be better than what she had believed possible.

*　　*　　*

Damien strolled down the candlelit hall with his three brothers. Dark-haired, blue-eyed, they each lived and loved hard and were openly committed to one woman, a fact that did not stop several ladies from issuing invitation to stray with a provocative stare or sly flirtation with a fan.

"Is it rather crowded in this hallway, or is it me?" Damien asked, coming to a dead stop as a woman in high-necked ruff dropped a deep curtsy that showed more of her cleavage that Damien wished to see.

"You are a fresh commodity on the market, married or not," his youngest brother Gabriel said.

"So is your wife," Sebastien said. "Keep a watch out for the young bloods."

Damien smiled coldly. "I intend to."

As they reached the end of the hall they balked and stood as one at the open doors to the ballroom. Damien stared at the figures dancing beneath the brilliance of a crystal chandelier. "Isn't there another way to reach the terrace?" he asked over his shoulder.

"There are several private corridors, my lord," said the tall footman standing at one of the doors. "I shall be glad to show you through them."

Damien stood back as a guest dressed as a highlander passed before him, a masked female gamekeeper in tow. "Do pardon us, please," the gentleman said, smiling beneath his domino. "I've walked a mile to reach the terrace. I miss the air outside."

Damien stared after them, the comment lingering in his mind. Did he know that voice? Did it belong to one of the innumerable Boscastle friends who had been introduced to him since his arrival? He had let down his guard since he had reached London. But now, without discernible reason, he felt his familiar unease return.

He glanced back at the footman. "I will take you up on your offer of a direct route to the terrace. Sebastien? Colin?" He glanced at his brothers. "Care to have your fortunes told?"

"We're going upstairs to gamble," Sebastien admitted with a grin. "If your wife cares to give us guidance, we'll share the profits."

Damien laughed. "I think you'll do better on your own. She makes mainly romantic predictions." At least she wasn't looking for a husband tonight. He was hers for life. And Winthrop had Iris, so Damien would not be disturbed by anyone except Emily.

"I'll go with you," Gabriel said. He was still shorter and bulkier than Damien, but he was no longer the headstrong boy Damien remembered. It was evident, from the family rumors he had heard, that Damien's three brothers had learned to harness their demons and force the self-destructive creatures to work for and not against them. As he had.

Sometimes that was all a man could do. Sometimes, with the right woman beside you, it was more than enough.

"Come up if you change your mind," Colin, the second-oldest brother, called back to him. "We'd like a chance to win some of that wealth you acquired."

Damien grinned and considered going up with them for a game, but only for a moment. He didn't feel right leaving Emily alone in that tent, where he couldn't see her. Even though nothing was likely to happen at a party of this class. Nothing except perhaps that there would be a man standing in line who'd push to the front and insist that the sultry lady inside read his fortune.

Most likely the man wouldn't care about his fortune.

He might have glimpsed Emily on her way to the tent and found her dark beauty alluring, believing her to be a woman open to romance.

He frowned at the thought as he followed the footman outside. There were plenty of guests and servants bustling past the tent. But there wasn't a pony at the back who could stamp a hoof when a customer grew too bold or asked an impertinent question of the fortuneteller. A hopeful guest might assume she was only the hired help for the evening, and not know she was a young countess who had a protective husband standing in the garden, where he could keep the tent in sight.

But he couldn't see *inside* the tent. He couldn't see *her*.

And he did have a good reason for his suspicious nature. Besides, this was London, and life moved at a faster pace here than in Hatherwood. Emily might not know how to deal with a passionate gentleman, one who found her as irresistible as her husband did.

Moreover, the line to the tent had grown smaller, and what would it hurt to pop inside and ask a beautiful soothsayer to read his palm? In the crush, it might be the closest he would get to her until the party ended.

Which would not be until breakfast. When the marquess gave a party, the guests did not go home until noon.

He couldn't wait that long. He would hold off another minute and stand outside the tent in Michael's place. And then when she was finished, he would whisk her away for an hour to one of the mansion's secluded rooms that had been designed for such secret meetings.

All he had to do was wend his way through the hundred or so costumed guests who thronged the garden and terrace stairs.

*   *   *

Emily had depleted her talent for telling people what they wanted to hear. She had also run out of patience for those who went into raptures over her predictions. It should be obvious to anyone with half a brain that she was an imposter making up fortunes as she went along, and that she was sitting here in the spirit of fun.

She reminded herself that she was also doing this for charity as well as to prove to the Boscastles that she had a benevolent heart. But honest to St. George, if one more debutante entered the tent and begged to know whether there was a titled husband in her future, Emily would put down her head and weep. How mortifying to remember that she had once longed for such words of reassurance.

And yet Emily's dream had come true. It seemed cruel to deny hope to another. What did it cost her to tell a young girl that a titled husband was in her future? It wasn't as if Emily aspired to be the Oracle of Delphi. No one would knock on her door years from now, denouncing her ability as a prophetess.

At last there came a lull. Perhaps the novelty of her predictions had worn off. Wouldn't it be awful if all the debutantes had met in the retiring room and discovered that she had foretold the same fate for each and all? She should have thought to end her readings with the warning, "Do not speak a word of this to another person, or none of it will come true."

A resounding cheer from outside the tent startled her. She rose from her chair and peeked outside to the terrace. Not a debutante in sight. However, there did appear to be some sort of fencing performance taking place in the garden, and it had drawn a large number of guests. Presumably Damien and his brothers had been attracted to the spectacle. She tried to pick out their figures in the crowd.

It was time to close up shop. She loved swordplay and she loved her husband. She didn't want to miss this party. Not when she'd come full circle and there was so much to celebrate.

She turned to extinguish the light.

A shadow fell across her chair as she leaned forward. Her hand hovered over the dimly burning lamp on the table. She looked up into the shadow's face, too stunned to say a word. It would be useless to pretend ignorance. Had he known all along who she was? How had she ever believed him to be a victim when he had not cared that innocent people would be killed for his cause?

"Why?" she asked, genuinely confused but also playing for time. Surely another guest would burst into the tent.

The fencing spectacle could not last forever.

Someone at the party had to seek her out before it was too late.

Iris was good and truly chafed. Here she waited in the private suite of a Park Lane mansion, a virtual palace of the gods, for her mistress to come upstairs and change out of that garish costume into one befitting a countess. Emily could have passed as a medieval princess in the brocaded skirts and heavily boned bodice that Lady Sedgecroft had left hanging in the spare wardrobe.

But did Lady Shalcross show any respect for her rank? Did she care that her maid would be judged on the countess's appearance? Not that Iris gave a care what others thought of her. Still, she had her pride. Masquerade or not, Iris did not approve of her ladyship's gypsy attire. It reminded Iris of their harrowing escape. And while the Boscastle family might consider the notion of a fortune-teller at a party to be amusing mischief, Iris felt it was taunting fate.

"Ah, I found you at last."

She glanced over her shoulder to see Winthrop slip into the room and walk toward the window.

"You aren't supposed to be here," she whispered.

He drew her into his arms. "Who's to tell?"

"There are nine days left before the wedding." She wriggled free and turned back to withdraw, hiding a smile. "Control your passions."

"Nobody else in this house does," he murmured, wrapping his arms around her waist, his chin propped on her shoulder to stare outside. "I wonder if his lordship will take a day to fence with Sir Christopher. He was damn good in his day. He had a way with his blade."

Iris had no idea who Sir Christopher was, but she had just noticed a man lurking at the back of the tent. He was wearing a mask, as were half the other men at the party. But even from here Iris thought he looked familiar.

"It can't be," she whispered.

"Yes, it could. I mean, his lordship could put on a decent show, even though he hasn't fought a duel in almost a decade."

"Look at him, Winthrop. Dear God, look at the man who is lifting the back of the tent. Don't you recognize him?"

Chapter 49

*D*amien had one eye on the sword-fighting spectacle and the other on the fortune-telling tent. The line on the terrace had dwindled to one last guest, and Damien wasn't sure whether that person had exited while his back was turned or not. He was surrounded on all sides by Boscastles, and while he was grateful to be accepted back into the clan, he wanted Emily to be part of his reunion.

He'd taken her away from her own family, and he knew she missed home. It was up to him to make her feel that she belonged.

His cousin Grayson elbowed him in the ribs. "If you miss her that much, then go and get her. It's not as if anyone will notice you're gone. To be honest, you aren't the most scintillating conversationalist at the party."

Damien laughed. "You always were a rude bugger. Why did I think that time would refine you?"

Grayson shrugged. "Did it refine you? I don't think so. Some of us, you being a prime example, only grow worse with age. Go on. You miss her. It's pathetic. I know the feeling. There is no cure."

Damien turned, unable to argue, his gaze lifting to the tent. *You miss her.*

Miss. "No," he said aloud.

A miss is as good as a mile. That voice. The viscount's voice. Had Batleigh meant to shoot Damien, not Deptford, that afternoon on the lake?

"Damien?" Grayson said, turning in concern.

He wheeled. He knocked a footman into a guest as he sprinted up the stairs to the terrace. From the corner of his eye he noticed Winthrop and the marquess's senior footman burst through the French doors of the mansion's ballroom. He heard Grayson call his name again. By now two other gentlemen had broken from the group to ask what was wrong. He had no time to answer.

Chapter 50

*A*n unexpected calm had come over Emily. She stared at the man holding a pistol in one hand, a mask in the other. Viscount Deptford. The traitor Damien had vowed to protect. The hapless victim who knew the names of every conspirator in England. A man who had used his lineage and advanced age as a weapon to deceive and betray.

"Lady Shalcross," he said as another figure slipped into the tent behind him. "I am not sure whether I prefer you as a countess or as a gypsy fugitive. Under other circumstances I might have welcomed your subversive tendencies. There might have been in place for you in our revolution. Rare is the gentlewoman who defies convention to make her own future."

"Why?" she asked, shaking her head.

His long, sallow face creased in a smile. "I do not have time to convince you of the wrongs the aristocracy perpetrates. You need only know that I am the heart of this rebellion. Ardbury was but an artery, and others have already taken his place. In the end only one of us could lead."

"But my husband risked his life to protect you at the castle," Emily said.

"My life was never in danger. The hunting accident was a ruse to deceive agents of the Crown and those who refused to follow me. Your husband was the intended victim on the lake. I suspect he was on the verge of realizing the truth."

"You're wasting time," the woman behind him said. It was the maid who had approached Emily at the inn, the maid whom she and Iris had caught at the castle. "We have to escape now, Papa. Either kill her or take her for ransom. We won't make it through the garden before the fencing display is over if you tarry."

The viscount held the gun steadily aimed at Emily as the other woman darted forward to grasp her arm. Emily considered her options. She could scream and be immediately silenced by the pistol. Her voice might not even be heard above the applause and shouts that drifted from the garden.

No one in the ballroom would hear her over the band. She wasn't about to be taken prisoner. She leaned away from the woman, casting a glance around the tent for a weapon. Her shawl lay across the small table. The long golden fringe glittered in the lamplight.

For the love of heaven, Emily, whatever you do, don't let the light fall to the straw.

The woman reached for her arm again, and in one impulsive move, Emily grasped the fringe of her shawl and swept it across the table toward the oil lamp. Within moments the straw scattered around the tent erupted into flames. The viscount's daughter gasped in panic as fire licked the hem of her gown.

She bent at the waist to beat out the flames with her gloves. "Do something!" she cried to the viscount.

He wrenched off his cloak and threw it at her, then

backed out onto the terrace from the rear of the tent.
Emily stamped out the flames that followed his escape.
She was a step away toward freedom when the woman
gave a hysterical scream.

Emily could not leave her alone in the fire. She pulled
off her wig and started to beat out the burning straw,
which by this time had filled the tent with banks of smoke.

Then there were other people crowding around her,
tossing buckets on the smoldering mess. She felt herself
swept off her feet and carried into the evening air.

"Are you all right?" Damien asked her in an unsteady
voice.

She nodded. "It was the viscount. And the maid who
isn't a maid—"

He set her down, taking a last look at her as if to reassure himself she was unhurt before he disappeared
from her sight. A moment later another pair of masculine arms enveloped her. She looked up into the blue
eyes of the handsome golden-haired marquess, whose
authority would have intimidated her at another time. "I
am Grayson, my dear. We met earlier in the week."

As if anyone who had met the Marquess of Sedgecroft once could forget his name.

Damien couldn't hold her close enough. He didn't give a
damn that they were sitting on a chaise lounge in
Grayson's Italian gallery, an infamous room that everyone who was anyone in society knew had been designed
for seduction. He was as oblivious to the family members who hovered about in concern as he was to the Roman statues that stood in the numerous recessed alcoves,
candlelight flickering on their sculpted faces.

A footman placed two glasses of sherry on the low Chinese table that sat beside the chaise. Damien drank them both, only to realize they had been refilled before his last swallow went down.

"Are you sure you weren't hurt?" he asked Emily, burying his face in her tousled hair, the odor of smoke on her skin arousing a fury in him that he fought to hide. "Can you breathe properly?"

He thought he heard her laugh. "Not when you're crushing the air from my body," she whispered. "Damien, you have to let me go."

"No."

"You have to. I must look a fright."

"You look beautiful to me," he said, his throat constricting. "But, then, you always have."

"Is Deptford dead?" she whispered.

He ground his teeth. "No, but he'll be tried for treason and that will be the end of him."

"And his daughter?"

He hesitated. "No one knows if she'll survive the night. Her injuries were severe."

"Oh. I can't believe how fast the fire spread."

"But you survived. For God's sake, Emily, don't ever do anything like this again."

She drew back slightly. "You aren't making sense, Damien."

"Is it any wonder?"

She caressed his cheek. "You're distraught."

"Distraught? I've lost my mind. I'll never be the same."

She glanced up at his three brothers standing in the corner. "I feel fine."

He expelled a sigh. "I don't. I should have recognized Deptford right away. It took Iris to identify him from an upstairs window."

"Shall we go back to the town house?" she suggested gently.

He released her with reluctance, realizing that they had an enrapt audience. "Yes. If that's what you'd like."

Her eyes held his. "If it isn't too much trouble."

"How can you say that after following me into hell?"

"We escaped, Damien. And you saved more lives than you'll ever know. Don't forget that. You overcame evil and you deserve recognition."

"Which I am confident he will receive," Lord Heath said from the doorway.

Damien glanced back at Heath in appreciation, then stood, drawing Emily to her feet. When had he come to need her this desperately? Why had it taken him all these years to find his perfect mate? Because he had not believed, as Emily did, that true love existed? Or because he placed too much value on his achievements to give anyone else the chance to understand that he might not have a heart of gold, but it wasn't made of stone?

He knew only that his heart belonged to Emily, and if he had lost her tonight it would not be beating now.

Epilogue

Emily was ecstatic. A letter had arrived from Michael. It was short and brought tears of relief to her eyes. The baron and Michael had come to an agreement that was Michael's duty as the firstborn heir to learn land management. In the baron's opinion that included building a breeding stable, the studs for which he and Michael would travel to London to select.

"They've made up," she told Damien wistfully. "And they didn't need me to help them. Maybe I was in the way all the time."

"We can visit them whenever you like."

"They're coming to visit us," she said, putting down the letter. "So are Lucy and her parents."

He narrowed his eyes. "To buy horses, too?"

"No." She smiled, taking his hand. "Lucy is on a husband hunt, and I've promised to help her."

"You haven't."

"Yes, I have. She's my best friend, and I can't abandon her to Hatherwood in her time of need. She tried so hard to help me find love."

"She helped you find trouble."

"Oh, I could have done that by myself."

He nodded his head. "You did. And look at how it ended."

"It isn't over yet."

"What do you mean?" he said, a scowl taking the place of his complacent look.

"You're not about to stay in the country, twiddling your thumbs until the children arrive."

He sat up slowly. "Are you pregnant?"

"Jane thinks I am."

He leaned forward, looking at her carefully. "Perhaps you should go back to bed."

"Damien, you are insatiable."

"I meant that you should rest."

Emily smiled, not moving from her chair. "I thought we were going to visit that villa outside Kent with the apple orchards."

He raised his brow. "There's a mansion two miles from Piccadilly that has greenhouses and a large nursery as well as a hundred acres."

"A marriage that began in deception," she said with a mischievous smile. "Who would have thought it would last this long?"

"It had better last forever," he said somberly. "I refuse to ever go through such a rigmarole again."

"You say that now. But look at the ladies who flirt with you and invite you with their eyes. London seethes with temptation."

"Well, I seethe for you, and I took vows to that effect." He knelt at her chair and took her hands. "You will have to trust me, and don't think I haven't noticed heads turning when you walk across a room. If I weren't such a polite and well-bred person I'd kick every one of them in the ass through the door."

"That was quite romantic until that last part," she said, sighing again. "It did not make you sound either polite or poetic."

"I have taken several false identities in my past, Emily. However, none of them has been particularly polite or poetic. I have told you this before."

"Well, if we're to be truthful to each other, I can't resist you when you're impolite, and I can live quite well without the poetry."

He smiled at her. "Can you live without me? I love you, Emily."

In time, perhaps, Emily and the earl might respect tradition and behave as befit their status in society. They would not linger abed late every morning, ignoring the punctual knocks at the door to announce the arrival of a breakfast tray or the earl's morning paper.

For now Emily could live without a lady's maid to dress her, while Damien insisted it was his right. And although she had no skills as a barber, she was enthralled by the sight of her husband shaving his face as he stood unself-consciously before his mirror in the nude.

In time, perhaps, Damien would again offer his services to England. Or he might buy a country house and invest in Baron Rowland and son's horse-breeding venture. He could not stay in bed all day with the goddess he'd married. He would read a month or two's newspapers at one sitting and catch up on the world and its attendant woes.

But for now, Damien and his wife could not live without each other, and their return to society would have to wait indefinitely, or at least until after their child was born.

Author's Note

Dear Readers,

I've been asked about Brandon's and Samuel's fates since the beginning of the Boscastle series. I know what those missing young soldiers mean to you, and I wanted to reassure you that they are alive and one day will come home. The trouble is, I'm not exactly sure what they've been up to, and until then Brandon's story will have to wait.

I took the liberty of changing two historical facts for the purpose of this book. In Regency times it generally would have taken two weeks for Damien to secure the special license that he needed for his unplanned wedding. Also, the tarot cards that Emily used were not printed at the time of this story, but they are based on a deck printed in the previous century. For the record, I do not use them.

As always, I love to hear from you, although I have fallen behind in replying to your questions and comments. I hope you will forgive me.

Warmest wishes,
Jillian

Keep reading for a special preview of
Jillian Hunter's next historical romance,
coming in early 2015!

England
1813

*I*n the five years since her father's death, Miss Ivy Prescott had held together a household of three younger sisters and a half dozen unpaid servants with the tenacity of the vine for which she was named. "We are a woeful lot," she said every night before the last candle stub was extinguished. "But as long as we live in Fenwick Manor, everything will work out for the best."

No one disagreed. No one had the strength. Any latent energy had to be saved for the next emergency. Another leak might spring in the roof, and rain would drip down the nose of an ancestor whose portrait hung in the Long Gallery of the Tudor house. A jackdaw's nest could clog the chimney flue. Hiring a sweep would be out of the question. As long as Cook managed to coax a kitchen fire to make tea and grill toast in the morning, one summoned the stamina to endure.

"Fenwick Manor will *not* be sold," Ivy insisted over her daily triangle of burnt bread. "I'll work my fingers to the bone to keep our heritage alive."

Rosemary Prescott, one year younger than Ivy but more an introvert, who scribbled stories in the dark, rallied to the cause. "I shall find work, too, and write of our struggles at the end of the day, no matter how weary I am."

The torch passed next to Lilac, as fair and as removed from reality as a fairy-tale princess. "I shall meet the perfect man yet. He will be rich and generous and kind. We'll have a French chef and each of us a lady's maid."

Young Rue Prescott's idea of contributing her part never failed to send her other sisters into disquietude. Rue rarely brushed her thick black hair. Her ink blue eyes mesmerized men young and old. The oft-mended gowns she wore only enhanced her natural curves. She was aware that other people considered her beautiful, even though she found their attention unmerited, if not embarrassing. Nonetheless, she understood the shallow values of society. "I will find a protector," she said, oblivious to the shock this suggestion induced in her elder sisters. "And with the allowance he gives me, I will rescue us all."

"Banish that repugnant thought from your mind," Ivy told her. "That is not an acceptable option. The reasonable choice for a lady of reduced circumstances is to become a governess in a respectable household. I will put a notice in the papers offering my services after I return from London."

Rosemary scoffed at this idea. "Do you realize we will probably end up waiting on people who once considered us their equals?"

"Perhaps we could let out rooms to wealthy travelers," Lilac said, her forehead wrinkling at the thought. "Some strangers might pay a heavy purse to pass the night in the bedroom where Anne Boleyn once slept."

Rue said, "Or to view the hiding place of King Charles the Second."

"Which is so well hidden," Ivy pointed out, "that none of us has ever been able to prove it exists."

"Of course it exists," Rosemary said. "What good would it have been to a hunted monarch if his hiding place was easily uncovered?"

Ivy could not argue. The house had witnessed revels and masquerades and political intrigues. The sisters considered it a crime to allow centuries of history to crumble into dust. And yet they had sold off one precious heirloom after the next. The harpsichord, a gold watch case, a ruby aigrette, and the silver ewer that had held the wash water of Queen Elizabeth's mother. Ivy would pawn her mother's baroque pearl necklace as a last resort.

Neither the interior of the house nor the nature of the Prescott women had followed any predictable symmetry. Their father's death in a duel in Hyde Park had plunged the sisters into immediate disgrace. Before the viscount had been laid to rest in the family vault, his daughters discovered that they had become social pariahs. Acquaintances who had courted their favor withdrew invitations to parties and balls. Former best friends snubbed the Prescott sisters in the shops and streets of London, where they had been admired.

Their father's sins had tainted the family name. And it was left to them to restore their own inheritance, a dilapidated Tudor mansion, to its original glory, using whatever talents were at their disposal.

ALSO AVAILABLE FROM

NEW YORK TIMES BESTSELLING AUTHOR

Jillian Hunter

THE MISTRESS MEMOIRS
A Boscastle Affairs Novel

When governess Kate Walcott is hired by
courtesan Georgette Lawson, it's not just to care
for her unruly children, but to help write
Georgette's shocking memoirs. Before long,
Kate is involved in a scandal all her own—
and one more dangerous and seductive than
she ever imagined...

**"We could all use a little more
Jillian Hunter in our lives."**
—*The Oakland Press* (MI)

**Available wherever books are sold or at
penguin.com**

facebook.com/LoveAlwaysBooks

LOVE
ROMANCE
NOVELS?

For news on all your favorite romance authors, sneak peeks into the newest releases, book giveaways, and much more—

"Like" Love Always on Facebook!

f LoveAlwaysBooks